"A SMALL DECEIT"

A novel by Peter Craigie

Published by Peter Craigie

ISBN 978-0-9559864-3-7

"I am not up to small deceit or any sinful games." Bret Hart

CHAPTER 1

'Terry, are you still in love with my daughter?'

It wasn't quite in the category of 'have you stopped beating your wife' but it was enough to stop me in my tracks. I took a deep breath and waited for some brilliant response to come to me.

Of course it was clever of her to have thought of me in the first place, given all the time that had elapsed. But she had always been a clever woman. Perhaps I should have remembered that. Especially when it turned out she was very successfully running her husband's businesses for him.

So I should have understood what was going on a bit sooner. But then you see, a client is a client. And in the consultancy business what's the worst a client can do to you, apart from refuse to pay your fees of course. Or so I thought at the time.

It was a sunny June morning. I was still in my bathrobe and feeling only slightly decadent. I had showered and shaved and worked through the exercises my physiotherapist recommended if I intended to go on walking upright. I have this back problem, a legacy of my rock-climbing days, so I do the exercises and convince myself they are doing me good. "After all," she says, "You can't expect miracles at your age. Things do wear out." I looked in the mirror. Forty-two, I thought, and things are wearing out.

I had just finished an assignment and had nothing very much to do at that stage except to send out a final fee note and I didn't anticipate any problems with payment on this occasion. But I was feeling a familiar sense of the depression that usually appears when the problem is solved and the adrenaline stops flowing.

Coffee, I thought. I headed into the kitchen, pausing to turn on a radio. The sound of Menuhin and Christian Ferras weaving their way hypnotically through the Bach Double Concerto filled the flat. I started to feel instantly better. I rescued the coffee from the fridge, measuring two spoonfuls into a cafetiere and poured on the boiling water. The odour of strong coffee surged into the kitchen. It's strange but true that decaffeinated does smell just as good as regular coffee. Just one of life's little deceptions.

I found my coffee mug, the one with the zodiac sign and the description of a typical Capricorn, including a list of suitable career options. 'Ambitious and careful, will work patiently and usually achieves what they want. Ideal career choices:- architect, bureaucrat, or civil servant'. I sighed. So that was where I had gone wrong, I thought. Which explained why I was still in my bath robe at 10-30 am, drinking coffee alone.

Still, there were worse ways to spend a Monday morning and

the assignment I was putting to bed had been interesting, in a grizzly way. The lead had come from one of the more enlightened of our banks. They had asked me to find someone to run a small foundry company; old established and family owned. The problem was that the family had run out of money and talent at about the same time.

Of course, it turned out to be more complicated than that---- these cases usually are. The decent candidates naturally wanted to see a plausible business plan and some evidence of funding and the very best wanted a share-holding; a piece of the action to make the risk worthwhile. Unfortunately giving away shares in a family business is usually the point at which the owners start twitching. Blood, as they say, is thicker than water--- and twice as nasty.

But in this case the situation was dire and when eventually I interested a suitable candidate I was able to negotiate a good package for them. In return the bank agreeing to refinance the family's currently unsustainable borrowings. The family reluctantly agreed to restructure the shareholdings and I took a small stake in the recovery myself, to show commitment.

"O.K." I said, taking a mouthful of coffee, "what can you do next to improve British management --to say nothing of your own cash flow?" Nothing obvious came to mind as I stood looking out of the window at the grey New Town buildings opposite. That was when the telephone rang.

I recognised her voice immediately; clear and cultured, a classless accent with just a trace of something else; a hint of the north, Lancashire or Yorkshire, giving an edge to the polished English tones. "Is that Terry Lennox? This is Helen van Eck. I hope you remember me. I'm--- Sylvia's mother?" A slight hesitancy in her voice? But behind it was an underlying assurance. Clearly she expected only too well to be remembered. And of course I did remember her--- instantly--- though I had met her on only two or three occasions and those some time ago.

Small, trim, finely boned with the same dark, almond shaped eyes as her daughter and the same delicate high bridged nose, the firm jaw line and the mouth perhaps a shade too thin-lipped. Her complexion had been flawless, even at the age of sixty. I thought back rapidly. It had been at least five years, or possibly six since I had seen her. That was when Sylvia and I were making a last, rather desultory attempt to build a relationship.

I had met her first a couple of years before that, along with her husband, a big, seemingly ponderous Dutchman, who was chairman of the largest international construction group in the Netherlands. He was of course a great deal brighter than he chose to appear, hiding the fact with home-spun Friesland cunning. I had liked him a lot.

Sylvia had been working for me then, and at that stage our relationship had been strictly business. Though with hindsight I knew that from the beginning there had always been an unacknowledged awareness between us of what might happen. But it wasn't until much later that Sylvia and I ---.

"Of course, Mrs. van Eck. How are you? How nice to hear from you. And what a surprise."

I couldn't imagine why she had called me. It was the first I had heard from her in all those years, though from time to time I had tried to contact her, usually when curiosity about Sylvia had overcome my inertia--- and my ego.

"Terry," she said quietly, "I'm afraid I have some very sad news for you." In a cold premonition I knew what was coming. "Sylvia has disappeared. It looks as though---. I mean, we are starting to fear the worst."

"Disappeared? How can she have disappeared?" But I was prepared for almost anything. For with Sylvia almost anything was possible.

"We're not certain, Terry. I haven't been able to go out to Florida to find out for myself. I only know what Carlos, her husband has told us." She paused. "Things have been very difficult here since Jan became ill." She seemed to be searching for the right words. Her voice faded and a long silence followed. I listened to the empty sound of the telephone lines, while I tried to absorb what she was saying. That was when she produced her show-stopping question. "Terry, are you still in love with my daughter?" I decided to ignore the question. The truth was I didn't know the answer any more.

"But what has happened," I asked. "How can she have disappeared?"

As I spoke I knew that if anyone could walk out on the luxurious life she had created for herself, it would be Sylvia. Impulsive and unpredictable had been her whole life-story. Well, when I knew her, unpredictable was an understatement. She drank heavily and her best friend, if she had one, would have admitted that she was more than a little unstable. Once we had gone on a memorable trip to Spain, and for the first time I saw some of her problems at close range. Not that she recognised it as a problem of course. But dry martini cocktails,

5

followed by a couple of bottles of wine at dinner was more than I could handle, at least on a regular basis.

Of course some people are nice drunks. But Sylvia became aggressive and very unreasonable-- and at that stage she didn't need much to top her up. There had been embarrassing scenes here and there and we were actually asked to leave a couple of restaurants. Well, we were thrown out really. On one occasion I walked out and left her sitting alone when she started acting up. After that the relationship really went downhill. At that point I remembered the old adage: never go to bed with a woman who has more troubles than you. So in the end we went our separate ways.

After that I heard she had settled down a bit. She married and moved to America. I saw her briefly one summer on one of her fleeting visits to Europe and she seemed happy enough then. That had been three or four years ago. But four years of marriage was probably enough for Sylvia.

I knew that before I met her she had spun out of control through two marriages, bailed out each time by her rich father. Along the way she had acquired a baby daughter, also called Sylvia. The child had come from her first marriage, to a Spanish officer from an old, traditional family of aristocrats who had been on the right side, in every sense, in their civil war. Sylvia must have been little more than a child herself at that time, seventeen or eighteen, and I could well imagine how she must have enchanted them. Young, beautiful and precocious--- and with money. She must have seemed ideal. But the conventions and the constraints of upper-class, rural Spanish life had driven her frantic. Sylvia must have been quite a shock for them too. Fortunately Daddy, shrewd old Dutchman, had made sure the wedding was in England, so that

6

when she ran, taking her baby daughter with her, it had been possible to arrange a divorce. The husband was furious of course and Spanish law had never recognised the divorce, which created problems over the child. But then Sylvia and problems were rarely strangers.

For me life with her had been an extra-ordinary experience, a flash of brilliance. Everything about her had seemed larger than life, like a movie in gaudy technicolour. But in the end it became just too exciting for me and so I kissed her goodbye. Could she really be gone forever?

Mrs van Eck went on, "I don't know the details, Terry. But it appears there was a sailing accident in the Gulf of Mexico. She is very fond --she was fond of sailing, as you know."

Sylvia was a superb yachtswoman. "When did this happen?" I asked.

"About six weeks ago. She vanished off the boat, in the dark one night."

"Six weeks! And there has been no word?" I said.

"No," said Mrs. van Eck quickly."Nothing. Not a word. We didn't know what to think. We have been waiting and hoping--- just hoping you know, that she had decided to go on a spree. You know how--- unpredictable she can be. But I suppose we must face the facts now."

I muttered something vaguely consoling. "Thank you," she said, sadly. Then her voice changed and she went on firmly, "Apart from the shock, Sylvia's disappearance has given me some practical problems with the business. You know about the company she has been running? The one she and I set up together?"

I thought back to what Sylvia had told me. "Yes." I hesitated, "You're in the art market, I believe. Tribal art --very fashionable I understand."

"That's correct. The company is called Ethnic Art Inc. and we, well Sylvia really, has built up a reasonable business. Turnover is almost three million dollars now".

I was impressed. She continued. "We have three galleries; Brussels, San Francisco and Boston and Sylvia has been planning another one in London." She added sadly. "The problem is that without her I don't think there is anyone capable of running the business. That's why I thought of you, Terry. I really need some assistance."

"What about Carlos? Can't her husband help?"

"Oh Carlos has his own business interests," she said dismissively. "And he doesn't seem to be interested in the art scene; though he has been helpful, up to a point." She paused. "I'm the principal shareholder you see. But Sylvia has handled everything. It was really her baby." She gave a strange little laugh and her voice trailed away. "Terry, what I'd really like is for you to take a look at the whole situation for me. Meet the people involved and tell me what I should do with the business." She paused. "If you're free, that is."

I took a deep breath. Well, I was free. But her very first question had really unsettled me--- and I wasn't even sure I wanted to find out the answer. "Well, I have to tell you that I don't know anything about the art business,' I said. "And this could be an expensive way to learn, for you I mean, at six hundred pounds a day, plus expenses. And it sounds as if there could be a lot of travel involved."

She interrupted me. "Oh, don't worry about that. Money doesn't matter, Terry. I really need help; help from someone I can trust. Look, will you come and see me at least? I'm afraid I can't get away from here. Sylvia's father is very ill. But I do need to give you more background."

Call me an old softy but I always begin to concentrate when a client says money doesn't matter. So I concentrated very hard. "You're still at the same place?" I said.

"Yes, " she said." We're in the same house in Vinkiveen. Of course you've been here. I'd forgotten." I let that pass, though it seemed unlikely that Helen van Eck had forgotten. "How soon can you come?"

"Let me call you back when I've checked on the flights."

"I believe there's a flight to Amsterdam every day from Edinburgh," she said. She gave an embarrassed little laugh, "I took the liberty of checking before I called you. I suppose I knew you'd help."

"Oh," I said." "In that case there shouldn't be a problem. I'm sorry to hear about your husband. Is the situation serious?"

"He had a severe stroke. Although his mind is still unaffected, thank god. Terry, you will come, won't you? It will be such a relief to know I can count on you. It's all so awful. "

CHAPTER 2

We were driving through the flat countryside of the polders, surrounded by views like a Van Meier landscape -- well manicured little fields, low hedges, freshly painted cows and dark church steeples with the occasional clump of rounded trees. Overhead was an over-arching expanse of translucent pearl-like sky. I had been met at Schiphol Airport by a uniformed driver and within minutes we were on the motorway, heading into the network of well maintained back roads and canals around the more expensive suburbs of Amsterdam.

The driver was a big, powerfully-built Dutch man, almost an archetype, with fair hair, blue eyes, square headed and strong boned. I thought he looked much as Jan van Eck must have looked as a young man. He wore a formal dark grey blazer and trousers, peaked black cap with a badge, and black leather gloves. In the rear view mirror I eventually worked out the initials "UCG" on the badge. He was very respectful. He offered to take my brief-case, held open the rear door of the big black Mercedes and maintained a discrete silence for most of the journey. But once I caught him scrutinising me carefully in the mirror. He'd certainly know me again, that was for sure.

As the car pulled up in front of the house I studied the building, trying to remember when I had been last there. It was a modern house, probably 1960's in construction and built of brick, wood, glass and steel, rising in a tall triangular gable, three floors high, with the slope of the slate-covered roof reaching almost to the ground. The entire frontage seemed to be of glass, with a huge drop of curtains within. Further back the house was lower -- onlytwo floors in height and on each side of the central apex were wings that curved away from the road like a Zulu impi. With all that glass and steel I hoped the central heating worked.

By one side of the enormous front door there stood the stone statue of an oriental-looking dog. Or maybe it was a lion. Richly carved and exotic, it seemed out of place in this ultra-modern setting. I guessed it was Indonesian; probably acquired by Sylvia's father on one of his business trips --the Dutch still had a strong presence in their former colonies. The driver gave me my case, rang a door bell that echoed in the depth of the house, touched the peak of his cap and took the car away round the corner of the house.

While I waited for something to happen I bent down and patted the little lion on the head. "Good boy," I said to it. "It's all right. I'm a friend of the family. "I straightened up, realising that the front door had opened. A middle-aged woman in a housekeepers black dress was staring at me.

"Good morning," I said, trying to pretend that I hadn't been speaking to a stone lion. "My name is Lennox. Mrs.van Eck is expecting me." The housekeeper opened the door wide and stood well back. She had a worried frown on her face and looked deeply unconvinced.

Inside was a deep hall that soared the full height of the building, like the nave of a cathedral. The floor was gleaming black slate, covered by about a dozen or more silk Afghan rugs that looked too valuable to walk on. The walls had a stark white finish on rough natural stone. Here and there, in recesses, were glass display cases, each with a single object, artistically arranged and illuminated.

Most of the objects looked African to me, darkly primitive images that were human in origin; figures and masks. But so strangely stylised that to European eyes the humanity had been twisted into something threatening and fearful. And yet, in this setting, as works of art at least, they were powerful and strangely beautiful.

Here and there between the recesses the plain walls were hung with paintings of the modern school. I thought I recognised some of the best living Scottish artists –Michie, Bellany and what might have been a John Houston. Above, at the level of the second floor, a long gallery with a stone balustrade ran on three sides of the house and opened into the upper rooms.

The housekeeper led me the length of the hall. It struck me that it would make a good badminton court but I decided not to confide the thought to her. She opened a pair of double doors and motioned me into a sitting room that ran across the rear of the house. Facing me was a wall of glass, hung with long drapes and looking out onto immaculately trimmed grass that stretched about fifty yards down to the edge of the water. The room disappear into the distance on either side, the space broken by little islands of expensive looking leather chairs and settees. At each end I could just see huge open fireplaces. There were more pictures on the walls. I wondered about the insurance premiums. Maybe I was under pricing myself at six hundred a day.

As my eyes adjusted to the bright light, a small slim figure rose gracefully from a bureau by the window where she had been working on some papers. "Terry," she said warmly. " How good of you to come".

CHAPTER 3

She floated across the room to meet me, as elegant as a young girl. The hair was greying now but beautifully groomed and her complexion at first glance still flawless. Her eyes, like her daughter's, were her most striking feature, with arching eyebrows and almost oriental in shape, the deepest brown in colour. The gaze was steady and cool. The glittering intensity of Sylvia was missing but the impact was immediate and strong.

Helen van Eck wore a simple scooped necked dress of very pale cream knitted silk. It looked as if it might have come from one of the top Japanese designers and probably cost a week's fees at my usual rate. It was loosely gathered at her waist by an open weave green belt tied in a casual knot. As she approached, I noticed that the green was echoed at her slender throat in a splash of colour from a necklace of large pieces of jade, each elaborately carved. I guessed the necklace cost about a year of my time.

She smiled and held out her hand. As I took it, she stretched up and lightly kissed my cheek. Even this close she looked more like late 40's than the late 60's I knew she must be.

"Thank you, "she said, with polished sincerity."I'm so glad to see you again ---it's been years, hasn't it?" I felt like a guest being received at a society wedding. But beneath the effortless charm I sensed there was a tension. "What a shame it has taken a tragedy like this to bring us together again," she went on smoothly.

My clients rarely kiss me, even at the start of an assignment and I realised I was having trouble getting into business mode, in spite of her practised warmth. "You are certain," I asked quietly, "that it is a tragedy?"

She gestured to a low table, surrounded by soft armchairs. On it was a tray of sandwiches and coffee cups. "I thought we might have a sandwich lunch while we talk." she said. "I'd love to talk longer but I'm afraid I must be in The Hague later this afternoon for a UCG board meeting." Otherwise, she implied, she would have chosen to spend the afternoon chatting to me about old times.

Only then she gave me a sad little smile. "Yes, I really fear something terrible has happened. Since Jan has been ill --". She shrugged her slim shoulders, "I've had to spend so much time helping with our business interests, I'm afraid I rather lost contact with Sylvia. Now--- I just don't know what to do. I'm hoping you will help."

"I'm sorry about your husband --please give him my regards."

"Perhaps you'd like to give him your regards in person. I think he'd like to see you. He was always a great admirer of yours." She glanced down at her watch. "We all were." she added automatically. That wrong footed me. For it certainly hadn't been my impression at the time. "Yes, I'm sure we have time." She stood up. "I'll take you through to see him--- he spends most of the day in our solarium, resting. He likes to look out at the water." She paused. "Don't expect too much, Terry. You may be shocked when you see him. He often finds it difficult to communicate. It's such a strain."

I didn't know whether she meant for him or for her. "And now there's Sylvia," I said.

"Yes, Sylvia." She looked at me silently. "It's been a nightmare, these past few months."

She led me through a small dark door in the corner of the room and along a corridor that ran down the west side of the house. Like the sitting room, the corridor was floored with light oak boards and littered with expensive rugs. The interior walls were white rough-cast and hung with more paintings ---mostly expensive old Dutch seascapes. The outer wall was glass from floor to ceiling.

At the end of the corridor we went through a set of double doors of heavy dark teak and into a rectangular room built onto the end of the wing. Its three external walls and roof were made entirely of glass, and the light level was brilliant. The room itself was a mass of greenery, with plants and flowers growing up and across the inside of the roof. Along the tops of the outside walls were electric heaters and in spite of the warmth of the day they were switched on.

The heat and humidity hit me like a wet towel. The intense light from the sky, the wide, unrestricted expanse of grass and water outside and the mass of greenery inside made the scene strangely exotic. In the furthest corner I saw a hunched figure in a wheel chair.

"I'll tell Jan you are here," Mrs.van Eck said quietly. "Then I'll leave you with him." She wrinkled her elegant nose. "I can't stand it in here. Meet me back in the sitting room when you're ready." She went forward to the old man and kissed him lightly on the forehead. "Terry Lennox is here, Jan." She said clearly and slowly. "He's going to help us with Sylvia's business."

In spite of her warning I was shocked to see van Eck. I remembered him as a big man --a heavy boned, square headed powerful old Frieslander who had seemed indestructible. Now, huddled under a rug in spite of the intense heat, he looked frail and shrunken. I could see his hands, thin and gaunt, gripping the arms of the chair. They were not the strong, workman like hands I remembered. "He tires easily." said Mrs.van Eck softly, and left us together.

The old man slowly turned his head. His eyes were unchanged, as blue and sharp as ever, but sunk in hollows in his skull-like face. He nodded slowly, indicating a cane chaise-longue beside him. I took off my jacket and sat down. I could feel the sweat trickling under my shirt. A faint smile flickered across his wasted face. He nodded again, this time towards a low table with some bottles of beer floating in a bucket of half melted ice. In another bucket stood a bottle of Dutch Geneva gin, also ice cold.

"For you?" I enquired.

He shook his head impatiently and I had a sense of the man's old strength of purpose. "Ring the bell," he said hoarsely, gesturing to a push button on the wall.

I leaned across and pressed the brass button and in a moment or two a young man in a white jacket came in. He looked Philipino and he was carrying a wicker tray. On it was a fine Chinese bowl full of cream and brown speckled eggs, slightly smaller than hens eggs. There was also a couple of delicate ceramic plates and a dish of coarse sea salt. He looked at us in a slightly conspiratorial way, his dark eyes askance.

"Patrice knows I'm not supposed to have these. But he's a good lad." Van Eck nodded to the eggs. "Seagulls," he said. "Hard boiled. Peel a couple. Then press them flat in the salt. Good with ice cold Geneva. And a cold beer to wash them down. Not good for me, they tell me."

I did as he had said, dropping the thin shells into a wastebasket. Then I carefully pressed the eggs down into the salt. They were curious in texture, firm with a slightly blue-tinted white and a very strong orange coloured yoke. But they held together nicely under pressure and were soon coated with the coarse sea salt.

I poured out two glasses of the Dutch gin and pushed one over to van Eck. Then I held out the plate. Carefully he picked up an egg and took it to his mouth. He chewed it slowly and a look of delight flitted over his grizzled face. He picked up the glass of gin and downed it in a single gulp.

I followed his example, chewing the egg tentatively. It wasn't at all bad. Strong tasting, with a definite sense of the sea; salt and sea-weed and it went down really well with the Geneva. Van Eck smiled at me. "Don't tell Helen," he said. "I'm not allowed these now. But they are good, no?"

"Good, yes," I said, repeating the process with another pair of eggs. He waived away the gin this time and instead I opened a bottle of pilsner and poured the contents into a tall glass. The outside of the glass beaded instantly with condensation in the steamy heat of the solarium. He shook his head but watched greedily as I raised the glass to him and took a mouthful of the cold bitter beer. I caught his eye and his face twisted in another half smile. It felt vaguely voyeuristic.

"Mr. van Eck," I said, "I'm sorry to hear of your difficulties." He jerked his head silently, almost angrily. "Of course I'll do what I can to help with Sylvia's company. But is there anything else I can do?"

He ran his tongue across his lips. I wondered if he was thinking about the beer. With a great effort he whispered something I barely heard. The effort was obviously tiring him. I leaned closer to him. "I'm sorry---," I started to say.

"Sylvia," he struggled, still scarcely audible even so close to me.

"Yes," I said, "Sylvia's company --." Again the old man shook his head, more violently this time.

"No," he whispered fiercely. "The Utrecht Group." He fell back into the wheel chair, his eyes closed.

I sat beside him for several minutes, sipping my beer in the heat and humidity, slowly dripping sweat into my clothes. I tried to speak to him again but he seemed to be asleep, his thin shoulders rising and falling regularly.

I rose quietly to leave. He must have heard me moving for his

eyes opened and he fixed me with a stare. He muttered
something. Leaning forward, I heard him whisper hoarsely,
"Being ruined," he muttered. "Not her company. Got to do
something." He slumped back.

"Yes, I know it's not Sylvia's company." I said reassuringly,
wondering exactly what was worrying him. His eyes stayed
closed. He gave his head a tired shake but he didn't speak
again.

I made my way back into the main part of the house. Mrs.van
Eck was sitting in the long sitting room, speaking Dutch on the
telephone. I had forgotten how talented she was. When she was
with me she seemed so completely English. She finished her
conversation and came over to join me.

"How was he?"She asked.

"Well, it was a shock, as you warned me. He seems to be a bit
confused." I said. "But tell me about Sylvia."

"I don't think there's much I can add to what I told you on the
telephone. Sylvia has simply vanished," she said bluntly. "She
disappeared from the house in Florida two months ago and
hasn't been seen since.

"And no one has heard from her?"

"Not a word," said Mrs.van Eck. "It seems she took one of the
boats out after dark one evening--."

"Alone?" I interrupted.

"Yes. Apparently she was accustomed to sailing alone; she

often went out on hot nights when she had trouble sleeping. The water was calm, with no wind to speak of." Mrs.van Eck paused while the female housekeeper brought our coffee. "But she didn't come back. The boat was towed back in next day by some tourists on an over-night fishing trip. They said they found it drifting about ten miles down the coast. The inflatable was still on board. It's a complete mystery. "

"Any sign of trouble? Was there any damage to the boat?"

She shook her head, "No, nothing."

I decided not to ask about tides or where a body might turn up along that coast. "It was in the Gulf?" I said. She nodded. "Yes. Near the house at Siesta Key." The name meant nothing to me. We sat in silence, trying to avoid the obvious conclusion.

"And there has been no word of any kind? Not even a ransom message?" She looked at me strangely and shook her head again. "And you haven't reported it to the police yet?" My obvious surprise seemed to sting her.

"I know you probably think that's strange," she went on hurriedly. "But you know what Sylvia can be like. At first we thought it was one of her sudden impulses. Just the kind of crazy, irresponsible thing she would do." There was a note of suppressed anger in her voice. She drew in her breath in a sort of half sigh and looked at me appealingly."You have no idea how difficult she can be," she said.

Oh yes I do, I thought.

"Sometimes I think ---." She stopped and shook her head."Of course we shall have to report it soon; if she doesn't show up somewhere."

"Did she take anything with her?" I asked.

Mrs.van Eck looked at me curiously. "What do you mean?"

"Well, passport, a change of clothes; that sort of thing."

"Oh, " she said, "I see. I don't really know. Carlos would know. Carlos is her husband. I don't think you know him." she added sweetly.

"No." I said "Do you have any reason to think that it wasn't an accident--any idea why Sylvia might want to walk out on everything; the marriage, the house, the business?"

"Mrs.van Eck looked at me steadily; her head tilted slightly, a little smile."That's just the thing," she said. "Would any of that be so very much out of character?"

I thought for a moment. "How was the marriage? No, forget that," I added hastily.

Mrs. van Eck smiled at me. She leaned across and patted my hand." It's a perfectly fair question, Terry, knowing Sylvia as you do. But as far as I know things were---," she hesitated," all right. But perhaps no more than all right, if you know what I mean. And of course recently she has had little Sylvia living with her. Since she finished college in Switzerland at Christmas."

She looked at me, her eyes serious." You know that my girls haven't seen much of each other; hardly anything at all while little Sylvia was growing up."

Thanks mainly to you, I thought silently.

She sighed. "They've never really hit it off somehow. Not as I should have liked them to do." She lowered her eyes.. "My daughter has many fine qualities, Terry. But Jan and I felt she wouldn't have been able to cope with a young child; not at that age. But even quite recently she seems to have had, well, no real maternal feelings."

She shook her head, sadly. "You see, we wanted her to be free of commitments; free to enjoy her young life. Maybe we were wrong about that." It was the first time I had heard Helen van Eck hint at a mistake."Of course it meant that Jan and I had virtually another child to bring up." She smiled. "Luckily we have been able to give them both a lot of advantages. But it's sad that the girls have never been close." She looked at me. "It is odd. But in some ways they acted more like rivals. Isn't that strange." She gave a nervous little laugh.

I had always thought the arrangement was unhealthy. I watched the pretty little girl treat her grandmother as her mother and behaving as if Sylvia was a friend or an older sister, all the time competing for attention and favours and I used to wonder at the emotional impact of it on all of them. I had some idea of the cost to Sylvia. It probably explained a lot---to be cast permanently in the role of child; never allowed to grow up and to take on her own responsibilities. Poor Sylvia, I thought.

"But they had seemed to be getting along so well together recently. To begin with, we wondered how wise it would be. But little Sylvia was anxious to spend some time out there with ---her mother." She sat bolt upright in her seat and looked at me sternly. "So I think it must be just what it looks like. Sylvia

23

must have had an accident of some kind. But we have to keep hoping, I suppose."

Suddenly she was all business. "However," she said, "in the meantime I really need your help with Sylvia's company. You see there simply isn't anyone around to look after things, now she is gone. As you can imagine, I have my hands full looking after Jan and his interests at the construction group."

She paused," It's particularly difficult now, as you will know, with recession almost everywhere. Projects have been delayed or cancelled in several of our markets. I try to keep in touch with our executives world-wide --wc've brought in a few new people, introduced some new ventures, and moved into new business areas that need close watching. And of course I do what I can with client entertaining and that sort of thing." She added casually, "Since Jan became ill I am acting as President of the group. It is quite a challenge." She gave me a smile that indicated she could probably handle it.

I was impressed. I knew the van Ecks had a substantial stake in UCG. But it was a big public company with some prestigious outside shareholders such as investment groups and other financial institutions. Old man van Eck had however dominated the business; he created it and built it up from scratch, by hard work and typical Dutch frugality. In the process he had earned a reputation for honesty and probity in an industry where that was not always so common. It would not be easy for Helen van Eck to maintain that kind of reputation and control.

I tried to recall what I knew about the company. Utrecht Construction Group had begun at home in the Netherlands, rebuilding after the war and then had developed overseas, initially in Indonesia and the Far East. Recently I had heard that they had moved into Africa, working with various governments on schemes for oil related infrastructure projects, using their experience in the off-shore European oil industry. At one stage that had been a highly profitable market, where price was secondary to delivery and quality. Now, with recession and lower oil prices things would be much tougher.

There would be even more top level wheeling and dealing, keeping political and business contacts warm, smoothing the path for the formal contract negotiations. From what I had heard about business in some of those countries, the old man could scarcely have enjoyed some of the things that had to be done. Still, by now the group must be turning over several hundred million pounds of sales. I looked at Helen van Eck with new interest. I remembered that her family background in England had been money, with both her father and her grandfather involved in banking. So she had the right pedigree.

"I have some information for you about the company," she said briskly. "Sylvia and I set up really just to give her something to do originally; a focus, you know. She took an interest in tribal art when she went to live in America. I thought it was just a fad. But she threw herself into it totally. You know how enthusiastic she can be." Mrs.van Eck looked at me a little wistfully. "It has amazed me how much the business has grown; how well she has done."

She handed me a bundle of glossy brochures, with photographs of exotic looking objects, all stylishly displayed. "These are the sort of things she buys and sells."

I glanced through the photographs. "You mentioned that turnover is around $3million." I said. "Where do you find this kind of material? And who do you sell to? And how?" I looked apologetically at her, "I did say that I didn't know much about this business."

"But you'll pick it up quickly, Terry." She smiled at me. "I know how you work. And of course I don't really know much about the business either. That is just the problem. I left things very much to Sylvia. I simply provided some initial cash for the start up the company. She wanted me to be chairman but really it's been her show. She did everything; opened galleries and show rooms, recruited staff who seem to know the art market. Then she set about learning from them. You know how clever she can be. She spent a lot of time building up contacts and promoting the company. Some of her openings made quite a splash in the society art world. Of course Jan and I were able to help her with potential clients; people we know who are collectors. But really she has done most of it herself."

Mrs.van Eck was in full flight now and I let her go on. "Mostly I think she bought from other dealers. That seems to be the way it's done. There are all types of specialists, experts in various fields,--Africa, Polynesia, North American Indian and so on." Suddenly she seemed surprisingly well informed. "I do know Sylvia was essentially aiming up-market, going for quality. And as you know she had friends and acquaintances all over the world --wealthy people who might be customers."

I noted the past tense. She continued. "I believe her husband was of help too. He has been a source of financial advice at least. He is technically a director, although he says he was never involved in day to day matters. He has his own business interests in food and wine importation and some shipping activities. She went on. "He arranged for Sylvia to have a local accountant in Florida and put her in touch with someone to provide legal advice. He helped her raise additional finance at one stage. But nothing more."

"Is Carlos a shareholder, "I asked.

"No. Not at all." she said sharply. "Sylvia and I own the business between us." I looked through the papers she had given me. "Can you let me have a set of accounts at some stage?" I asked. "I don't see one here."

"All I have here are some rather old accounts almost two years out of date. You should speak to the accountant. Carlos will put you in touch with him. I suggest you contact Carlos."

"Mrs.van Eck---" She leaned forward earnestly."Please, Terry, call me Helen."

"Helen," I said. "What exactly is it you want me to do?"

"The immediate problem is to find someone to manage the business in Sylvia's absence. We have to continue to buy objects, decide on selling prices, authorise payments, deal with staff, all the usual day-to- day things."

"Perhaps one of the existing staff could take over, until the situation is clarified. Until we are sure what really has happened to Sylvia"

She looked at me with a strange little smile."Terry, I think we have to assume the worst. Perhaps you will learn more when you meet Carlos. But meanwhile I simply don't know enough about the company or the people to make any kind of sensible decision. That's why I need your help. I have so much to deal with here" she said, gesturing around her vaguely. "And I know

27

it's the sort of thing you do well." She looked at me helplessly.

I tried to look modest.

"I'd be grateful if you would meet the staff and make your assessment of them; let me know what they can contribute to the business." She hesitated. I knew there was more to come. "Also it would be useful to have your view of how the business is placed. I wonder for example if we really need all the galleries. They must be very expensive." I nodded and she went on. "But you're quite right. Ideally I should appoint someone on an acting basis until we know how things are. Until we know what really has happened to Sylvia. You see, if she has gone for good I might want to take a very different approach to the business."

Suddenly she was the sorrowing mother again. "There may be no point in going on," she said sadly. Then she paused. "In any case," she ended briskly, "if I do decide to sell I'd like to have your opinion about how to dispose of the company and what it might be worth. Does that make sense?"

I had to say it made a lot of sense. If it hadn't been for the circumstances, it would have been a pleasure deal with a client like Mrs.van Eck and I said as much. Then I glanced at my watch. "Why don't I take this information away and study it. I can drop you a note later in the week with my thoughts on how I can help, and how much it is likely to cost you."

Helen van Eck put her hand on my arm, leaning towards me. She lowered her voice. "Terry," she said, "I have complete confidence in you. I understand that you want to do everything very professionally. And I appreciate that." She smiled at me sweetly. "But let me make myself quite clear. I need you to take this problem off my hands and as quickly as possible. It will be such a relief to know that I can count on you." She straightened up. "So I'd like you to make arrangements to see these people as soon as possible." She pointed to the papers in front of her. "You have a list of their names, addresses and telephone numbers and any personal information we have on them."

I started to speak but she held up her hand and pushed a cheque across the table. "I know it's going to be an expensive exercise, but within reason money is not an issue. I took the liberty of preparing a cheque for you. This is an initial retainer to cover your expenses.

It was drawn on her personal account at an exclusive private bank in London and if I needed any convincing the number of noughts made up my mind for me. I picked up the cheque and glanced at it to confirm that it was actually in pounds sterling. Then I folded it carefully into my wallet.

"Look, Mrs.van Eck---"

"Helen," she insisted.

"Helen," I said obediently, "I will of course do what I can to help. Let's just hope that none of this will be necessary and that Sylvia will turn up safe and sound."

"I can't tell you how much I hope she does," said Mrs van Eck sincerely. "Perhaps you will be my lucky charm." She leaned forward towards me." But I do want you involved as quickly as possible," she stressed. "How soon can you get out to the States?"

I took a deep breath. "Well, if I rearrange a few things ---" That meant a dental appointment I wanted to miss anyway and a visit to the gym that I needed but could do without.

"You should see the Brussels gallery first" she said firmly. "Book yourself onto a flight to Brussels from Edinburgh"

"Sure." I said. It was obvious my mind had been made up for me." I'll call you from Edinburgh and let you know my plans. But I think I can get to the States this week-end, via Brussels."

"That's wonderful, Terry." She rose and rang for the housekeeper. "Just one thing, please." She smiled at me. "Do be sure to let me know where you are at all times. I'd like to feel that I can contact you if I need you."

As we walked across the echoing hall towards the front door I asked her how much she had invested in Ethnic Art Inc. "I gave Sylvia about 1.5million Dutch guilders as initial equity---for premises and stock and so on. And I understand that she has some additional bank borrowings. But Carlos or his accountant will give you the details. She took my hand. "Thank you so much, Terry." she said. "You have no idea how much this means to me. But do please keep in touch."

Then I was on my way back to the airport. Half a million pounds to keep Sylvia amused, I thought. I would have been cheaper---if only I had been able to stand the strings that came attached to the deal. But maybe Mrs.van Eck knew what she was doing. She seemed a woman who usually did.

CHAPTER 4

Two days later I had decided who were the possible candidates, agreed my programme with Mrs.van Eck and was on an early morning flight to Brussels, en route for Florida. As assignments go, it seemed straightforward enough. Certainly, she seemed a touch obsessive about needing to know exactly where I would be and how she could contact me. But clients are like that sometimes; afraid that if they don't hear from you every day you're off lying on the beach. Or working on another assignment. Not that it hasn't been known.

My first stop would be the Ethnic Art gallery in the square of the Grand Sablon in Brussels, where I had arranged to meet a man called Paul Friden. According to my information Friden was an Austrian national who ran the set up in Brussels. I wasn't sure what I'd get from him, but he seemed a likely candidate with good international experience. The other contenders were Americans; Jerry Prescott in San Francisco and Dave Wilson, who managed the gallery in Boston. On paper they all three seemed well qualified, with academic credentials and experience in the art world. How good they were commercially was another matter. That I would have to find out.

I had decided that Carlos, the husband, sounded as if he would be the best starting point in America. He had clearly been an influence on Sylvia, so far as the business was concerned, and I hoped he could tell me more about the financial background to the company. I suppose too, if I was honest, I had more personal reasons for wanting to meet the latest of Sylvia's husbands, if only to find out more about her disappearance. It seemed strange to me that an experienced sailor like Sylvia could disappear from a boat she knew well, in calm weather and familiar waters. Which left me with some disturbing thoughts. Had she been drinking--- and had she really been alone? Would Carlos know? And would he tell me? These were questions without answers, at least for the moment. It was a waste of time to speculate, so I put them on hold and concentrated on some useful thoughts.

The first thing I needed to find out was what the business was about and how it should be managed. When I told Mrs.van Eck I knew nothing about the art business it wasn't just my usual modesty. I had a lot to learn. That, of course, was nothing new. Finding your way through unknown territory is how an assignment usually starts. Either it's a trackless desert, where you have to dig for every drop of information or else you're swamped with a morass of confused detail that seems to lead nowhere. But sooner or later the way forward becomes clear. It has to, otherwise the client doesn't pay you.

What bothered me most was that so far I didn't have any useful financial information about the business. Not that this was so unusual either. Clients like to keep their cards close to their chests, even when you're supposed to be helping them. All the agendas are not always on the table. Even so, Mrs.van Eck had been surprisingly vague. Maybe she had other things on her mind.

From Brussels airport I took the train into the Gare Central. Meeting Friden would at least give me a chance to pick up some background and the jargon of the trade before I had to meet Carlos and the others. Too late as usual, I thought of people I might have consulted before getting this far into the unknown. There were people on the fringe of the art markets who might have briefed me on the scene. I made a mental note to contact one of them, a woman at the museum in Edinburgh who was actually an authority on tribal art. But Helen van Eck had left me little time for preliminaries.

Brussels was a town I knew quite well and the Grand Sablon was close at hand as I walked out of the terminal and down the Boulevard de L'Empereur. I went past the steps up to the Musee des Belles Arts and turned left up a steep narrow street that opened suddenly into the wide Place du Grand Sablon. Ringed by medieval buildings, mostly converted into slightly less than fashionable shops, galleries and cafes, the square had a down-at-heel charm. The address put the Ethnic Art gallery just behind the massive Eglise de Notre Dame that dominates the top end of the Grand Sablon.

I made my way across the cobbles. The gallery was in a heavily restored old building that had acquired a stylish modern facade, with big plate glass windows in which a few choice objet d'art were displayed. I didn't know what they were but they reminded me of the objects I had seen in the entrance hall at the house in Vinkiveen.

Some were grotesquely shaped human groups, female figures

33

with pendulous breasts and disproportionately long upper legs. Some were masks, carved or painted with elongated and strangely inhuman features. One or two looked like metal castings, probably of bronze, with fine detailing that any of my clients in the foundry industry would have been proud to produce.

I pushed open the door and went in. A tall well-built youngish man, probably in his mid-thirties rose from his seat at a small antique desk set in the corner of the brightly lit room. He had a shock of fair, untidy hair, a fresh open face, wide mouth with slightly coarse lips and a broad ,high forehead. He beamed at me, his eyes blue, large and emotional behind horn-rimmed spectacles. He wore corduroy slacks, with a checked cotton shirt and a plain knitted tie and a cut of tweed sports jacket that looked British but was fashioned and fashionable in Milan and Paris.

This was Paul Friden. He immediately whisked me round the gallery, pouring out information about the objects on display. In minutes I was reeling under a torrent of exotic names; Chokwe masks, Hemba figures, Yombe fly whisks. From time to time I managed to stop him long enough to ask a question. Most of the material was African, much of it from West Africa.

"The Europeans carved states out of different ancient tribal communities, more or less ad hoc." he explained, "And usually quite violently." He looked at me solemnly "Colonialism." he said. His English was perfect, almost too perfect in fact, with the purity of pronunciation that only a foreigner bothers to achieve. His enthusiasm for his subject was obvious. Eventually I persuaded him to sit down and show me his sales figures. He seemed to lose some of his enthusiasm at that stage.

"Oh," he said, his blue eyes widening. "No one tells me anything about the business, not officially anyway." I could just detect a trace of a central European accent now. "I have an MBA in finance and marketing," he said peevishly, "but I'm never told what is going on."

"What about monthly accounts?" I asked. He shook his head.

"So what information do you have to supply to the people in the States?" I made the question deliberately vague.

He laughed. "Mr Lennox, it doesn't seem to be that kind of a business. I don't know what the accountants are supposed to do over there. It isn't like a proper company, with reports and accounts and business plans."

"So who authorises purchases?"

"I do," he said. "Or Sylvia. It's all very informal. If it's African tribal material I can spend up to about $100,000. And usually I am consulted, if Sylvia or one of the others comes across something interesting in my area of expertise." He looked at me and grimaced. "Not that it always works like that. She can be a law unto herself, at times." He shrugged. "But it works well enough between the others; Prescott in San Francisco, and Dave Wilson in Boston. We keep in touch. If I find anything Pacific, or Inuit, or Native American, I'd consult one of them, to see if they wanted to make the purchase." He shook his head. " But it's strange. The company seems to have money to burn."

"Who do you sell to, mostly?" I asked.

"That depends on the quality." Friden said. "If it's very good I have contacts in most of the European museums, public and private, like the Musee d'Afrique here in Brussels." He went on, "Also I keep a record of wealthy collectors. I know what might interest each of them. Also we hold exhibitions and receptions."

He waved his hands around. "Either here or, occasionally, at the house at Vinkeveen. It's all low key, but mostly they do buy, sooner or later." He hesitated, "Sylvia's family is well connected. So that helps. Industrialists, politicians and so on. Utrecht Construction does a lot of work overseas, in Africa as a matter of fact." He grimaced at me. "We seem to be putting on a show for some visiting Nigerians at the moment." He sounded disapproving. I decided to let it go.

"It's an interesting business," I said mechanically, waiting for him to relax," So what problems do you have?" I looked at him innocently.

"What do you mean?" He looked startled, his blue eyes widening.

"Well, you know," I said with a casual shrug," the kind of things that worry you. Poor sales, stocks too high, poor cash-flow, high property costs, theft and pilfering."

He looked thoughtful. "No, nothing like that. We don't sell much but we don't need to. Not with the cash these items generate. And stock doesn't appear to be a problem for anyone. Certainly no-one has complained." He glanced around. "Although, God knows, we have a lot of stuff here." He beamed happily at me "But it's as good as money in the bank."

He paused and leaned forward towards me, confidentially

"There is only thing I find annoying. The way the family move objects around. I have so little control over the stock that sometimes it's hard to know who's got what."

I must have looked puzzled. He went on, slightly awkwardly now. "Of course I realise Mrs.van Eck owns the business, so I suppose she can do anything she likes, at the end of the day. You see she often asks for some of the best pieces for the house at Vinkeveen --if she's entertaining someone they want to impress. "

He hesitated, "Of course usually the objects come back eventually. But occasionally she actually gives them away." He shook his head. "As gifts, to people she and her husband are doing business with; people they want to, well," he hesitated again, "to influence in some way. People who can help them in the business somehow." He shrugged." I suppose it's common enough in business. But it does make life difficult. And it's been getting worse. Since Mrs.van Eck has become more involved with the construction company."

Friden smiled at me a little ruefully "Still, it is her business isn't it? Her's and Sylvia's. How is Sylvia anyway? I haven't heard from her for weeks." Without waiting for a reply he plunged on. "But it's all a bit, well, unbusinesslike, if you know what I mean."

I nodded. It was beginning to sound as if Ethnic Art was being run as a hobby rather than a real business.

"And now Sylvia has started to do the same," Friden went on petulantly, encouraged by my silence. "In fact last time she was here she took away a valuable Benin bronze --a rare 15th century Princess Head."

"A princess head? "I asked. "What exactly is that?" Friden's eyes lit up behind his large spectacles. I could tell another lecture was on its way. "It's a very fine casting from an area known as Benin, that's part of Nigeria now. Produced by a process called the lost wax method, if you know what that is."

I indicated that I did know about the lost wax method of casting. Friden looked impressed for a moment. Then he went on. "When the first Europeans arrived in West Africa --they were Dutch or Portuguese traders in the 15th century, they found highly sophisticated civilisations there with well developed social structures. In some cases with advanced metal-working techniques."

"Such as the cire perdu method of casting?" I said.

"Exactly." Friden nodded."The Europeans were amazed -- the dark continent and all that sort of thing. There have been all kinds of theories to explain away the existence of such technology in societies we considered primitive." He laughed. "Everything from lost Roman legions to visitors from outer space. But the truth seems to be that these societies had developed the technologies indigenously."

"Fascinating." I said. For once I meant it, thinking of how difficult lost wax casting is even today, with modern chemical and heat control technology.

"Yes, isn't it," he said eagerly, "Some of the very finest castings are of human heads, made to commemorate members of the royal family. Decorations for the altar of a deceased Oba, or king, for example. They are beautiful objects in their own right --as works of art. And beautifully made, with incredibly fine detailing." He went across to a window . "Here, let me show you the quality of work were talking about."

Carefully, he lifted out a small group of figures, cast in metal and about nine inches high, on a flat base. The elaborate detailing on the clothing and head-dresses was remarkable, cast in a bronze-like metal with a dark patina of age."This is actually from lower Niger – of course," he said apologetically, "but it will give you an idea of the skill of the craftsmen." He gazed at it proudly. "But the altar heads are my favourites." He paused, "Especially the old ones."

"And you have one?"I asked. Friden nodded, his big eyes gleaming." Yes," he said, "A Princess Head ---the head of a young woman, almost certainly a high noblewoman or a Benin princess. Delicately cast, in very thin bronze, with a fineness of line, a realism in the face that makes it almost certain she was a real person. It is very special. We think it's extremely early Benin--probably from the earliest period of European contact, or even before."

"And valuable?" I enquired. Friden nodded," Very, very valuable. An elderly German lady from Hamburg called me one day out of the blue and said that she had found it in the attic of her father's house. He had just died and he had lived in that house all of his life and his father before him."

"But how would something like a princess head end up in Germany?" I asked.

"We think our bronze may have arrived in Germany with the old lady's grandfather. We know he worked in Africa, as a trader when he was a young man. He may have acquired it then."

"You mean he took it from a tomb?"I said .

He shrugged. "Well, possibly. Or he purchased it from someone who did. It was probably brought to the coast after a big European military campaign that was organised against Benin at the end of the 19th century. But we may never know for sure."

"How much is it worth?"

Friden shook his head. "It's hard to say, precisely. In one sense it is priceless. After all, it represents the artistic apex of a vanished culture--a culture that was deliberately destroyed by the Europeans. Who can say what that is worth?" He gazed at me intently. "There are literally only a handful of these fine bronzes known to exist. Mostly they are in museums. There's one in Berlin--a very fine example, and one in your National Museum in Edinburgh, as it happens. And there are one or two in museums in Lagos-- in some ways that is where they should be, of course. Oh, and in the United States. But they are all more recent examples--16th century the experts think and not so fine as ours. Our Princess Head is very special." He grinned at me proudly.

"So how much is it worth?" I persisted.

"To anyone collecting in that field? Perhaps half a million pounds. Or maybe even a million."

I whistled. "My God! What did you pay for it?"

Friden shifted uncomfortably. "I don't want you to think that I cheated the old lady. I explained to her exactly what I told you

40

about its value and importance. But she sold it to us for $300,000. She had no children or relatives left, and she doesn't seem to need the money." He paused, "I think she felt a little uncomfortable about how it had come into her family. I think the idea of her old grandfather storming into an African city, shooting down the natives, looting their temples and grave sites made her feel guilty."

"But $300,000 made her feel better?" I smiled.

Friden threw back his head and laughed. "Let's say it was an acceptable deal all round." He looked down at his hands."I may have said something to her about the Princess Head finding its way back home--into a collection in Nigeria."

"Is that really an option?"

Friden shrugged his shoulders. "Who can say? But anyway I don't have it to sell now."

"You mean, because Sylvia took it away?" I asked.

Friden looked puzzled. "Yes. It's odd. When Sylvia was here last--about two months ago-- she took it away with her. I understood that her mother, Mrs.van Eck, wanted it at Vinkiveen. I was annoyed, of course, because I had just circulated details to possible buyers. But she had a car and a driver with her---and the house is very secure. So I didn't worry too much. The van Ecks have a wonderful collection of art -- very valuable. Anyway, Sylvia took it away in a special carrying case."

I looked at him enquiringly. "So what's the problem?"

Friden looked uncomfortable. "It seems she didn't give it to her mother. I know that, because Mrs.van Eck telephoned me a few days later to ask me where the Princess Head was." He shifted uneasily. "She said she had asked Sylvia to tell me to take the bronze up to her. It was all a bit of a muddle," he said. "And now I can't seem to contact Sylvia. She's been very elusive these last few weeks." He laughed weakly.

"So half a million pounds worth of bronze has gone walk-about?" I said thoughtfully.

Friden looked at me in sudden surprise. "Oh, I'm sure there isn't a problem," he said hurriedly. "It's just a mix up between Sylvia and Mrs.van Eck. And that's not unusual, I can assure you!" He gave a nervous laugh. "Though I was a bit worried when I heard you were coming to ask me some questions. I know how anxious Mrs. van Eck is about it. She has some big shots coming from Nigeria and wants to show them something special from their heritage." He grinned at me wryly. "I believe it's supposed to convince them that Utrecht Construction is terribly concerned about the culture of the countries where they do business." He cocked his head sideways and smiled. "If you can believe that!"

I told him my visit had nothing to do with the Princess Head. Then, before I headed back to the airport, we walked together across the Grand Sablon to have lunch at a cafe I remembered. I asked him a few more questions but it was more for form than substance. For I had learned what I wanted to know. The investment in stock was colossal and Mrs.van Eck's initial equity of $500,000 would not have gone very far.

I wondered about the level of borrowings needed to finance stock at that level. I also wondered how those borrowings had been secured. I wondered about the slow sales and the poor cash-flow the company must have. I wondered about Sylvia and the missing Princess Head. Especially, I wondered about Mrs.van Eck--and why she had told me so little.

Then I left Friden and made my way back to the airport.

CHAPTER 5

The next seven hours or so went easily in business class on the flight from Brussels. There was time for a drink and a leisurely meal, and time to read a chapter or two of a book before dropping of into a couple of hours of restless sleep. I was half way through "A Distant Mirror" by Barbera Touchman, a dismal but fascinating account of 14th century Europe. It made depressing reading; plague, a war that lasted a hundred years and impoverished the survivors and a papal schism that crippled society. I looked out of the aircraft window at the sun on the white cloud tops and felt an irrational, secret delight creep over me. I was heading for the New World, where all would be bright and shining. Well, maybe.

It was afternoon when I arrived in Florida and very hot. With only hand baggage, I passed quickly through immigration and customs at Tampa International, collected a hire car and headed south over the soaring Sunshine Skyway toll bridge across the bay. Down the coast pelicans zoomed off the piles of the bridge like air borne prehistoric monsters. The early summer sun was high overhead, the air was heavy with salty humidity and I was glad to close the car windows and switch on the air conditioner.

On the map Siesta Key was a long sliver of land that ran down the Gulf coast just south of Sarasota. It and a string of others like it, mostly sand and concrete, sheltered dozens of bays, anchorages and inland waterways that were the playgrounds for millions escaping the cold of northern United States and Europe. In certain secluded areas there were the private beaches of the well-heeled. It was down at the lower end of the Key that Carlos di Giorgio and Sylvia lived.

The drive down US41 was relatively quiet, once the congestion of central Sarasota was cleared and after about half an hour I turned off the highway onto a low shipbridge over the channel and then south down Siesta Key. The road was a leafy-lined pleasant blacktop, through a dense wood which on each side hid exclusive housing developments and scattered large private houses.

For a time, here and there were big gaudily coloured hotels and condominiums fronting onto the popular beaches but as I drove on these became less frequent and I realised that the land was narrowing rapidly. Soon I was on a road called Midnight Pass, almost at the tip of the Key, and now I could see glimpses of water on each side, gleaming through the lush greenery. Mrs van Eck had told me to look for a house called Pelican Cove. I slowed down, examining each driveway and gate entrance for a name. I seemed to be running out of Key. Just when I had decided that I must have missed the house, I saw it.

A discrete cast-iron figure of a pelican, with the name of the house above it, was swinging on a bracket attached to a large stone gatepost. Below it was a painted wooden sign saying

"STRICTLY PRIVATE--KEEP OUT". Di Giorgio obviously liked privacy.

I pulled off the road and parked across the wide entrance. Now I saw the other gate post and a high fence half hidden by overgrown shrubbery. In front of me a black metal gate, about eight feet high shut off any access. The gate was solid metal up to about half way, with heavy bars above, topped by a set of unwelcoming spikes.

I got out of the car and walked up to the gate. Through the bars I could see a long, gravelled driveway curving away to the left, disappearing into more trees and tall shrubs. It was very hot and humid, even in the shade beneath the trees. I stood for a moment, listening to the drone of insects and smelling the sweet heavy perfumes from the flowering shrubs. Far away I could hear the sound of a motor-boat engine and, much closer, a light whirring noise. But there was no sign of life.

I looked around for some way to open the gate or at least to attract attention. Then I saw a small grill set in the right hand pillar. Above it, a miniature TV. camera was looking at me. It tracked me with a faint purr as I walked across to the pillar. I was feeling slightly foolish and wondering how to proceed when the pillar spoke to me.

"Yes?" it said in a metallic voice.

"Hi," I said casually. "My name is Terry Lennox. I'm here to see Mr Carlos di Georgio." I hoped no one came past and saw me. "Do you have an appointment?" the voice said.

"Yes, I do," I smiled at the grill and then up at the camera, trying to look reassuring. "He's expecting me." There was a pause. "One moment sir."

I waited patiently for a minute or two, listening to the sound of the distant boat engine and thinking about the blue water and Sylvia. Then there was a loud whirring noise and the camera swivelled sharply, panning swiftly across me and on to the front of the hire car, refocusing as it went. I guessed it was recording the license plate number for some reason. Maybe Carlos collected car license numbers.

"Please drive in, sir and park at the front of the house. Someone will meet you there." The gate slid silently open on heavy metal runners I had not noticed before. I drove under a thick canopy of trees along the driveway. It was only slightly narrower than the main highway and seemed almost as long. Then suddenly I was clear of the trees and out into the hot glare of the sun.

The house was long and low and built in the Spanish hacienda style with red tiled roofs and pink stucco walls and it was surrounded by terraces, lawns and flower beds that stretched in every direction, running down to the sea at the rear of the house.

The front entrance was a wide cool porch of adobe and tile, set in the middle of the long side of the roughly rectangular building. From it a stone terrace with a low balustrade ran to the left and round the house towards the sea as far as I could see. Outside there stood a collection of large black limousines and a group of uniformed drivers, lounging against the cars or talking casually. They stopped talking and watched me as I drove up.

In the shadow of the porch there were two other men, wearing smart business suits, white shirts and dark ties like IBM executives. They were watching me too. As I stopped the car one of them came down the steps and slowly round to the driver's side.

I opened the window. "I'm Terry Lennox-- to see Mr di Georgio?"

"Just park over there, sir." He directed me away from the other cars. He was waiting for me as I walked back to the porch. He was big, at least my height and weight but he looked in better shape, moving with the balance and ease of a good cornerback. His hair was dark and well groomed, his complexion swarthy. From behind the sunglasses his eyes studied me carefully. Well, maybe he had a problem with faces, I thought. But I decided not to ask.

With this kind of security I was beginning to understand why Sylvia might have wanted to go awol. "This way, sir" the man said. He led me up the steps and opened the heavy wooden front door. A cold blast of air conditioning hit me from the dark interior of the house. I followed him across a stone flagged entrance hall, down a long passage illuminated only by small, head high strip windows, and into a room that filled the entire end of the house. The two outside walls seemed almost all glass. One had a sliding door onto the terrace and looked out on a swimming pool beyond and a terrace dotted with sunbeds and parasols. The other side of the room had a view of more terraces and gardens, leading down to a landing stage with a small boat-house. In the distance there was a seemingly unlimited vista of the Gulf of Mexico, stretching away into flawless blue sky in the west.

"Mr di Giorgio has another meeting in progress," the IBM type said to me. "But he'll be with you presently. Please make yourself comfortable. If you would like something to drink, please help yourself." He gestured towards a professional looking bar set up in the corner of the room. "Feel free to move about the terraces," he added. "The doors are opened from this consol." He pointed to a set of switches beside the bar. Then he left me alone.

It struck me that at no time had he taken his eyes off me since I got out of the car. Maybe he was wired up to the camera. The idea cheered me up and I mixed a long gin and tonic, with lots of ice. I looked around the room. It was long and low, with a white ceiling and pale cream walls and a polished natural stone floor. It was furnished in Spanish style and tastefully, with old dark wooden tables and heavy leather chairs, simply made from sheets of tanned hide fastened by brass studs to the wooden frames. The floor was covered by a scattering of small woven rugs, in natural colours and bold geometric patterns. It all looked genuine and expensive, and knowing Sylvia I was sure it would be.

The glass door opened silently at a touch. I took my drink out onto the terrace and found a lounger in the shade of a parasol at the corner of the house. I lay back, enjoying the cooling bite of the tonic. The pool looked invitingly clear and cool in the glare of the sun.

Beyond the pool was a low wall and beyond that a kind of summer house, a bower of open trellis overgrown with purple bougainvillea and clematis. Nearby a young man, tall and athletic, wearing a pair of cut-off jeans and a sun hat was playing water in a steady stream from a garden hose onto a colourful bank of flowers.

I sat quietly, letting the stress of the journey soak away in the heat. Then, further down the terrace behind me I heard a door open and a man's voice, low and peevish. "God damn it Rich," he hissed. "I don't like being told to take a walk in my own house."

"Don't take it like that Carlos," another man's voice said, soothingly."They have one or two things to talk through. You know how careful Marcus is about the organisation."

"Sure," Carlos said petulantly, "but why can't he talk in front of me? I've nothing to hide-- there's nothing wrong with my operation. So what's the problem?"

"No problem, Carlos. You heard what Marcus said--- he wants a few words with Nico, to go over some figures. It's nothing to do with you. So don't take it personal." There was a pause. Then, firmly "Listen, he wants me in there. I'll let you know when Marcus is ready for you."

I heard the door close again and the sound of Carlos walking along the terrace towards the corner where I was seated. He stopped directly above me. "God damn it." I heard him mutter. I realised that from his position he couldn't see me and I was beginning to feel embarrassed. I wondered if this was a diplomatic moment to stand up and introduce myself to Sylvia's husband. I decided it wasn't.

On the other side of the pool the young man was moving slowly round the garden, thoroughly soaking each area in turn. As he approached the little bower there was a stir. A girl stood up, stepped out of its shadows and stood in the hot sun, stretching her slender arms up over her head. She was tall and darkly tanned and her white one-piece swimming costume, cut high at the thighs, emphasised her slim athletic figure. A big floppy sun hat hid most of her face and all her hair.

She turned her head slowly, and looked across the pool towards where Carlos and I were watching. Her face was still in shade and against the glare of the sun I had a brief impression of a half familiar profile. Then, deliberately, she stepped forward in front of the young man, turning her back to the house. The boy stopped in his tracks, the hose spurting a stream of water at her feet. I was too far away to hear what was said but I saw him shake his head and start to turn away.

Smoothly, the girl stepped closer and slid her left arm round his waist, at the same time reaching up to place her right hand on his naked shoulder. For a brief moment it seemed an intimate little scene. Then suddenly the young man pushed her away, the water from the hose in his hand splashing out in a wide arc across the white costume. I heard her laugh as she half stumbled and fell against him, grabbing onto his shoulders. He dropped the hose and seized her wrists, pushed her off and turned away. I heard her laugh again and call something after him as he strode away across the garden in the direction of the beach.

Behind me I heard a sharp intake of breath. "Little bitch." Carlos said and then walked quickly away down the length of the terrace. As if she had heard him, the girl turned in our direction. Under the shadow of the hat I saw her smile. She swept off the hat and shook out her shoulder-length reddish brown hair. Then she started slowly round the pool, glancing up at the retreating Carlos with a knowing little smile. With her head slightly bowed she came towards the corner of the terrace where I was seated.

As she drew level I stood up out of the shade. "Good afternoon." I said. "I love your garden. Is it difficult to get staff here?"

The girl jumped back in real surprise. "Christ!" she said. "Who are you? One of Carlos's pals?" At close range I could see how young she was--- no more than nineteen or twenty, but already with the fine features and some of the same intensity as her mother. But her eyes different, an unusual shade of green and hazel, and there was a touch of youthful petulance there that I had never known. The hair was different too, dark but more auburn than jet black. Even so there was no doubting her pedigree. The wide mouth, straight nose, the direct challenging gaze all spoke of the Sylvia I used to know.

I smiled. "No." I said. "I don't think you could call me that. But I am here to meet him. My name is Terry Lennox. I used to be a friend of your mother."

"My mother?" A puzzled look appeared and then her face darkened. She stared at me, and seemed to see me for the first time. "Terry Lennox," she repeated. Then the amused little smile returned. "Terry Lennox!" she said again. "Of course. I know about you."

CHAPTER 6

She looked at me with interest. I was suddenly very aware of
her gaze. Where she learned to look at a man like that I don't
know but it wasn't at finishing school in Switzerland. Or maybe
it was. I reminded myself hastily that she was just a kid--- I
could have been her father, literally. The situation needed
defusing. I laughed and said "Well, there isn't that much to
know."

She smiled at me, holding me with her eyes. "That," she said
slowly, "isn't the way I heard it." She tossed her head back and
ran a hand through her long fine hair. "You and Sylvia were
pretty close--- for almost two years, wasn't it? You must be
something special to keep her interested that long"

Her voice, and some of the mannerisms, contained a subtle
echo of her mother that I found oddly disconcerting. I shrugged
and looked across to the distant figure of Carlos. He was
standing at the edge of the little pier, looking towards us. "How
is your mother?" I asked casually. I wondered how much she

knew.

"My mother?". The same hesitation as before. "Oh, you mean Sylvia. She's away somewhere on a buying trip--- or something. She's always on the move. I never know where she is." She pouted slightly, suddenly the little girl. "Not that that's anything new. I've hardly seen her since I came here." She shook her hair again. "Not that I care." she added defiantly. "But why are you here to see Carlos," she paused and shot a look at me, "or is it Sylvia you want?"

It was a good question and one I had been trying to avoid since Helen van Eck had called me. I avoided it again. "I'm here on business." I said firmly. "Your grandmother asked me to take a look at the art business she owns--- the one Sylvia runs."

"I see," she said absently. Suddenly she smiled up at me. "What a shame you've missed Sylvia." she said lightly. "Maybe I can do something to help." She fixed me with another steady gaze. "I mean, in her place. I'm sure Mummy would want me to help you in any way I can."

It was all nicely ambiguous. But the look left me in no doubt. I became uncomfortably aware of the hot Florida sun. In a still moment I listened to the sound of birds nearby in the shrubbery and the distant drone of a power boat off shore somewhere. The girl moved imperceptibly closer, looking up at me innocently. Suddenly I realised it was a rerun of the scene with the young boy.

Out of the corner of my eye I saw Carlos striding back across the grass towards us. I swayed back slightly away from her. "Who was your young friend with the hose?" I asked. She flicked her head again, like a filly deflecting a stray fly. "Oh, that's nobody," she snapped. "Just Tom Ambrose. He works here sometimes. He's a bore. How long are you going to be around?"

Before I could answer, Carlos arrived. It wasn't the way I had planned to start the assignment. In the consultant's hand book there isn't anything about being caught in compromising situations with the client's pretty young relatives. But generally it's considered a bad idea.

Carlos reacted just how I expected. And just how she intended him to. What the little charade really signified was more difficult to understand. "Hey, who the hell are you?" He was still twenty feet away from me but I had no trouble hearing him.

He was a big man; a couple of inches over six feet, which made him a couple of inches taller than me and he was powerfully built, but carrying a bit of extra weight now. I seemed to recall that he had played quarter back at college, which explained the shoulders. Still, I noted with satisfaction the bulk round his middle, the developing paunch and the jowls that had blurred his jaw line. In his prime he had probably weighed in at around fifteen stone; say two hundred pounds, but that was a distant memory now.

He had a square, heavy-boned face and head, with a solid looking chin and strong, good-looking features. Overall, I had to admit the impression was still attractive, with tanned complexion, curly, short, fairish hair slightly greying, and blue eyes with just a tinge of red around the whites. I wondered fleetingly about the blue eyes and fair hair, and a name like di Giorgio but decided his connections must be in the north of Italy. Or even Sicily, where once they had their own Norman

Conquest

"Mr di Giorgio." I said, with my best consultants smile,
reaching out a hand. "My name is Terry Lennox. I believe Mrs
van Eck told you I was coming."

He stopped dead in his tracks and stood, looking from the girl
to me and back again. I could see him mentally changing gears.
I wondered how good a quarterback he had been. The scowl
vanished as he looked back at me. "Hey, yes," he said,
suddenly all warmth and welcome. "Terry! Good to meet you. I
know about you." I was beginning to wonder what it was that
everyone knew about me.

"So what can I do for you, Terry?", he went on. "Is little Sylvia
entertaining you?" he said, with a sideways glance in her
direction."

"I was just about to," she snapped, throwing on her sun-hat. As
she turned away, in her best finishing school manner she said "I
do hope we'll have a chance to talk later" She brushed past me.
Carlos and I silently watched her go. "Lovely girl," I said.
Carlos nodded slowly. "Yeah" he said thoughtfully. Then he
remembered me.

"Say, Terry, I'm a bit tied up for about another half hour with
another meeting. I've got some guys here I do business with
from time to time." I indicated that I was happy to wait. "Good,
good." he said. "Tell you what. One of them may be able to
help you with Ethnic Art Inc. His firm does some accounting
work for the company--- he gave Sylvia advice on funding and
stuff. His name's Rich Pantuliano. He has an office in Tampa.
Helps me with some of my business interests too. Nice guy.
You'll like him."

"That sounds great." I said. "I really don't have a feel for the business yet--- Mrs van Eck didn't seem to have much information. I haven't even seen a set of accounts."

Carlos shook his head sympathetically. "You haven't, eh? Well, it's a real seat of the pants business, so don't expect there to be too much available. But you can rely on Rich. He'll help you, I'm sure." He hesitated and glanced around quickly. "Look Terry, I'd like to ask you a favour too." I wondered what he meant by "too". So I smiled and tried to look co-operative. "You know the family has decided not to go public yet; I mean about Sylvia being missing."

"Yes," I said, "I was surprised to hear that, as a matter of fact."

He nodded. "Sure," he said vaguely. "Well there are reasons." He shrugged "We didn't want to alarm little Sylvia, for one thing---and we're still not quite certain what happened." I looked at him enquiringly. "I mean, I know what it looks like. But Sylvia can be--- kind of unpredictable." Yes, I thought, that's the truth.

"But say, let's discuss that later. What I wanted to ask you was--- I wanted to say---. Well, Rich and the others don't know about the situation. Not exactly. Or why you're here. So I'd be glad if you would be discrete when you're talking to them, you know."

I nodded."Of course," I said. "I'm acting for Mrs van Eck primarily. My precise brief is no one else's business. But why the secrecy?"

He put a heavy arm round my shoulders as we walked back

towards the house. "I'll explain it all later. But in the meantime I thought it would be best to tell them you're doing a general review of the company for Mrs van Eck. You know, don't say anything too specific. If that's o.k. with you?" He went on rapidly, "You see, as I said, I do a lot of business with Rich and his friends and I don't want to rock the boat right now"

I glanced sideways at him, wondering if that was some kind of black humour. I decided it wasn't. "All right," I said. "I don't see why that should be a problem at this stage."

"Great, great," he said. He gave my shoulders a squeeze. "Really appreciate it, Terry. It's been difficult for us all here. See you later." His words strangely echoed what Helen van Eck had said. I watched him make his way back down the terrace. He knocked on the door of the room before he went in to join his colleagues. That seemed strange in his own house.

But then the whole set up was getting stranger by the hour.

CHAPTER 7

I went back into the house. Carlos seemed friendly enough. But clearly he would have preferred me not to be there. I sat down in one of the old Spanish chairs to wait. I thought about the girl and Sylvia and Mrs van Eck. I thought about Carlos and what he might have to worry about. Then I thought about the girl again. She was easy to think about. But it seemed strange that she still didn't know that Sylvia had vanished, when apparently the rest of the family did.

I hadn't been at the house an hour and already I was involved in some game that was being played out. Maybe more than one. Well, my brief was clear enough and Helen van Eck was my client. On the other hand it would do no harm to go along with Carlos, so far as it was possible. And it was convenient to find Pantuliano at the house--- I needed some real financial information and he seemed the most likely source. Just why Sylvia's disappearance was being kept so quiet, I didn't understand. The family's natural reluctance to expose their personal problems? Well, maybe. But why did the girl seem to be unaware of the problem? Well, families are queer. Perhaps I didn't need to know.

Just as I was getting restless Carlos reappeared. With him was another man; medium height and plumpish in build with glossy dark hair brushed straight back over a rounded head and receding from a high forehead. His complexion was at the Mediterranian end of tanned and his dark eyes glinted behind round, old-fashioned looking gold framed spectacles. His plump jowls had just the shadow of an early evening beard developing and he looked as if he could do with a shave. I decided he probably looked like that most of the day.

Otherwise he was well groomed, wearing in a smart dark blue shirt with a button down collar, a Brigade of Guards tie and a three-piece business suit. I thought the tie was probably an oversight and decided not to mention it. "Hi Terry!" he beamed at me. "I'm Rich Pantuliano. Carlos tells me you're looking at Mrs van Eck's little art business. Say, if I can help---," he paused. "But really, all we do is produce some accounts for her from time to time. Still---, if I can help?" He took a seat opposite me and crossed his legs, carefully adjusting the crease in his trousers. He sat kicking one foot casually, an arm over the back of his chair. His moccasin shoes looked Italian and must have cost him six hundred dollars at least.

"It's good to meet you, Rich." I said. "I was hoping to speak to someone who could let me have a set of accounts for the company. How's the business doing?"

"Well, you know, it ticks over" he said. "I'm not that close to it myself. Sylvia really runs the show. Like I said, we do a bit of accounting for her." He turned towards Carlos, "How is she anyway?" he asked.

"Can you let me have a copy of any recent accounts?" I interceded.

Carlos said nothing. Pantuliano nodded. "Sure, I'll get some stuff to you. How long are you going to be here?"

"Just a day or two. Any chance of me getting it tomorrow? Or you could fax it to me in the U.K." I fished out a business card. "No problem," he said automatically. We exchanged cards. "And if you have any detailed management accounts, those would be useful" I added. Rich laughed. "Not much of that, I'm afraid. Maybe a set of half year accounts. Otherwise it's been seat of the pants stuff." I nodded understandingly. "Still," I smiled, "anything would be helpful"

He put his head on one side and looked at me enquiringly. "What exactly are you doing for Mrs van Eck?" he said casually. "You an accountant, or what?"

I laughed. "Mostly what" I said. "No, I'm no accountant. I give general business consultancy--- mostly small private company strategy and organisational advice. You know, whether to buy, or sell--- that kind of thing. But mostly looking at the people side--- strengths and weaknesses, and what to do about them." I hoped that would satisfy him.

"So what's your background?" he persisted. "Well, I used to work for one of the big international firms. But not as an accountant," I added. "Then I decided to go independent. What about you, Rich. What's your background?"

Carlos broke in eagerly, "Rich is a CPA."

Pantuliano smiled. "But I'm not really an accountant either. I moved into corporate finance with one of the big New York investment banks, putting deals together, arranging finance, that sort of thing. Then I decided to go it alone--- like you." He gave me a beaming smile. "Moved here to Florida for the climate." He looked around. "Great life-style" he said.

The door opened suddenly and another man appeared, closely followed by the two I had seen standing in the porch. Pantuliano glanced up and his expression changed. He and Carlos leaped to their feet. "Marcus", Pantuliano said. The newcomer stood by the door, holding it open, and silently looked at the three of us, a little smile on his lips. He was older, maybe fifty-five or so, of medium height, with bushy greying dark hair and a square head and face. Strong dark eyebrows contrasted vividly with his grey hair, and his eyes were so dark they seemed to have no pupils. In spite of the smile they showed nothing as his gaze flicked over us. When he looked directly at me his eyes were like two black pebbles at the bottom of a cold stream.

Carlos rushed forward. "Marcus, this is Terry Lennox. He's here from Europe to look at the Ethnic Art company for my mother- in law--- just some general business advice" he added quickly. "Terry, this is Marcus Cuneo. We, we, have some business interests in common; isn't that right, Marcus."

Cuneo ignored him. The impenetrable dark eyes moved over me and then on to Pantuliano. I stood up and held out my hand. "Good to meet you, Mr Cuneo" I said. He looked back at me without moving and for a long moment I thought he was going to ignore my hand. Then he touched it briefly with his. "You and Carlos got much to discuss?" he asked quietly.

"Just talking about the background to the business," Carlos said, "nothing too detailed." Cuneo continued to ignore him, staring at me. I realised he was waiting for me to speak.

"I'm at the stage of trying to understand the business, so I can advise Mrs van Eck on what she should do with it." I hesitated, "You may know, she's the main shareholder and she has a lot of other pressures at the moment, business and personal, so she's asked me to help." I hoped that was a sufficiently bland answer.

"And what about Sylvia?" Cuneo asked. He turned to Carlos now. "I haven't seen her around. Is she O.K.?"

"Oh sure, Marcus, no problem. She's away on a buying trip to Europe right now." Cuneo nodded and half turned away.

When do you expect her back?" he asked over his shoulder.

"Oh, in a week or two. But you know how Sylvia is!" Carlos laughed uneasily.

The little smile reappeared on Cuneo's lips. "Yes, Carlos but you can handle her, can't you." He inclined his head towards me. "I hope you enjoy your visit to the United States, Mr Lennox. Rich here will help you all he can. He'll let me know if we can do anything else for you. We value Carlos and his family--- I wouldn't want them to make any wrong decisions."

That began to irritate me. "Well Mr Cuneo, I hope to be consulting closely with Carlos." I said, "But of course you will appreciate that my client is Mrs van Eck." I decided to lighten it a touch, and laughed. "The first rule of consultancy is always to know who your client is."

Cuneo's expression didn't change. "Appreciate that," he said thoughtfully. Then he nodded. "Yes, I do appreciate that, Mr Lennox. But I'd like you to keep in touch. You can get to me through Rich here."

I decided it wasn't worth debating the issue with him at this stage. "I'll bear that in mind" I said. There seemed no point in asking him what his interest was. Cuneo nodded again and almost smiled. Then he turned away. His two silent companions followed him down the corridor. A few moments later I heard car doors slam and the sound of tires on the driveway.

Carlos was the first to break the silence that lay on the room. "Hey, quite a guy, Marcus!" he said awkwardly and went quickly across to the bar. He mixed himself a drink, holding out a glass to me enquiringly. I shook my head.

Pantuliano looked from me to Carlos and back to me. "Marcus Cuneo is a big man in the business scene around here" he said. "He doesn't like loose ends." So now I was a loose end. I decided to let that go, too

CHAPTER 8

Pantuliano asked me where I was staying and offered to drop some Ethnic Art accounts off at my motel. In fact, I had made no accommodation arrangements but Carlos called a motel up the coast, not far from the airport, and made a reservation for me. Then Pantuliano left in a rush, apparently to catch up with Cuneo, shaking my hand and promising me any help I needed.

Carlos and I sat down again. He seemed to relax, full of bonhomie and clutching a large whisky and water. "Tell me what happened to Sylvia." I said, leaning forward towards him. He looked at me over the edge of his glass. "What do you mean?" he said, "I wish I knew--- no one seems to know what happened."

"Well, tell me what it looks like" I persisted.

He shrugged his heavy shoulders. "Some people found one of our sailing launches--- her favourite boat in fact, floating down the coast south of here. She must have taken it out late one evening or in the early hours of the morning. It looks as if something went wrong. Just what, I don't know."

I frowned. "Isn't that strange?" I asked. "Did no one hear her leave?"

Carlos looked away. "It wasn't unusual for her to go out alone. She was a very experienced sailor and she often went out at night, to cool off when it got too hot for her." He glanced back at me. "She never really adjusted to this climate, you know." I didn't know but I could imagine.

"And nobody heard her go?"

He looked down at his drink. "No. You see, some nights she used to sleep down at the boat house. She--- she liked to watch the sunsets across the gulf. And I was up at the house. I didn't hear anything that night."

"What about little Sylvia?"

He shot a sudden glance at me. "She was away at some all-night party with friends on one of the Keys." He paused, and went on. "Anyway, when we found the boat it was in good shape. Nothing missing. Not even the inflatable dinghy. It was still on board. I still haven't figured out what happened. And all her clothes and jewellery were still in the house. The only thing we haven't found is her passport."

"So she did take that? Do you think that's significant?"

He shrugged. "Who can tell?" he said with a grimace.

I shook my head. "What about the police?" I asked.

Carlos sucked in his breath. "Well, I talked it over with Mrs van Eck and we decided not to make an official report just yet." He stared at me almost defiantly. "There is a chance that she's gone off somewhere and we didn't want to scare people unnecessarily." His expression changed. "You have no idea how difficult Sylvia can be sometimes" he ended lamely. He looked at me sadly. "She and I haven't been very close recently. I assumed she had just taken off in a pique."

I shrugged my shoulders. I wasn't entirely surprised. It explained the nights in the boat house. "And now?" I asked."What do you think now?"

He shook his head. "I just don't know, Terry. She seems to have really vanished this time. I've made enquiries, but there's no trace"

"Look, Carlos, you know my brief is to advise Mrs van Eck about who might look after the business in Sylvia's absence--- whether temporary or permanent. Can you tell me anything about the company that might be helpful?"

He shook his head. "Don't know much about it. I fixed her up with some financial advice and helped with transportation and shipping. That's about it. You know some of that stuff is pretty expensive." He stopped and shot a glance at me. "And sometimes it's difficult to get things in and out of certain countries. My contacts were useful." I looked at him questioningly. He went on "There are government controls in some places to stop the removal of cultural objects. It can get quite political. So it helps if you know the right people. People like Marcus Cuneo have contacts" He grinned at me. "There can be exceptions made, if you treat them right." He looked at his watch. "Say, Terry, I don't think I can tell you much more about the situation. Why don't you look at the information Rich is pulling together for you. What's are you planning to do next?"

"I plan to meet the guys who run the branches and see how they measure up--- get a better idea about the business at the same time.

"Sounds good" he said, "I'm sorry I can't ask you to stay here but I'm leaving for Miami tonight. There's a plane coming to pick me up in an hour or so." I must have looked puzzled. He laughed, "Around here we use boats and sea-planes like taxi-cabs--- it's the easiest way to get around."

I nodded. "I'll head back up to the motel. I could do with a shower and some rest after the flight." Suddenly it seemed a very long time since my discussion with Paul Friden in Brussels.

Carlos told me how to find the motel and walked me to my car. As I slid behind the wheel he put his hand on my arm. "Terry, I appreciate your co-operation--- over Marcus, I mean." He hesitated, "It's just that we have some big deals cooking up together and he---, well, he doesn't like surprises."

I smiled at him. "I know, Carlos. He doesn't like loose ends either." I looked up at him through the open window. Then I pressed a switch and as the window slid silently up, I said," I'm not keen on them myself." Then I drove away down the long driveway. In the mirror I could see him standing in front of the house, watching me. "Good exit line," I nodded to myself.

CHAPTER 9

I found the motel easily enough, south of Tampa Bay and just off the state highway. It was imaginatively called the Sunshine Motel. A middle aged blue rinse refugee from New York City took my credit card details, gave me a room key and showed me on a big wall chart how to locate my cabin. I turned down a free polystyrene cup of coffee but noted that it was available, with donuts at breakfast.

Then I drove round the tree shaded development until I found my new home. It was all it needed to be to satisfy the weary traveller--- spacious, clean and cool, with a sitting room with big glass sliding doors, a large bedroom with a bed big enough for four people, a well equipped mini bar, a T.V. set and an efficient shower and bathroom.

In the literature I found the telephone number of a local restaurant and ordered a pizza delivery, stripped of my sticky clothes and headed for the shower. By the time I had dried off and got into my bathrobe the pizza had arrived. I opened a cold bottle of Rolling Rock from the mini bar and settled down in front of the T.V. to watch the Giants and Cincinnati play an afternoon game at Candlestick Park. After three innings I was having trouble keeping my eyes open. It had been a long day. I had just finished brushing my teeth when the door bell rang. I glanced at my watch. It was still only just after nine o'clock but my body clock was convinced it was about two a.m.

When I opened the door the slim dark figure stood in the darkness, illuminated by the overhead security light. For an instant the resemblance fooled me again. Then she spoke and I knew it was little Sylvia. "Hello," she said, flicking her hair sideways with a move of her head. She leaned one shoulder nonchalantly against the doorframe, like a young Laureen Bacall. "Western Union," she said, "I have a message for Mr Lennox."

"Sylvia," I said, "what a surprise." We stood in the doorway, facing each other, while I tried to think of something urbane and polished to say. Without moving from the side of the door she gave me a look she must have practised in front of a mirror. "Aren't you going to ask me in?" she said in a low voice. She raised her perfectly shaped eyebrows a fraction. It was beautifully done.

I stood back and she slid past me into the cabin, moving with the coltish grace of a well-bred young filly. She turned towards me as I closed the door. I looked her over. Apart from the colour, she had her mother's wide set eyes and the same perfect jaw line, but somehow subtly changed. Definitely worth looking at in her own right, I thought. One day she would be a real beauty. Come to that, she was pretty good now.

She was wearing a simple, expensive looking linen wrap around dress, pale cream in colour with dark blue trim, and on her feet a pair of blue open weave sandals. Her long auburn hair fell loosely over her shoulders. The hazel-green eyes gazed coolly at me, meeting my appraising stare. I suddenly became aware of my bath robe. Unconsciously I tightened the belt a touch. "I'm afraid I'm not dressed for guests," I said. "Just getting ready for bed."

She gave a giggle and raised the back of her hand to her mouth. For a moment she looked like a school-girl. "Don't let me stop you," she said, again with that slight lift of the eyebrows. I looked at her closely. She didn't appear to have been drinking. But I realised that I was enjoying looking at her.

"What can I do for you?" I asked. "I mean, why are you here? Does Carlos know you're here?" I hoped I was making sense. She gave a little snort and touched her mouth with the back of her hand again. "Carlos," she said dismissively, "Who cares about Carlos." It was a good point but still I felt uneasy.

"Sylvia, you know I'm working on an assignment for Mrs van Eck. I don't know why you're here but I'm certain she wouldn't expect you to be in my hotel room at this time of night. To say nothing of your mother" I added, as an afterthought. "Why are you here anyway?"

She lowered her head, her hands behind her back, and took a half step towards me. "Oh surely there's no need for Mummy to know," she said demurely, looking up at me through her dark lashes. "Anyway, she asked me to give you a message." She took another step. "And she's a dear--- she and daddy always understand whenever I really want something." She looked at me again "And who cares about Sylvia. She always gets what she wants."

71

I heard myself saying, "And what do you want?", as if I'd been programmed.

She gave another giggle and moved closer still, at the same time pulling loose the tie that held the front of her dress together. As the dress swung open I caught a glimpse of her young breasts and her long firm tanned body. She was wearing little or nothing under the dress. "Why you, silly," she said softly. She was very close to me now. "If Sylvia can have you, so can I."

As she moved against me I put my hands on her shoulders, to stop her I suppose. I felt the slim warmth through the material of the dress as I held her at arms-length for a moment. "Look," I started to say, "this won't do--" With a practised little shrug and a slight twist she slid out of the dress, letting it slip to the floor, at the same time pressing her body close in against me.

Suddenly I found myself with my arms round the neck of the half naked girl. She stood surprisingly tall against me, the high heels bringing her dark head to my eye level. She smelled faintly of cederwood, and something else, musky and more animal. Her arms went around me and she leaned against me, looking up into my eyes. "Believe me, Mummy won't mind" she murmured, as I kissed her. "But won't Sylvia be furious," she said softly and closed her eyes, sinking against me. Somehow it didn't seem the right time to ask her to explain. Besides, I think I knew what she meant.

We made it to the big double bed. Of course I knew it wasn't a good idea. But I excused myself with the thought that clearly it was not the first time she had been in this situation. And I have to be honest--- even in my tired condition she made it something special.

By eleven thirty she was gone, leaving only a shambles of twisted bedclothes and the faint smell of cederwood lingering in the bedroom. Once she decided to go she had dressed rapidly, what little there was to put on. She borrowed a comb and casually pulled it through her hair, grimacing at herself in the mirror, seemingly oblivious of me now. I lay back in the ruin of the bed with my hands behind my head, watching her move around the room. Before she left she paused at the door of the cabin. "I'm going to be back in Europe soon. Shall I contact you?" she asked me.

"That would be nice" I said. Well, what else could I say?

She smiled at me. "I thought you must be something special," she said. She gave one of her little giggles and touched her lips with the back of her hand. "Won't Sylvia be furious! By the way, Mummy wants you to telephone her at Vinkiveen when you can." Before I could think of a reply she had slipped out into the warm dark Florida night.

I lay for a moment trying to think rationally about what had happened, and why. It seemed clear she still had no idea about Sylvia's disappearance. For some reason Carlos and Mrs van Eck wanted to keep it secret. For the same reason? Marcus Cuneo didn't know either. But I had a feeling he'd find out if it was of interest to him. I was finding it hard to think straight. In spite of myself I couldn't keep images of the girl my mind. If I'm honest, I suppose I felt pretty pleased with myself. I rolled over and pulled a sheet over me, drifting quickly into an exhausted sleep.

CHAPTER 10

Very slowly, from some black hole of oblivion, I was dragged back by a persistent ringing sound. I switched on the bedside light and looked at my watch. Five minutes after midnight. I had only been asleep for a few minutes. "What next?" I groaned. I found my robe, slipped it on and went to open the door, half expecting to see her standing there again.

Instead, it was a tall fair haired young man. At first I didn't recognise him. Then I realised it was Tom Ambrose, the young man from the garden at Pelican Cove. In the glare of the overhead light his strong features were set grimly. I blinked at him, half drugged by lack of sleep.

"Is the girl gone?" he said abruptly.

Oh Christ, I thought. Now I'm part of a love triangle. "What do you mean" I said. It seemed to be my night for sparkling repartee. "Anyway," I added, beginning to feel annoyed, "what the hell do you want?"

The boy slightly recoiled. "It's OK Mr Lennox, I know she was here. But I need to talk to you." I stood aside and motioned him in with a sigh. It seemed to be my night for visitors and I was beginning to give up on the idea of sleep.

We went through to the lounge and sat facing each other. "Young Sylvia was here, wasn't she?" he half whispered.

"Look, son," I said, "I hope I haven't upset anything."

For an instant he looked puzzled. Then his face cleared. "No, no! Nothing like that. The kid means nothing to me." He gave a contemptuous smile."She's a nut--- a spoiled brat. No, it's Sylvia I want to speak to you about. I know that you were a good friend of hers at one stage." He paused. "Maybe more than that", he added wistfully, looking me frankly in the face. "She often spoke to me about you."

"OK," I said, opening the minibar and pouring out a Scotch. It was a good single malt and I approved. "Drink?" I offered him.

He shook his head. "No thanks, I don't," he said, "I'm in training for the athletics team at college."

I nodded, "What's your event?"

"Pole vault, mainly. That's my best event. Also I do a bit of rock climbing back home in Colarado." I can believe it, I thought as I looked at his powerful chest and upper arm development. "You've done a bit of climbing too, haven't you" he added. "Sylvia told me about it."

I sipped my malt, starting to revive a little. "Nothing too serious," I said, thinking of a night spent in a rock chimney on

75

a mountain east of Loch Torridon. Only three thousand feet, which in Colorado would sound like sea level. But with low cloud and freezing rain driving in on a south-westerly it had been nasty enough for me. That was the time I fell--- and decided to give up climbing in favour of drinking Scotch. "Tell me what you want to see me about."

"Mr Lennox, I just need to tell somebody. I need help. Something weird is happening--- and there's no-one I can talk to at Pelican Cove. They're all weirdos over there," he continued bitterly. "That's why Sylvia--- " he stopped and stared at me. I saw the doubt creep into his clear eyes.

"It's OK," I said encouragingly, "I'm on your side." I still didn't know what side that was. But he was the first person I'd met on this assignment who seemed to want to tell me something.

"That's why Sylvia took off," he spat out. "I don't blame her --- what with Carlos and that kid," he added.

I frowned "I'm not with you. Tell me what you know."

He paced to and fro across the room. Then he turned and glared at me, his blue eyes defiant. "I helped her to get away. She asked me to help her and I did."

"But why? And why you?" I asked.

"Because she knew she could trust me," he said, simply. "I'd do anything for her. She's the most wonderful--- ." He stopped, a look of embarrassment on his face. "Don't think there was anything going on between us," he said fiercely. "It wasn't like that. Although I would have gone with her if she'd wanted me to. Gladly." He paused again and stared at me, challenging me to say something. I looked at him and nodded my understanding. "Anyway, we--- she wanted to make it look as if she had had a boating accident. She expected Carlos to contact the police. I don't know why. But I think that's what she really wanted him to do for some reason." By now he seemed to be thinking aloud, pacing around the room.

"But he didn't" I said quietly.

He stopped in his tracks and looked at me as if he had only just remembered me. "No," he muttered. "That's right. He didn't. I don't understand why. But Carlos is covering up for some reason. He's pretending that she's away on a buying trip--- that the accident didn't happen."

"Which it didn't," I said.

The boy stared at me. "But how does he know that?" he asked.

He had a point there. I tried to get my frayed mind around the question. "He obviously knows something we don't," I said wearily. Mrs van Eck had sounded reasonably convinced about the accident. OK, so she was dependant on what Carlos had told her. But for some reason he had not told the girl anything. To spare her feelings? Perhaps. But equally he hadn't told Pantuliano and company. And I doubted if they had feelings of any kind. Maybe Carlos was simply hoping for the best. Or was there something more? Something that the young man standing agonising in front of me didn't know about?

"Like what?" he asked.

"Maybe Carlos is used to Sylvia doing crazy things--- " I started. "

There's nothing crazy about her" he almost shouted. "She's the kindest, most intelligent woman I've ever met. You don't know her."

I decided not to give him a resume of my experiences with Sylvia. "All right," I said, "tell me why she wanted to leave and why she did it that way."

"She used to talk to me at nights, down at the boat house." He ran his fingers through his hair. "She was teaching me Spanish," he said suddenly, as if that explained something. "She's been just about everywhere--- Europe and everywhere." I made an encouraging noise. "Anyway, I learned a lot from her. And she told me some of her problems." I looked at him with what I hoped was an eager expression on my face.

"She's always been miserable here. In Forida I mean. And she knew she had made a mistake about Carlos." He glowered at me as if it was my fault. "I reckon he was always a crook. Then Sylvia discovered something--- something to do with the company. Her art business."

Suddenly I was fully awake. "What do you mean?"

He shrugged. "She didn't tell me exactly what. Or not so I could understand. It sounded complicated. I'm not even sure she understood it all herself."

"Did she say anything specific?"

He shook his head helplessly, "Something about funding? Does that make sense?"

"It might do."

"Anyway it really pissed her off. I've never seen her so angry."
I half smiled. I could imagine Sylvia pissed off--- she'd been
that way most of the time I had known her.

"But why the vanishing act?" I persisted. "Why not just leave
the guy. Divorce him. Or separation?"

"I think she was planning to confront him about it", the young
man said, "but then the other thing hit her. She seemed to go to
pieces. She just wanted to run," he added miserably. "And I
helped her." He looked at me pleadingly, "It was what she
wanted."

I took a deep breath. "What other thing?" I said gently.

"Carlos and the kid," he said.

The light began to dawn for me.

"Sylvia was so pleased when the kid said she wanted to come
here and stay with her for a while." He gave a bitter laugh.
"From what she told me, she and the kid had a strange kind of
relationship. I think she always felt kind of left out of things---
the kid being brought up by her grandmother." He raised his
eyebrows. "It sounded pretty strange to me." I knew exactly
what the boy was saying. With the best of intentions,
presumably, Mrs van Eck had taken over Sylvia's role and left
her free to--- do what?

Tom went on, "Anyway, Sylvia seemed to think this was a
chance to spend some time with the kid--- sort of be a mother
to her again. To make up for lost time, I suppose. But---"

"But it didn't work out like that?"

Tom stared at me. "No. It turned out real bad--- about as bad as it could." I kept quiet. "The kid saw Sylvia as a kind of rival. Sylvia tried to make it work, but it seemed hopeless as far as the girl was concerned." He hesitated, "Just because Sylvia liked me--- well, anyway, because she spent some time with me, and talked to me--- the kid made a dead set at me from the start." He looked at me and flushed. "I mean, I could see what she was up to. She was really callow. It was just a try on." He gave a little laugh. "Normally, I'd have been glad to make something of it." His face set hard again. "But not when it was like that. Not when it was really about getting even with Sylvia. Anyway I refused to play."

I looked at him with more interest. And now I understood the events of earlier in the evening, I felt a little less pleased with myself. "You said something about Carlos and the girl?"

"Yes." He looked me square in the face. "That's what pushed Sylvia over the edge. When she discovered that Carlos was screwing her daughter."

The light was flooding in now. "So that's why she ran! But to do what? Think things over on her own? What? And where?" But as I spoke I knew that Sylvia had nothing much to think over.

"No, I think she was leaving Carlos for good."

"So why the fake disappearance?"

"I don't really know. She never told me that." He thought for a

80

moment. "But there was something else going on, more than just Carlos. Something she didn't tell me."

"Trouble with the business?"

He shook his head, "No. Well, maybe. I just don't know." He gazed at me in bewilderment. "But I think she took something with her" he blurted out. "Something important. But I don't know what."

CHAPTER 11

I stared at the young man. He was slumped forward in his seat, his strong hands clasped between his knees. "Tell me what happened that night," I said gently.

"It was easy enough". He sounded confident suddenly, now he was on firm ground. "She took out one of the sailing cruisers and met me off the Key. I was in my dinghy. Then I put her ashore up the coast, at a marine I use. It's deserted at that time of night. She used my car to get to the airport and left it at the car-park. I picked it up next day, using my spare key."

I nodded. It seemed logical enough, in a crazy sort of way. "But you have no idea where she went? Has anyone checked on flights out?"

He shook his head. "I don't know. She does have a friend in San Francisco--- a woman friend. She mentioned her several times. They seem to be close. And I think she saw her on her way back here from Europe recently. But she didn't tell me what her plans were."

"But she wanted Carlos to think she had drowned. Hoped he would contact the police." My mind was like a soggy sponge again. The whisky hadn't helped that much. "Maybe she was just angry and confused--- wanting to create as much of a drama as possible."

"She seemed pretty clear headed to me. Excited, but I think she knew what she was doing. Determined too."

"OK," I said. "I think I understand what happened. Up to a point. What is it that's bothering you? It seems to me Sylvia is playing this her way. I don't see what you or I can do to change the situation.

"What worries me is that Carlos knows the accident was faked. He's not just hoping. He really knows." He bit his lip. "He doesn't know I was involved." He swallowed hard. "At least I hope he doesn't. But he has people looking for her now."

"People? You mean police of some kind?"

He shook his head vigorously. "No, these guys were definitely not cops--- not even the private kind. They were pretty rough looking guys."

"How do you know all this."

"I was in the garden, under the terrace last week. I work part time there when I'm not at college. They didn't know I was there."

I knew that was possible. "Did you hear what was said?"

"I heard him say as they were leaving, "Just find her and find her fast. I want it back or destroyed. Or her somewhere where she can't use it."

"You thought he was talking about Sylvia?"

"Sure. What else?"

I couldn't think of what else, of hand. My brain had seized up with fatigue. "The men," I said, "were they connected with the people I met today? Pantuliano, or Cuneo?"

"I don't think so. These guys were toughs. I know about Cuneo. I mean, I've read stuff about him. He's a class act, in his own way. He has connections--- politicians, businessmen, even senators. The men I saw were small time hoodlums. The kind you see around the water front. Not in Cuneo's league."

"What did they look like?"

The boy thought for a moment. "One was kind of, nondescript. Like I say, just the type of guy you see lounging around the working harbours--- big, tough looking, dark hair and wearing a leather jacket. The other one was smaller and lean built. He looked a real nasty type. Kind of strange looking, a narrow face and close set eyes with long hair, tied in a kind of loose pigtail. But the hair was really weird. It was pulled right back, maybe even shaved, so that his forehead ran onto the top of his head. The hairline was back behind his ears. And then he had let it grow long at the back. Like those old Chinese pictures you see. But he was an Anglo of some kind."

I smiled at him. "Sounds unappetising, I must say. But at least he should be easy to recognise."

"What I want to know is, do you think I should go to the police? Tell them the story. Get them to find her--- to warn her that Carlos has these men after her?"

I finished off my whisky. "Why not," I said thoughtfully. "That's what Sylvia seemed to have in mind in the first place. On the other hand, Tom, there's only your word for all this."

He leaped up angrily. "What do you mean? Don't you believe me?"

"Take it easy. I'm thinking how the police might see it--- and how Carlos might play it. You say Sylvia used to spend evenings alone with you at the boat house." He started to say something. I held up my hand. "And you admit being involved in her disappearance--- and keeping quiet about it for almost two months? Imagine what the cops could make of that." He slumped down, his hand across his mouth.

I watched him closely. "Maybe you made advances to her. At the boat house or on the boat--- unwanted advances--- there was a struggle and accidentally she went over the side. Something like that."

He sat there in horror, silently shaking his head. "But I thought you would help. I wouldn't have done anything likethat. I loved her." He collapsed forward, his head in his hands.

I leaned towards him and patted his shoulder. "No, I don't think you would. But you can see how it might be made to look," I said quietly. "Let's sleep on this. Don't do anything until we've spoken again. Do you have somewhere I can contact you? I've got things to do in the morning," I looked at my watch and groaned inwardly. "And I'm due to fly out to San Francisco, as it happens, in mid-afternoon, so let's talk around lunchtime."

He gave me the telephone number of the marina where he kept his boat. "It's the coffee shop, actually. Just ask for Raoul. He'll find me. I rent a room over one of the old boat houses. It's still a working harbour--- hasn't been gentrified and turned into boutiques yet." He gave a wry grin."They all know me there."

I showed him out. He took my hand. "I guess you're right, Mr Lennox. I'm glad I came to see you. She always said you were someone to trust."

As he stepped out into the night I said, "Do you know the name of her friend in San Francisco?" He paused for a moment. "No. But it was a woman's name. Linda, or Lorna. Something like that."

I closed the door behind him and leaned on it wearily. Maybe it is a woman, I thought, but Sylvia has never had any difficulty finding a man to help out when she needed one.

It was two a.m. when I fell into bed again--- I'd given up thinking about what time it was in Europe. Then I lay awake, thinking about the Princess Head that Friden had told me about that morning--- yes it was that morning--- in Brussels But what could it have to do with Carlos? Or little Sylvia? And why might Sylvia have wanted it. For the money? Not likely, I thought drowsily. That was something Sylvia could always get. I fell into a long, deep sleep, if not of the just, at least of the physically exhausted.

CHAPTER 12

I woke surprisingly early. The sun was high and the air outside already warming up. I switched on the bedside radio and scanned through the usual selection of local stations playing pop music interspersed with travel, weather and news bulletins. Suddenly the sound of chamber music filled the cabin. I had tuned into an all-day classical music channel

I did some light exercises, showered, shaved and dressed to the elegant intricacy of a harpsichord sonata. It sounded French and quite early. Couperin, I thought, and had my first success of the day when the presenter, in reverential tones confirmed my guess. What a country, I thought--- 18th century baroque music before breakfast. I drove round to reception for my donuts and coffee. The coffee was served in a polystyrene cup. Well, who said life was perfect?

Overnight I had decided not to waste time waiting for Pantuliano to send round the information. I had a feeling it wouldn't arrive. Instead I went back to the cabin and called Mrs van Eck. She wasn't available. It was too early. But her answer phone was, so I left a message to say I had called. Then I fished out Pantuliano's business card and rang his office in Tampa. He wasn't available either. The telephone can be a wonderful aid to communication.

Instead, his secretary put me on to someone she described as one of Mr Pantuliano's assistants. To my surprise he seemed to know who I was. "Yes, Mr Lennox. I know about you. I'm putting some information together for you at the moment." So I arranged to pick up the papers on my way to the airport. He also told me that Ethnic Art had banking facilities at a branch of Lloyds International in Miami.

I called the branch manager and told him who I was and what I was doing for Mrs van Eck. He didn't know anything about me. He was polite but firm. It was impossible for him to discuss a client over the telephone. I must appreciate that. I did appreciate that. So we agreed that a fax from Mrs van Eck might be helpful.

Then he unbent sufficiently to tell me that monthly statements were not sent to any of the Ethnic Art addresses or indeed to Mrs di Giorgio. Instead they went to a firm of accountants in Tampa, a firm called Bay Financial Services. I hung up and looked again at Pantuliano's card. He was Senior Partner of Bay Financial Services, in Tampa.

I called the house in Vinkiveen again and left another message, asking Mrs van Eck to contact Lloyds Bank in Miami to request that copies of the past year's bank statements be sent to my home address in Edinburgh. Then I headed for downtown Tampa and Pantuliano's office. It was located in a modern office block that was bland and unremarkable on the outside.

Inside was like entering the Tardis of Dr Who. I was shown into an expensively furnished waiting room, with pink velour covered seats big enough to swallow an unwary client. There were acres of grey carpets and the walls were done in matching pink and grey and covered with tasteful photographs of diving pelicans, posing egrets and strolling grey herons, all against the famous Florida seascapes. Maybe Pantuliano was a nature lover.

An attractive receptionist, tall, slim, blonde and highly polished gave me a smile like a Doris Day movie. No, regretfully, Mr Pantuliano was not available. However, to my surprise there was a package waiting for me from someone called Merritt. I glanced through the papers. At first sight the stuff seemed useful, but I needed to study it. I noticed that there was no information about bank transactions. Just a balance sheet and profit and loss statement for the previous trading year. Still, it was a start.

I asked the receptionist if I could speak to Merritt and in a few minutes a middle aged man with thinning dark hair and a worried expression appeared from somewhere and sat down beside me. He was wearing lightweight grey trousers crumpled around the knees, a pale blue polyester shirt of the drip-dry variety, short socks of the same colour and a pair of scuffed tan loafers.

"Hi," he said tersely. "I'm Bob Merritt. You wanted to see me."

I smiled my re-assuring smile and reached across to shake his hand. "Hello," I said, with lots of eye contact and personal charm. "Good of you to see me--- and thanks for the information about Ethnic Art." I patted the papers beside me. "I take it you work for Mr Pantuliano?"

He grinned nervously and ducked his head. "Well, he's the boss. I just do some book-keeping and stuff for some of the firm's smaller clients." He hesitated, "But, yes, Mr Pantuliano asked me to pull something together for you." He fiddled with a pen clipped into the pocket of his shirt. "Is everything OK?"

"I'm sure it is," I said. "I haven't had a chance to look at the figures yet. But I will. And then maybe I can get back to you."

"Well," he said doubtfully, "I'm not sure I can tell you much more. Maybe you should speak to Mr Pantuliano if you need anything clsc."

I nodded, "Yes, of course. I will. But it is you who prepares the accounts for the company?"

"Yes, but I don't get that much information, really. Just enough to pull together some year-end accounts." He shrugged. "No-one seems too interested in seeing detailed accounts." Until now, I thought. He went on, "It isn't a complicated business of course." Still I said nothing. "Though it sure seems to eat cash," he blurted out. "Of course I don't see the whole picture," he went on hurriedly. "Listen, I have to go." He stood up abruptly.

I didn't get up. "Interesting," I said, leafing through the papers he had given me. "I don't see any cash flow information here. Or a trading statement. Do you do any projections or reports for Mrs di Giorgio? Or for anyone else?" I added.

He looked down at me uneasily. "I--- I'm not too sure. I'll have to check. Can I get back to you on that?"

I told him I was leaving for the west coast in a few hours time and that I would call him if I had other questions. He looked relieved. I watched him dart away across the pink and grey fantasy like the white rabbit in Alice. There, I thought, goes a nervous man. I left a note for Pantuliano, asking for details of cash flow projections and reports and a recent trading statement. But I was not hopeful.

Then I headed for the airport. Just before check-in I called Tom Ambrose at the coffee shop at the marina. Raoul found him so fast he must have been sitting at the counter. I told the young man to sit tight and do nothing meanwhile. He agreed but didn't sound too happy and I wondered if he would really hold off.

I gave him my address and telephone number in Scotland, and my contact numbers in San Francisco and Boston and I asked him to let me know if he needed help or if he heard anything about Sylvia. Then I promised to keep in touch with him and hung up. There wasn't much more I could do for him. I thought about calling the house at Pelican Cove to see how the girl was. But I decided against it. Coward, I thought.

CHAPTER 13

A few hours later I was looking down from the aircraft window as the plane banked around the lower East Bay, over the bleak salt flats at the bottom end of the San Francisco peninsula. It was late afternoon and the westering sun was illuminating the glittering pinnacles of the city like a stage set. Now and then I caught strange fleeting glimpses of the bridges that linked the whole area together. A milky summer fog was starting to ease itself in from the Pacific, through the Golden Gate and across North Beach and the business district.

Then we were making our final run up the peninsula. Far away to the north-east I could see the wide, winding expanse of the Sacramento River, still gleaming in the sun. Just across the bay was the network of freeways, already heavy with commuting traffic that holds together the complex of attractive satellite communities dotted around the San Francisco Bay Area. White sparkling houses and highways were interspersed with dark empty spaces; hills, parks, woods and lakes that made the place such a delight.

I passed quickly through arrivals and within minutes was on my way by cab up the Bayshore Freeway, part of Highway 101. I lay back, watching like a dream the progress of the rush hour commute. Curiously it seemed equally busy in both directions. I wondered vaguely about that. Apart from its obvious inefficiency I came to no real conclusion. Get a grip, Lennox, I thought. I realised I was beginning to slump after the exertions of the past few days. My biological clock was trying to tell me something.

I had a reservation at the Hyatt on the Embarcadero. I assured the well-groomed receptionist that I didn't need help with my bags and then I glided slowly up to the seventh floor in a space-age glass fronted elevator. Beneath me in the great canyon of the hotel concourse little people scurried about and ate and drank. Above in the greenery that filled the glass roof of the atrium there was an alternative scene going on, with scores of birds swooping and chattering. I tried to work out if they had got into the building by design or accident. And what did they live on? The crumbs from breakfast trays? Another of life's mysteries I seemed destined not to solve.

The hotel had upgraded me to a business suite. This turned out to be a glamorous affair, with a triangular shaped room about the size of a squash court set in the apex of the building. It looked out through two walls of glass to the Golden Gate Bridge on one side and on the other to the more workman-like Bay Bridge to Oakland and parts east. On both bridges a seemingly endless flow of traffic drifted soundlessly in and out of the city.

I decided to take a preliminary look at the accounts Pantuliano had given me and then to have something to eat. I got out of my travel clothes and lay on the king-sized bed to relax for a few minutes. I listened to the vague sound of the city and the regular boom of fog horns that were starting up around the bay.

It was mid-morning next day when I woke, relaxed and ravenous, but with the hazy dissociated feeling that jet lag creates. I sweated my way through my exercises, to shock myself back to normal. Then I ordered a huge breakfast in my room and tuned the radio to a classical music station from Palo Alto. I ate, listening to the balance and order of an early Mozart violin concerto and my spirits rose. Maybe life was civilised and reasonable after all.

I cleared away the dishes and picked up the accounts. I'm not much of an accountant and it's hard to tell much about a company from one set of figures. But this one looked odd. The profit and loss statement showed a big loss on trading, with high operating costs. I made a note to check the detailed trading account, if I ever got one. Current assets were substantial--- that was to be expected in view of the very expensive stock they carried. But the balance sheet showed long term liabilities were even higher. The accounts were sprinkled liberally with notes. Which seemed odd for a business that was supposed to be so simple and straightforward.

I consulted the notes and quickly found myself in deep water. I went back to the figures. Borrowings were unexpectedly high, almost three million dollars. But what surprised me most was that they were not in the form of bank loans or overdrafts. Instead, the debt originated from a finance company called Southern Commercial Lending Corporation, and seemed to be in the form of a private placement of low interest bonds secured on the assets of Ethnic Art Inc. Securitization? I studied the notes again. There was a covenant agreement which gave Southern Commercial Lending first claim on the assets of Ethnic Art in the event of the company ceasing to trade. I couldn't imagine why this method of funding had been chosen. But the bottom line was clear enough. Shareholders funds were negative, and by quite a margin.

I shook my head. Maybe I hadn't got the jet lag out of my system. I needed a real accountant to look at this. An old friend of mine, Donald Lynch, lived in Boston and he was a specialist in corporate finance. I decided it was time to call in a favour he owed me. I caught him just as he was going out to lunch. "Donald?" I asked. "This is Terry Lennox. I have an interesting little problem for you."

He groaned down the telephone, "Oh no. I can't afford any more of your little problems. What is it this time?"

We had been colleagues once in consulting and still exchanged information from time to time. But he loved to give me a hard time. I visualised him sitting in his office in the Hancock Building, looking out onto Boston's Back Bay.
He'd be lounging back with his feet up on the desk, his waistcoat unbuttoned, his premature paunch bulging over well cut trousers.

"Actually, I have two interesting problems for you. Maybe three."

He groaned again. "Terry, have you any idea what it's like here? I'm in the middle of orchestrating a hostile take over bid." That didn't surprise me. Donald was always orchestrating a take over bid--- or organising resistance to a hostile bid. That was how he made his living. And he was one of the best there was. "And do you have any idea how much the firm charges

95

for my time?"

"Of course I do--- and you're worth every cent," I said soothingly. "I remember how much you earned in bonus from that steel foundry deal I passed to you last year?"

There was silence. "OK," he sighed, "if you're going to appeal to my better nature, that's different. What's the story?"

"Look, I'm going to be in Boston in a day or two and I need your opinion on some company accounts."

"Fine," he said. "Just let me see them when you arrive. Or fax them to me."

"Also, I'd like you to find out all you can about a finance company called Southern Commercial Lending, based in Florida."

"Is that all? You wouldn't like me to work out your tax liability for last year. While you have me retained?"

"Don't be ironic, Donald. It's very unbecoming for a man of your stature." He blew a raspberry down the telephone. I went on, "Besides, my tax liability doesn't take that long to work out. But I need that information by the day after tomorrow." There was a long silence.

"You realise this will cost you," he said finally.

"Naturally. I was thinking of dinner at the Harvard Club on Commonwealth Avenue."

"Ah," he said brightly. "Why didn't you say so? It will be a pleasure to act for you."

I arranged to call him when I arrived in Boston and in the meantime would try to get the papers to him as soon as possible. "There is one other thing." I said.

Donald sighed. "I thought I was getting off lightly. What is it?"

"I'd like to know as much as possible about a European company, Utrecht Construction Group." Even over the telephone I could feel his mood change. I could almost see him swing his feet off the desk and sit up in his chair. "UCG" he said thoughtfully. "All right, what have you heard, you sneaky bastard?" He sounded serious.

"Nothing much, Donald. I'm doing some work for a client called Mrs van Eck. She owns the company whose accounts I want you to look at. She is also involved with Utrecht Construction. Why do you ask? Are you working on something for UCG?"

"Professional confidences, old son. But maybe we'll talk about it over dinner at the Club." As I was about to hang up I heard him chortling, "Lennox, you really are amazing. I don't know how you do it." Then he hung up on me.

CHAPTER 14

Ethnic Art's west coast gallery was located close to Ghirardelli Square, a stylish commercial area near the tourist traps of Fisherman's Wharf. It was run by a man called Jerry Prescott and according to my information, he was a local from the Bay Area who had a degree in Art History from Berkeley and a Masters in Business from St Mary's College. He sounded brisk and business like when I called him and we arranged to meet at mid-day. My cover story was that I was an old friend of Mrs van Eck whom she and Sylvia had asked to look at the business with a view to future strategy. Obviously, there was no reference to assessment of people or any possible succession problem.

I took a cab from the Hyatt up the Embarcadero and along Bay Street, stopping the driver at the corner of Leavenworth. I walked the last couple of blocks down the hill, enjoying the clear air, the sunshine and the cool breeze. After the heat and humidity of Florida it felt like heaven and the view of the great orange bridge across the Golden Gate to the highlands of Marin County was like a scene from a movie.

Near the end of Leavenworth was a big multi-story brown brick building that had been a fish cannery in the last century and had since fallen on hard times. In recent years however it had been restored, with a mixture of market speciality shops and one or two discrete little restaurants. I found Ethnic Art Inc. at street level on the city side of the building. As I approached, a white car was just pulling away from in front of the gallery.

Through old-fashioned small paned windows with thick traditional glazing bars I could see a collection of strange and expensive-looking objects: rugs, exotic carvings and a display of silver and turquoise jewellery. I pushed the low, panelled front door. It didn't open. Obviously it was kept locked for security.

I glanced about and found a small brass plate set in the door frame, with what seemed to be a bell-push. It produced a discrete buzz somewhere. I peered into the interior. It was a big space--- bigger than seemed probable from its street frontage--- and dimly lit. I sensed a movement inside and a man's face appeared at the window beside me. I stepped back, smiling disarmingly, and mouthed "Terry Lennox" at him, pointing to my watch. The man stared at me closely and then looked all around the street, as if to make sure I was alone. This seemed to be taking customer security a bit far, I thought.

He opened the door cautiously. "Jerry Prescott?" I said brightly. "My name is Terry Lennox. I spoke to you on the telephone?"

"Oh! Yes! Right!" He scanned the street nervously again. "Come in. Come in."

I stepped into the gallery and he immediately locked the door behind me. "High security," I said pleasantly.

He shook hands with me in a distracted sort of way. He was a man of medium height and wiry build, with small hands and finely-boned wrists. I looked him over. He was clearly disturbed, tension showing in his long, fine featured face and brown eyes. He tried to compose himself, running his fingers through his thinning curly brown hair.

"Yes. Well. Not usually. But I've just had a bad experience." He was wearing a pair of crumpled brown tweed trousers, a checked cotton shirt and a short-sleeved pull-over with a Shetland or Fair Isle pattern. Overall the impression was of an Oxbridge antiquarian book-seller of the casual sort. "It kind of shook me up."

"Tell me about it."

He stared at me for a moment. "Yes, I will." He wandered into the back of the gallery. "Coffee? It's instant, I'm afraid." I refused the coffee and sat down in one of a pair of matched cane-backed Vermont rockers, watching him potter about a small kitchen area. Then he came and sat opposite me, clutching a mug of steaming caffeine. It didn't seem the time to tell him what it was doing to his nervous system.

"I just had a visit from a couple of very strange guys who said they were looking for Sylvia. Wanted to know when I had seen her last--- did I know where she might be?" He gazed at me in puzzlement. "I mean, why should I know where Sylvia is? I haven't seen her for months. Not since she came here on her way back from Europe. Anyway, I didn't like the look of them. So I told them to push off." He winced. "That turned out to be a

mistake. They started to threaten me. One of them in particular
--- a very nasty piece of work--- started to push me around." He
shrugged his shoulders. "With two of them--- .Well, what could
I do." He pulled up the sleeve of his shirt, massaging his wrist.
I saw the reddened skin under his fingers.

"What did they look like?" I asked curiously.

"The really unpleasant one was about my height, with a weird
looking hair style: bald at the front and long and greasy at the
back tied in pony-tail." So Tom Ambrose had been right.
Carlos was anxious to see his wife again. Prescott went on, but
I was barely listening to him. "The other one was much bigger.
Dark haired and rugged. Tough but pretty ordinary.looking"

"And you say they were only interested in finding Sylvia?"

Prescott nodded. "Yes. At first I thought it was just an excuse
to get in; that it was a robbery. But I don't think they took
anything. I locked up after they left. I was just checking to see
if anything was missing." He hesitated. "I hope Sylvia isn't in
some kind of trouble."

"Yes," I said. "I hope so too. Did they say anything else about
Sylvia? Why they were looking for her?"

He shook his head. "Not really." He paused, "Except, when
they were leaving, the smaller one said to tell her they would
find her unless she gave it back. I had no idea what they meant.
And I said so. But they just laughed and said Sylvia would
know."

"And do you have any idea where she is?"

He shook his head again, rubbing his bruised wrist. "No. I hardly ever see her to tell you the truth. Although," he looked thoughtfully at me, "recently she has been putting in an appearance here more often than usual."

"Why do you think that is?"

"I believe she discovered some old friend is living in the city. An old girl friend called Linda Polk." Good old Tom, I thought. He was going up in my estimation all the time. "But I don't know much about her," Prescott said, "and I sure didn't say anything to these guys. But she lives somewhere up on Mount Davison, at Chavez Avenue I think. Sylvia stayed with her a couple of times. She seems to be a potter of sorts. Maybe that's how Sylvia met her."

"Listen, Jerry, I know this is not a good moment but I do need to talk to you about the business. And I don't have a lot of time. I take it you will be reporting the incident with the men to the police?"

"Yes," he said slowly, "I had better do that. For Sylvia's sake. At least I got a good look at them." He stood up. "What do you want to know about the business?"

In the next hour he took me through the place. He was surprisingly organized. "This is just like any other business," he said. "It's all about stock, suppliers and customers. It looks glamorous because of the stuff we handle." He waved his hand vaguely around the room, "And the kind of people we deal with. But basically it's just buying and selling to make a profit."

"And do you?"

"Make a profit? Well, that's difficult for me to say. I don't ever see any financial information. All I know is what I sell here. I understand that Sylvia gets her financial and business advice from someone local in Tampa. I expect he can give you chapter and verse." I smiled and nodded.

He showed me some of the stock. It was mostly old and expensive. "I kind of specialise in Native American tribal art," he explained, "plus the Pacific area--- Polynesia and so on. It's a real privilege to be able to handle this quality of material." He pointed out a group of beautiful old Navajo rugs, woven in pale and lovely colours. "These are all 19th century, and with good provenances." He glanced at me. "That means we know where they came from and who owned them. Without a proper history even a fine object can be questionable--- and less valuable of course."

I stopped in front of a large, grotesque mask, carved in wood and covered in feathers and fringes, with crudely painted semi-human features. "That's Papua New Guinea. You can have it for thirty thousand dollars."

"And these?" I asked, looking at a display of small doll-like figures. "Ah," he said. "Old Zuni Kuchina dolls, carved from solid cotton-wood root. You'll see the cheap and nasty version in the tourist shops in the south-west, but these are genuinely old dolls. They represent the Zuni gods and spirits. They were only given to young girls: to teach them how the world really works. These are very rare, and very valuable."

He took me through the rest of the collection, area by area; jewellery and pottery, some of it by famous contemporary potters from the pueblos up the Rio Grande, and some rather plain looking brown pots that he said had been made a thousand years ago by the ancestors of these modern pueblo Indians, the ancient Anazazi. Very rare and very expensive.

I asked to see his records of sales. Within a few minutes I could see the same pattern as in Brussels; a great deal of very expensive stock and, to judge from the two trading periods he showed me, sales that did not seem to be covering costs. "Do you get the impression this is more of a hobby than a real business?"

He shrugged his shoulders. "I don't see the whole picture."

That was the same phrase Merritt had used and I was beginning to wonder who did see the whole picture. "But if it was my business I'd certainly run it differently." He shot a glance at me. "Of course, maybe it's really run as a kind of tax loss."

I nodded, thoughtfully. "Yes, that's possible of course. How safe is the stock here?" I asked.

"No problem" Prescott said promptly, "I keep a record of everything on my computer and we never have any troubles. Nothing ever goes astray here." He unlocked the front door for me. "Take a look outside and tell me if there's a white Buick parked anywhere around. I don't want to meet these guys again if I can avoid it." I could see nothing outside to worry about, so I thanked him for his cooperation, wished him well with the police and headed back to my hotel.

CHAPTER 15

Back at the Hyatt I called Mrs van Eck. She wasn't available. I left another message to say where I was and that I'd call her later. Then I looked up Linda Polk in the phone book. A woman's voice answered without giving her name. "Yes?"

"I'm looking for Linda Polk."

Her voice sounded hard and challenging. "Who wants her?"

I told her who I was and why I was in San Francisco. "Terry Lennox," she said. I thought I detected a slight east coast accent. "I've heard of you," she said. Another one, I thought. Some of the defensiveness seemed to have left her voice.

"I hope it wasn't all bad."

"No, as a matter of fact Sylvia said you were one of the good guys."

I laughed. "I wonder why she didn't ever tell me that."

"Can you hold on, Terry," she said. It was clear as I listened that she had covered the mouthpiece of the telephone. So she has company, I thought. In a minute or two her voice returned. "What can I do for you, Terry?"

"It's Sylvia I want to speak to you about. I suppose you've heard that she has disappeared?" I said casually.

"Yes," she said, "some kind of sailing accident. I--- I could hardly believe it."

"No, me neither. By the way, how did you hear?" There was an awkward moment of silence. "Oh I think someone in Florida called me," she said. "Someone who knows her."

"I see. Well, it was quite a shock when her mother told me," I said. "Then I heard that you and she were friends, and as I'm in town I thought I'd like to meet you--- just to see what you can tell me about her. I've almost lost touch in recent years. But we were close, as you know."

There was a longish pause. "Well, I don't suppose I can tell you much you don't know." The defensive note seemed to have reappeared. "But I don't mind meeting you," she added.

"This afternoon? I'm not in town long."

"Sorry, no," she said quickly. "But maybe this evening. Come here for a drink before dinner. I'm afraid I have a date tonight." I agreed to call on her at Chavez about six o'clock.

The traffic was heavy on Market Street and up over Portola Drive, but just before six the cab turned into Chavez Avenue, a quiet street that runs around the lower slopes of Mount

106

Davidson. Above us, the hill with its giant cross dominated the southern city sky-line. The driver dropped me off outside number thirty-five. It was a street full of big detached houses, set back from the road in large gardens, with flights of steps up to first floor entrances. At street level were the garages and here and there an entrance to a lower level more modern apartment.

Linda Polk's house had a short driveway up to a double garage beneath the house. A white painted staircase led up to the front door and at the top was a small balcony with decorative wrought iron railings. The place was classic 1900's San Francisco, stone built with an almost alpine pitch to its tiled roof and it seemed to run a long way back into the hillside. I could see a stretch of grass down the side of the house, overhung by big old willows. The back of the house must be pretty quiet and dark, I thought. I pressed the door bell and waited.

After a long wait the door opened a couple of inches, still held on a security chain. Through the gap I caught a glimpse of a face and a flash of red hair. Then, down at waist level I saw a hand, a woman's hand holding a very small chrome plated automatic pistol. The neat black muzzle was pointing up at me. "Who is it? What do you want?" It was Linda Polk's voice, sounding weak and frightened.

"It's Terry Lennox. You said to come at six." There was a moment's silence.

Then, "Oh yes, thank god. You're alone?"

"Yes, I'm alone. What's going on? Can I help?"

There was a rattle as the chain was released and the door opened slowly. She was a big woman and in her prime must have been quite a beauty. Now, the fullness of her figure had blurred and thickened, leaving an impression of flesh only just under control. Whatever colour nature had given to her hair had been transformed into a deep rich red. But she had retained some of her looks, with wide set dark eyes, a good nose, slightly snubbed and a generous mouth. Dressed up, she would have looked good in most circles.

Now however she was wearing a thin cotton robe that fell apart to reveal plump knees and her long hair was tumbled in disorder. She looked pale. But she lowered the little automatic, jerked the robe closer around her and stepped aside to let me in. Before she closed the door she looked quickly around the empty street. Then she replaced the chain and turned to face me, swaying slightly.

She leaned back against the door frame and then I saw the vivid red weal on the left side of her face. Her eyes were red and swollen and it was obvious that she had been crying. She began to tremble. I put my arm around her shoulder and felt her slump against me. I gently took the gun out of her hand. It was a small calibre Browning that probably made her feel better but was unlikely to do much damage, unless she was very close or very lucky. I helped her into a big sitting room that ran across the front of the house. "What's been going on?" I asked."What's wrong?" Linda sank down into a deep, soft armchair and buried her face in her hands.

I glanced around. The room looked as if a bomb had exploded in it. Cabinets had been emptied and drawers lay tipped out around the floor. A glass-fronted bookcase was standing open, its books scattered about, some of them lying broken-backed. I frowned. I hate to see books destroyed. The air was thick with the smell of alcohol and the smashed remains of some bottles lay in the wide stone fireplace. I hoped it hadn't been a good malt.

I put my hand gently on her shoulder. "What's happened, Linda?" She straightened up and took a deep breath. Her hands went automatically to tidy her dishevelled hair, with her eyes lowered. When she spoke she seemed to have recovered most of her assurance. "Two men." she said. That sounded familiar. "They forced their way in. I didn't have the chain on the door. I usually don't. Not in this area. I should have known--- should have expected---." She stopped and stood up quickly. When I straightened I realised how tall she was.

"Listen Terry," she said. "I could do with a drink now. I think there's a bottle they missed in the kitchen." She led the way into a medium-sized, slightly old-fashioned kitchen with a small window looking out onto the overhanging trees and the hillside. Like the sitting room, the kitchen had been ransacked. Even the refrigerator had been emptied, with salad and plastic containers tossed on the floor. Linda sat down heavily on a 1950's chrome kitchen chair and leaned on the formica-topped table. She waved a hand in the direction of a row of head high cupboards. "There's some Scotch in there. They missed these somehow."

I found a bottle of 12 year old Glenfiddich. It looked like duty free, in the one litre size. Things were looking up at last. I took down a couple of glasses and poured her a generous dram, then a smaller one for myself. "Water?" I asked. She shook her head. I went across to the kitchen sink and put a splash of water into my glass. I watched her as she gulped down half the neat whisky, holding the glass tightly in two hands. She gasped as the spirit bit.

I sipped my drink. "Do you want to tell me what this is all about?" I asked.

She was almost fully recovered from her shock now. She stood up, shook her head and wandered out of the kitchen. I followed her across a dark little hall and paused at the door of her bedroom. It too had been turned upside down--- the bed pulled to pieces and the mattress ripped open. The drawers of the bedside chests were tipped upside down on the floor. She surveyed the wreckage silently, apparently looking for something. Then she stooped and picked up her handbag, lying half-empty in a corner. She fished inside and brought out a packet of cigarettes.

Still staring absently about her, she shook out a cigarette and put it between her lips. She looked at me, seeming to notice me properly for the first time. "Cigarette?" she offered. I shook my head. "I don't."

Linda gave a little smile. "Very wise. You probably don't carry matches either?" I shook my head again. Somewhere in the corner of the room she found a flip-top pack of cardboard matches of the kind bars and restaurants give away.

Calm now, she struck a match and lit the cigarette, throwing back her head as she did so to blow the smoke into the air. I was becoming irritated. "Linda, do you want me to go?" She stared at me silently for a moment, her eyes narrowed against the drifting smoke. Still she said nothing.

Then as I started to turn away, exasperated, I saw something in a small niche beneath the bed room window that made me stop.

I gasped. It was a near life-size head of a woman, sculpted in clay. I knew the model. The strong, fine lines of the jaw and nose were unmistakable and the sculptress had caught perfectly the tilt of the head and the slightly mocking smile. I could almost see the quizzical sideways glance from the intelligent eyes.

It was Sylvia, more or less as I had seen her last.

I stopped. "My god that's good" I said and turned back towards Linda Polk. She drew again on the cigarette.

"Yes, I think it's one of the best things I've done. You really like it?".

I nodded. "I think it's superb. You did it?" She sat down on the edge of the bed, surrounded by the shambles of her room. "Well," she said, "I had a beautiful model, didn't I?"

CHAPTER 16

I went across and sat beside her. "Linda, tell me what this is all about. Do you want me to call the police? Did you know the men who did this?"

Linda looked at me steadily. "Sylvia said I could rely on you if you came." I tried to look reliable and I must have been successful, for she suddenly stood up and strode across the room. "Maybe you can help." She stubbed out the cigarette and threw it down, angrily. "But, no, I don't see what you can do. Not with these people. They're really rough guys."

Something faintly out of place snagged my thoughts for a moment. But then I followed her through to the sitting-room. She stood staring out into the darkening sky, looking westward across the aptly named Sunset area of the city. "No. It's not your scene. These people are dangerous." She seemed to be talking as much to herself as to me.

"Try me" I said gently. "Tell me what these men wanted." She swung round to face me. "They were looking for something that belonged to my ex-husband." I felt a vague sense of anticlimax. "So this," I waved my hand around aimlessly, "this is some kind of personal thing. It has nothing to do with Sylvia."

Linda smiled ironically. "Oh yes," she said, "It has everything to do with Sylvia." I shook my head. "OK. I'm confused. Explain."

She leaned back against the window frame and looked me in the eyes. "I used to be married to Carlos di Giorgio. That's how I met Sylvia in the first place."

I put on my professional face and said quietly, "Tell me more."

She didn't even try to hide her anger. "Carlos is a complete bastard. Of course I thought he was a nice guy when I married him." She gave a wry smile. "I suppose Sylvia did too. Then I found out how he made his money. I mean the kind of businesses he was involved in--- the kind of people he worked with."

I interrupted her, "People like Cuneo? And Pantuliano?"

She raised her eyebrows at me. "So you've met them already." She went on quickly, "Yes, his importing operation was a front for other imports--- and exports. Illegal stuff."

"Drugs?" I asked.

She nodded. "Yes, and weapons too, shipped using his legitimate companies as cover."

I whistled. "So it's big stuff?"

"Yes. I don't know how for sure how big. But big." She paused.

"Of course Carlos isn't the top man or anything like it. He's always been pretty small beer," she disdainfully."But he's close to some important people, like Cuneo. Anyway, when I objected to it, he became nastier and nastier. So I threatened to leave him. Several times." She shrugged. "He didn't like that. His bosses don't like people with personal problems. He started to use violence. He beat me up a few times. Then there were other women." She hesitated. "Say, is there anything left in that bottle?" I found the Glenfiddich and splashed some in each of our glasses. She gulped down a mouthful. "Finally I took off one day when he was away. He didn't know where I had gone."

To lose one wife is a misfortune, I thought. But to lose two? She went on. "Then I started divorce proceedings. I think it was around then that he met Sylvia, so he went along with it. As soon as the divorce was finalised they were married." She grimaced " Sylvia must have been crazy. I'm sure it was her money or her family money he was interested in." She shrugged and smiled at me. "But you know how it is sometimes."

I rather thought I did, remembering what had happened at the motel in Florida. "How did you meet her?" I asked. Linda smiled. "I was suing Carlos for non-payment of alimony--- I still am, come to that," she added ruefully. "That cheap crook still hasn't paid me what he owes. Sylvia contacted me when she began to realise what he was like. She thought we had something in common." She smiled bitterly and shot a glance at me. "I didn't contact her, if that's what you were thinking. All I want is what he owes me."

"Tell me what these men were looking for."

Linda hesitated, "When Sylvia left she took something with

her. Something that belonged to Carlos. Something important. Something that he wants back."

The Princess Head? But surely that didn't belong to Carlos. Something he wanted badly enough to send hired hands all the way to San Francisco to find," I said. "Linda, what was it she took? What does Sylvia have that he wants so badly?""

"She called me a few weeks ago to say that she was leaving him and that she had a private diary of his. It is apparently a record of some of his less legal business activities. She read some of the stuff to me. Details of meetings; the names of people involved--- the amounts of money, and where it went. Instructions he was given by the others."

"Cuneo and Pantuliano?" I wondered why Carlos would keep a record like that. It sounded dangerous.

"Yes. I had no idea the diary existed when I was with him. Maybe it didn't. It would be dynamite in the wrong hands, Terry." She shrugged and looked around aimlessly for another cigarette. "Anyway Sylvia thought I could use it to force Carlos to pay up. But as soon as I found out what it was I knew it was too dangerous play around with. I told her to get rid of it. I don't want that kind of trouble: not with Carlos and his friends." She laughed sourly, "I don't need the money that bad."

"And of course Carlos realised Sylvia had taken the diary." I said. "But how did he connect it with you? Have you seen her recently?"

"He must have known Sylvia had been to see me from time to time. I suppose he assumed she had passed the diary on to me. Or at least that I'd know what happened to her.

"But you don't," I said.

She shook her head. "No. But he sent his thugs to call on me anyway. And I'm not sure I've seen the last of them." She shot a glance at me. "He won't rest until he has it back. Or knows it's destroyed." I remembered young Tom Ambrose's account of the conversation he had overheard in the garden.

"Linda, what did these men look like?"

"There were two of them. A dark haired guy and a smaller man with an unusual haircut." It all sounded horribly familiar. Any doubts I had about Carlos melted away. She went on, "The front part of his head was shaved right back, and then his hair hung long down at the back--- in a kind of loose pig-tail." She shivered. "He was the nasty one. The other one was a big slow moving type. Not too smart. But it was the smaller one who hit me." She rubbed the side of her face. "He seemed to enjoy hurting me."

"What about the diary? Have you any idea what Sylvia did with it?" There was just a momentary hesitation. Her eyes left mine for an instant. "No. My advice was to send it back to him and get him off her back. And mine too," she added sardonically. "I certainly didn't want it around here."

"You say she called you? Do you have any idea where she was intending to go? You do know the accident was a put up job?"

Linda hesitated. "She did say something about making it look like a sailing accident. To give her time to disappear, I suppose. But it's hard to say where she might be now. She could be anywhere. All she told me was that she was leaving him and was going somewhere to lie low for a while. To lick her wounds. That was how she put it. She said she needed time alone. I think she said something about it being just a matter of time, whatever that meant."

I wondered too. "So you've no idea where she is?"

Linda Polk shook her head. "No," she said firmly, "All I know is what I told you." It sounded genuine. But there was something that still worried me. Something she had said earlier. Something I couldn't quite drag back into the front of my mind. Maybe I was still jet-lagged.

CHAPTER 17

She started to clear up the mess in her bedroom. "Look," I said, "Why don't you get out of here for a while? Or at least call the police? You did say these men might come back. Do you have somewhere else you can go?"

"I don't want to involve the police," she said sharply. "But I have a sister up in Seattle. I could hole out with her for a while." She stopped. "No. Maybe that isn't such a good idea. Carlos would think of that."

I thought for a moment. "Maybe I can help." I looked at my watch. "What time is it in the UK?" I added eight hours and came up with three am. "What the hell. It's an emergency." I smiled at her. "I have a friend in Edinburgh who owns a condo somewhere in the East Bay area." Odd but true. Well, that could be his motto. He was a wealthy lawyer who had been attracted by the condo's proximity to the San Francisco gay scene. And he was a good friend. "If I can use your telephone I'll see if the place is vacant. Maybe we can park you there for a while." She nodded her agreement.

I listened to the telephone ring for what seemed like an eternity. I was beginning to think he was spending the night away from home, not unknown in the gay community. At last I heard his voice, crisply public school even at the crack of dawn. "John Boyd. I explained the problem, without too many details. When I mentioned Sylvia's name he broke into a familiar braying guffaw. "My dear boy, are you quite mad? I thought you were cured!" He never had approved of Sylvia, although with typical discretion he had said nothing about his feelings until the two of us were well and truly separated.

I explained it wasn't for Sylvia. I didn't dare tell him it was for her husband's former wife. I wasn't sure even John's razor-sharp mind would make sense of that at three o'clock in the morning. I wasn't even sure I could. But yes, the condo was empty. He gave me the address. The keys were with the lady who managed the complex and he promised to call her to say we were on our way. I thanked him and hung up.

The place was over the Bay Bridge, beyond Berkeley and just off the eastbound freeway, on the fringes of Pleasant Hill, one of the many communities that ring the Bay Area. Linda Polk went to put on some clothes and pack a bag. I studied the map and then wandered into the bedroom to watch her throw some essentials into an overnight case. She had transformed herself with some make-up and a comb, in the way women can. She was wearing a pair of jeans and a white shirt, with short leather boots. She looked twenty years younger, her red hair pulled back and held with a simple headband of suede.

I went over to the clay head of Sylvia and ran my fingers down the cold, rough surface. Linda watched me. "You liked her, didn't you," she said quietly. I thought for a moment. Liked seemed inadequate to describe the turbulence that Sylvia had inspired. But I looked up and nodded, silently.

Linda lit another cigarette. She glanced from the head to me and back again, as if making up her mind about something. Abruptly, she said, "Take it." She smiled. "It will remind you of her. And maybe of me too. Yes, why don't you take it, Terry." She sounded certain now. "Take it and keep it safe. I have a box I use for mailing my work to customers. I'll pack it up for you"

I was touched, and I said so. At last, I thought, I'd found a version of Sylvia that wouldn't give me a lot of trouble. I looked at my watch again. "Let's get out of here, Linda."

She nodded. "O.K." She said, "my car is outside." I went over to the window and looked out at the darkened street. That was when I noticed the white Buick parked about fifty yards down Chavez Avenue. Sitting in the car were two men.

CHAPTER 18

I turned back to Linda. "I don't think it's such a good idea to use your car." She looked at me questioningly. "Our friends are sitting out there in a white car. If we want to get away from them we'll have to think of something else." I grinned. "I'm not up to a car chase around this city. I saw it once in the movies and it scared me then," I hoped I was sounding insouciant. Her eyes showed real fear.

She peered cautiously out into the street. "Yes. That's their car." She glanced at me, puzzled. "But how did you know? And what are we going to do now?"

I shook my head. "It's a long story. And it doesn't matter right now. But I'll tell you what we're going to do. We're going to call the police. All you have to do is tell them the story. Raise a complaint and have them removed." She looked scared. "No," she said quickly. "I can't--- I just can't. I promised Sylvia,"

I broke in, "Why does it matter now?" Her mouth tightened.

121

"And you don't know Carlos. I don't want any more trouble from him."

I thought quickly. Why do some clients always resist good advice? I reached for the telephone book. I remembered that there was an Alamo car rental office near the Hyatt. I called and arranged an immediate pick-up. While we waited I explained to Linda what I wanted her to do.

When the cab arrived I walked carefully down the stairs, carrying the box containing Sylvia's head. The men in the car showed no sign of moving. As far as I knew, they had no reason to be interested in me. I had a feeling that was about to change. I opened the rear door of the cab and slid in.

The cabbie was a distinguished looking man with a cultured west coast accent. Probably an out of work accountant caught in the recession or an academic from Berkeley moonlighting. I told him where we wanted to go. Then I asked him if he could see the white Buick parked up the street. He adjusted his rear view mirror, and nodded. "If that car follows us I'd like to lose it. Can you do that?" He glanced at me in the mirror. "I can try. They're not cops, are they?"

I shook my head. "No. It's nothing illegal, I promise you." I searched rapidly for an explanation that wouldn't seem too bizarre. "There are some friends of the lady's ex-husband in the white car and they want to know where we're going. You see, we're eloping."

He looked at me in the mirror again. "How romantic," he said dryly. I don't think he was convinced. "How well do they know the city?" I told him I thought they were from out of state and he laughed. "In that case I can probably lose them. Have you ever tried driving in San Francisco?" I signalled to Linda. She came down the steps in a rush and jumped into the cab beside me.

The driver took off down Chavez. Behind us the Buick's headlights abruptly lit up the street. Our cab weaved through the maze of residential streets round the side of Mt.Davidson. Most of them seemed to dead-ended at the dual-carriageway of Portola Drive, a main through highway downtown. A couple of times I thought we had lost the white car. But as we finally swung onto the highway I could see that it was still behind us. Our driver spotted it in the mirror. "These fellows really want to know where you're planning to start your new life," he called back to me, breezily. I think he was beginning to enter into the spirit of the thing. "I thought I'd get rid of them in there. It's not going to be so easy downtown."

Time for the fall-back plan. We swooped at speed down Portola with the lights of the city beneath us, through the hilly inner suburbs and into the sleazy lower end of Market Street. Suddenly there was traffic all around us, with busy cross streets and lights that broke up the flow.

From time to time I lost sight of the Buick but always it reappeared, sometimes a block or so back, but never far away. Between the tall buildings, Market Street stretched flat and even into the distance. Somewhere up ahead was my wonderful hotel room and a well-stocked mini bar. What am I doing, I thought in despair. I could be watching the ball game on TV.

As we passed the Civic Centre I leaned forward. "Can you pull over at Powell Rapid Transitstation? We're going to split up."

"Hey," the driver said. "That romance didn't last long."

123

I decided to ignore him. "Look, Linda. As soon as we stop, get down into the station and take a train to the East Bay. Any train. I'll take your bag. Just get away from the station. If they follow you, double back. Change trains, change lines, do anything. Use the system. They probably don't know how the rapid transit system works. But whatever you do, lose them. And end up at Pleasant Hill B.A.R.T. station. I'll meet you there as soon as I can. Then I'll take you to the condo and we'll be in the clear. Have you got that?"

She nodded. "There's a big Nordstroms store on top of the station. If anyone follows me I'll lose them in there and then slip down to the trains later."

The cab stopped under the towering post-modernist department store. Linda scurried out and across the wide side walk. "Go," I said to the driver. As we eased back into the traffic stream I saw the white Buick pull over and stop. We turned down Fourth and into the grid of one-way streets south of Market. In a couple of minutes we were at the Alamo depot. The cab driver looked at me blandly as I paid him. "Say, I hope you too get together again."

"Thank you," I said solemnly. "So do I." I hoped Linda would know her way around Nordstroms better than the heavies from Florida. Somehow I thought she would.

Half an hour later I was driving up the slip road onto the Bay Bridge in a new Pontiac and heading for Interstate 80 East. Traffic was light on the long two-tiered bridge that links the city with Oakland and I drifted easily along through the darkened lower level with only a few cars behind me. I began to relax, with only a passing qualm about the last big earthquake that brought the top deck crashing down on the east bound lane.

As I plunged into the tunnel through Treasure Island I thought momentarily about R.L.S. and Edinburgh. Maybe one day I'd get back to being a management consultant there. I shook my head at my image in the mirror. What was it about Sylvia that created this kind of chaos? And I hadn't even seen her for years! I was beginning to regret the call from Mrs van Eck.

Suddenly I was out of the Bay Bridge and into the sweeping maelstrom of the big interchanges around and above Oakland. I concentrated hard as the road signs reared up over me, trying to remember John Boyd's lucid directions, almost oblivious to the rest of the traffic. I slipped onto Highway 24, climbing steadily up into the Berkeley hills, with the street lights of small communities on each side. Then another tunnel, artificially bright, driven straight through the hillside.

The other side of the tunnel seemed a world away from Oakland and San Francisco. Traffic thinned out rapidly and on each side were high dark hills, thickly wooded. Alongside the freeway the scattered, brightly lit B.A.R.T. stations shone out like good deeds in a wicked world, most of them deserted at this time of the evening. Now and then the blaze of car head-lights swept past me.

I took the Pleasant Hill exit and shot down into the local road system. The streets were wide, well illuminated and clearly signed and after only a couple of passes I found the entrance to the B.A.R.T. with it's vast parking lot almost empty. I cruised around and finally pulled up near a deserted bus stop. As I stepped out of the car the night air hit me, dark and warm, filled with the dry perfume of some semi-tropical plant. In the silence there was only the occasional distant swish of traffic on the freeway and the regular piping of the cicadas. Overhead the sky was clear and full of high stars. I had been told that east of the hills the climate changed. But this really did seem to be a different world.

I locked the car and walked into the well-lit concourse of the station, towards the automatic gates that controlled entrance and exit from the rapid transit system. The only sign of life was a small glass cubical with a bored-looking attendant who was there in case someone's ticket failed to work the computerised controls. I stood in the middle of the station, looking around. Then the door of the ladics toilet opened and Linda appeared. Why had I worried?

CHAPTER 19

The condo was only a couple of blocks from the station and I found the manager's office easily. She was a lanky, slow-spoken lady with a southern accent and a willingness to chat. I pleaded a long journey and reluctantly she gave me the keys and let me go. The complex was old and rambling development of apartments in two storeys, built of a kind of creamy adobe plaster. The buildings were all surrounded by sheltering trees, with here and there attractive little swimming-pools for the use of the residents, most of whom apparently were at work during the day. It seemed an ideal place to lay low for a while.

John's condo was small but well equipped. There was a large bedroom with a king-sized bed, and a big sitting room with a Futon-type sofa that folded down to make another double bed. I had decided not to leave her alone at the condo so we found some blankets and pillows and together we made up both beds.

In the little galley kitchen I found the usual pots and pans, some basic dishes and cutlery and odds and ends of foodstuffs.

Definitely enough for survival. I remembered I hadn't eaten since lunch and decided to heat up some tinned beans and sausages. Not exactly haut cuisine, but it would have to do. Linda made coffee. It was all beginning to seem very domestic, considering I had only met her three hours before.

She was starting to relax and as we ate she told me what had happened when she left me. "The tall one got out of the car and followed me into the Nordstrom building. But I managed to slip down into the station. I had an old ticket with some credit on it, so I gained a few minutes on him getting onto the platforms. But still he came after me." She grinned excitedly. "I did what you told me and took the first train. It was going to Fremont but I took it anyway and changed at Oakland. That's a big station and I thought I'd be able to avoid him there. He only just missed getting on the train so he probably saw the destination. I was scared. But I was lucky again. The next train was for Concord, and he wasn't on it. So here I am."

I touched her hand. "Well done. We should be in the clear now. But what are we going to do with you? We can't stay here for ever."

She nodded. "I've been thinking about that. I have some friends in Denver I could stay with. I can take the Amtrak from Oakland tomorrow. \the Zephyr leaves every morning about ten. If you can you drop me off there tomorrow?"

We decided on an early night. She took the bedroom and I curled up on the sofa-bed under a blanket and listened to the sound of the occasional car swish past on the road outside. I lay there thinking about Sylvia. Linda knew more about her than she had told me, that was obvious. I was certain Sylvia had visited the house on Chavez; maybe even that day. The two men from Carlos probably knew something. Why else would they have been there? But there was still that elusive something. Something that Linda had said. Something that I couldn't quite bring into focus. Then I must have dropped off to sleep.

I awoke with a jump. Linda's voice whispered in my ear, "It's only me." It was dark but I felt her warm plumpness as she slid in beside me. "It was a bit scary in there on my own. I hope you don't mind." Her voice sounded sleepy. Well, what can you say? I wrapped my arms around her and held her against my chest. It felt nice, in a friendly sort of way. We drifted off to sleep together.

In the early hours of the morning we woke again. Daylight was just starting to seep in at the windows. She burrowed her face into me shoulder and pressed her body against me. This time we didn't go to sleep, at least not right away.

When I woke again it was broad daylight and I could hear her moving around the condo. It was seven thirty am. I showered and shaved, using a cheap plastic throw-away razor that I found in a drawer. I wiped the steam from the mirror and examined my face. The razor had seen better days but it did the job. Not a bad paradigm for myself, I thought.

We gulped down a cup of hot coffee. Neither of us mentioned what had happened the night before. She was still wearing the same clothes but she had done something to her hair and she looked relaxed and poised. "The sooner we get to the Amtrak depot the better," she said. I nodded. "Maybe I'd better drive," she said, "I expect I know my way around the roads better than you." I nodded again and we started out towards the car.

I wandered up to the condo exit and looked around. There were trees everywhere; young redwoods, larches, olive trees and the occasional palm. Through the greenery, on the other side of the broad street I saw the white Buick parked. There was a man sitting in it. "How the hell?" I started to say. Then it dawned on me. He hadn't followed Linda here. He had followed me.

I met Linda by the car. "Don't panic, but one of our friends is sitting outside in the white Buick." Her normally pale complexion went paler still and she half slumped against the car. "Don't worry," I said, "Are you O.K. to drive?" She nodded and slid behind the wheel.

I made my way back to the manager's office. She was just opening up and she seemed glad to see me. "Listen," I said. "There's something I'm worried about. I've spotted a car, a white Buick, sitting across the street with a man in it. I think he's been there all night, watching the place. Have you had any trouble with break-ins here? Maybe I'm worried unnecessarily, but---"

She picked up the telephone. "You did quite right to tell me. We can't be too careful these days--- with so many of the folk away all day. The local police will send a patrol round right away. They're real fussy about keeping undesirable elements out of this community. Exactly where is this car parked?" I told her and left.

It was about two minutes later that I saw a car with the markings of the local Sheriff's Office glide up alongside the Buick and two large cops emerge to saunter over to the driver.

"OK Linda," I said, ""Let's go. I think your Florida friend will be tied up for a while." Quietly, she drifted the car out of the condo and onto the highway. Within minutes we were on the freeway headed back towards Oakland and the city.

At the Amtrak depot Linda got out of the car. She leaned forward and kissed me. "Sylvia was right. You are one of the good guys," she said softly.

I stared at her. Suddenly the question that had been nagging at me became clear. "Tell me something, Linda. When I first arrived at the house on Chavez you said that Sylvia said you could trust me if I came to see you. Why did she think I might come to see you? What made her think I would be involved in this at all?"

Linda looked puzzled. "I've no idea why."

"But you have seen her, haven't you? And quite recently." I asked.

She nodded. "Yes. She came to my place yesterday. But I promise you I don't know where she is now. Or even what she's trying to do." She hesitated. "I have a feeling there's more to it all than just Carlos." She smiled at me. " Anyway, take good care of her head. At least you've got that. Maybe you'll find the rest of her one day!"

She blew me a kiss and I watched her walk away from me. She didn't turn round. Why should she? It had only been a small deception.

CHAPTER 20

By the time I had dropped off the car and got back to the Hyatt it was lunch-time. I ordered some sandwiches and a bottle of the local Sierra beer from room service and started to make a few phone calls. Mrs van Eck was unavailable, as usual.

I decided to call Carlos at the house at Pelican Cove. At least I think it was Carlos I wanted to speak to. I didn't know exactly what I was going to say to him. "Tell me Carlos, is it true you're a crook, with Mafia connections and that you have been screwing your step-daughter?" Or, "Your former wife tells me that you sent two thugs to beat her up and threaten her." Or even; "Is it true that Sylvia disappeared with some incriminating evidence you might kill for?" I decided to see what developed and to play it by ear.

The telephone rang several times. Just as I was about to hang up, I heard young Sylvia's voice. Had I expected that? "Hello," I said weakly, ever the master of the quick quip. "How are you? This is Terry Lennox. Remember me?"

"Terry," she said calmly. "How sweet of you to call. Is there anything I can do for you?"

I restrained myself. "Ah, no; not really. Well, I mean---."

I heard her give a little laugh."That doesn't sound very promising."

"I was really calling to speak to Carlos." I decided to brazen it out.

"Worse and worse," she murmured. "I hoped you might want to see me again."

"Look Sylvia, about the other evening--- I'm afraid I acted rather badly."

I heard the familiar little giggle. "On the contrary," she said, "I thought you behaved beautifully." She was obviously enjoying herself.

But this conversation was getting out of hand and she was beginning to irritate me. "Can I speak to Carlos?" I asked resolutely.

"No. He's in Miami. Some boring business meeting with Mr Cuneo. When am I going to see you again?"

"I don't think that's such a good idea, Sylvia. Besides, I'll be back in Europe soon."

"Perfect," she said calmly. "I'm going back to stay with Mummy at Vinkiveen. It's boring here without Sylvia to tease. I'll make a point of seeing you there."

I took a deep breath. "Sylvia, I said I didn't think that would be a good idea."

She giggled again, but this time there was a touch of spite in her voice. "What a bore! I can't see what Sylvia saw in you. Not that she ever had much taste." Her voice hardened. "But don't think I'm going to let you get away just yet."

I struggled for a reply. How could I let the kid wrong foot me so easily? "Sylvia, what happened was a mistake. It was my mistake. But just think how your mother would feel about it. And your grandmother."

"To hell with Sylvia!" The voice was unpleasant now, harsh and ugly. "She has never been a mother to me--- why should I care what she feels?" She went on spitefully, "And just you think of what my grandmother, as you call her, would feel about it."

I winced. She had a point. "Now I do have to go," I said hastily. "I have other calls to make." As I hung up I heard her give a little giggle and shout out, "Remember, I expect to see you again." I stared at the telephone, beginning to realise I was in some game with rules I didn't even know and might never fully understand. But little Sylvia could obviously be as much trouble as her mother. I cursed myself again for letting it happen.

I fished out the business card Pantuliano had given me. It had the telephone number for Bay Financial Services and a home number. I tried it and waited. Almost immediately I heard Pantuliano's voice. I introduced myself. He actually sounded pleased to hear from me. "Terry!" he said, "How are you?"

I decided to take it head on. "Rich, I may have a problem."

"OK," he said, "Tell me about it."

"Well, the reason I'm calling is that Marcus Cuneo asked me to keep you informed."

"Sure," he agreed, "Glad to hear from you. What's the problem?"

"It's about the Ethnic Art accounts you gave me, Rich. There are some things in there I don't understand, and I wondered if you could help me."

"Go on," he said. A little of the warmth seemed to fade from his voice.

"It puzzles me that the company has such a high level of debt."

Pantuliano was silent for a moment. "OK," he said. "Anything else?"

I went on. "Yes. Can you let me have a trading statement and a detailed list of debtors and creditors, long and short term. I need to understand what's going on." There was another slightly awkward silence.

Then Pantuliano spoke. "Terry, I think you and I should meet to talk this over. Are you coming back this way soon?" I thought quickly. "I don't have any plans to do that."

"Like I say, I think we should talk face to face. It's important. Where are you now?" I told him and said I was on my way to Boston and from there back home.

"Right," he said. "When you finish your business in Boston route yourself back to Europe through here. I'll have you picked up at the airport if you call me." I agreed to change my plans. Just before he hung up he said, "Terry, this is quite a delicate situation. Marcus would want us to handle it with discretion." I told him discretion was my middle name. It wasn't true, but it seemed to satisfy him, for the moment.

So Marcus Cuneo thought the situation was delicate. Didn't someone say that when a man wants to speak to you on a matter of delicacy, it's probably a matter of no delicacy whatsoever? I was glad I hadn't mentioned the Carlos problem. I decided to save that one for him later.

I didn't want to carry Sylvia's head around with me for the rest of the trip so I called Jerry Prescott at the gallery and asked him if he could ship it back to Scotland for me. He did that kind of thing all the time it seemed and was no problem. I took a cab to Ghirardelli Square and gave him the box. He seemed pleased enough with Linda's packaging. "Look," I said, "I'm not sure when I'll be at home to receive it." I gave him John Boyd's address in Edinburgh. I only wished I could have seen his face when he unpacked it. On my way out I asked Prescott if he had told the police about his trouble with the two men. He hadn't, so I told him I thought he should. "And give them the descriptions. That could be important if they come around again." He looked scared. But it seemed a useful precaution. And what harm could it do? By now it was too late to fly to Boston in a civilised fashion, so I spent the rest of the day doing tourist things around the waterfront. Then I had an Italian meal in North Beach and went back to the Hyatt and an early bed.

CHAPTER 21

Next morning the Golden Gate was filled with an opaque milky mass of sea-fog that bubbled and billowed up to the tops of the famous bridge. To my right, the city lay still bathed in clear golden sun-light, its tall buildings sparkling and clean. Before long it looked as if the fog would take it over, turning it into a typical mist-shrouded, dripping summer day in San Francisco. I tuned the radio into the classic music programme. It was playing something modern and chaotic. I sighed and switched it off. Bad start to the day. I did my exercises, showered, shaved and dressed.

By then it was eight thirty. I added eight hours and decided to try Mrs van Eck's number again. This time amazingly she was available. I heard her cultured English tones clearly in spite of the distance between us. "Terry!" She sounded pleased to hear from me, her voice low and rich.

"Good morning Mrs van Eck, "I said. "Or rather good afternoon."

She gave a charming little laugh. "Helen, please" she replied.

"How are you getting on with the assignment? Do you have any news for me?"

"Well," I said, "I've been trying to contact you. But you've obviously been very busy." She was silent for a moment.

"Yes," she said, her voice calm and relaxed. "I'm sorry. I did get your messages. But there is such a lot going on here. I've been very much occupied with a big Nigerian contract we're trying to land. But it was good of you to call. Now tell me your news, Terry."

"As far as the company is concerned I'm still assessing the overall position. I need to look at those bank statements and cash-flow details when I get back. You were able to contact the bank in Miam?" I asked.

She said "Yes." And she sounded a touch irritated. "Yes. They are going to send the information directly to your home. It should be waiting for you. But, tell me. Is there anything else significant to tell me?"

I hesitated. "I have to say, I'm concerned about the finances of the business. But I must do some more analysis." There was no point in telling her about Donald Lynch. "But I'd prefer to discuss that with you face to face. I should be back early on Wednesday morning. If I call from the airport perhaps you can have me picked up. I'm on my way now, via Boston and Florida."

"Florida?" She sounded surprised and interested. "You're going back to Florida?"

"Just a few loose ends," I said. "It won't add significantly to the costs."

"Terry," she said reproachfully, "I explained to you that costs don't matter in this case. Of course I'll arrange a car to meet your flight on Wednesday. Is there anything else?"

There was an awkward silence. "Mrs van Eck--- Helen," I said, "I don't want to raise your hopes unduly, but I have some reason to think Sylvia may be alive after all." There was a longer silence this time. I tried to imagine how she was feeling, but at this range I had no idea. In fact with Helen van Eck I had trouble up close.

When she spoke she seemed cool and controlled. "Has she been in touch with you?" she asked, almost casually.

I corrected her hastily. "No, I'm afraid not. But I have spoken to some people who seem reliable." I paused, thinking of Linda and young Tom Ambrose. "Well, more or less. And they claim to have seen her since the incident with the boat." I thought that was about as far as I should go.

"I see," Mrs van Eck said. She sounded disappointed. "Well, you will keep me informed Terry?"

I stared at the receiver in my hand and shook my head in amazement. "Well, of course. But if she is still alive and well somewhere is there any need for me to identify anyone to run the company."

"But I still need your advice on what to do with the business. No, keep at it, Terry. Now, if there isn't anything else for the moment, I'll look forward to seeing you soon." She was about to hang up on me, when I intervened.

"Mrs van Eck, one other thing. Carlos di Giorgio says he told you he thought Sylvia might be alive--- might have gone off somewhere for some reason. Is that true?"

There was a long pause. "I'm not sure. He says so much. He may have said he hoped that was the case. But does it matter? Goodbye, Terry." I was left holding the dead receiver as the line hummed emptily. So much for Mother Love.

Two hours later I was on the flight to Boston's Logan Airport. I made a note to call John Boyd to warn him about the package that was on its way to him. Then I settled back to watch the sun on the Sierras and the hot dry plains slip away beneath the wing of the aircraft. I already had a tight schedule in Boston and now I'd agreed to fit in another trip to Florida. I sighed and began to flick through the pages of "A Distant Mirror".

But the problems of medieval Europe quickly palled and I found myself wondering again what had happened to Sylvia, and what she was trying to achieve. I thought about Linda Polk, down there somewhere. I hoped they were both safe. Then I fell asleep. Just as well, I thought, as I drifted off. I had better get all the sleep I can. Tomorrow I'm buying dinner for Donald Lynch.

Boston's airport must be as close to the city centre as any in the world. The harbour and the tall buildings downtown seemed almost an extension of the runway as the plane plunged down to the flat scrubland and the waters of the Atlantic, rolling in from the east. Somewhere across there, I thought, is Scotland.

Logan was hot, crowded and sticky. Outside in the concrete parking area the sky above the town was darkening already and the air hung heavily, moist and full of fumes from the scores of coaches, cars and cabs that slowly edged their way around the inadequate approaches of the airport. Eventually I was in a cab and racing the short distance into town through the tunnel under the harbour.

I had booked a room at the Harvard Club on Commonwealth Avenue and the driver deposited me there in under twenty minutes, negotiating the appalling early evening traffic with style and panache. He shot straight up onto the John Fitzgerald Expressway and round to the dual carriageway of Storrow Drive along the side of the Charles River before cutting across to Commonwealth. The river looked lovely. Sailboats drifted along in a light breeze against the backdrop of Cambridge and the MIT buildings.

By the time I had checked into my room in the august halls of the Harvard Club and had a quick shower it was late evening in Boston. I was still in afternoon mode however and so I decided to drop the Ethnic Art accounts into Donald's offices near the John Hancock Building in order to to give him a flying start tomorrow. I added a note asking him to do a data base check on Cuneo and Pantuliano. I knew there were people who provided personal details of individuals, for a fee. By accessing computer records nowadays just about everything about anyone could be discovered, from theoretically confidential tax returns to their credit card records. Very useful if you wanted to discredit the personalities in a take-over battle and Donald was bound to have used the facility. I was curious to see what was known about my friends in Florida.

Then I had a date to meet Ethnic Art's local manager, Dave Wilson, at the gallery in Newbury Street, in the fashionable Back Bay. I had the familiar frustrating feeling I get at this stage in an assignment that the law of diminishing returns was working and that I would learn very little that was new from Wilson. Still, it had to be done and I needed to take a view on the man.

I strolled down Boylston in the dark humidity of a Boston summer evening, enjoying the faintly European feel of the city. I left the envelope of papers with a security guard at Donald's office block near the old Trinity Church and headed across to Newbury Street. The Ethnic Art gallery was at the stylish end of the street. I climbed the stone steps in front of what had been a terraced 19th century house. To one side was a shop selling Japanese haute couture. The dresses had no price tags, a bad sign. On the other side was an expensive looking jewellery store, its windows empty and shuttered at this time of the evening. Ethnic Art was closed up too but there was a light gleaming in the interior. The old-fashioned door had a delightful brass knocker in the form of a whale. When I knocked, Dave Wilson opened the door quickly.

He was a small man, trim and dapper, with fair hair cut short and fashionably tinted, a fresh youthful complexion that made him look younger than the late thirties I knew him to be. He had neat pleasant features and a relaxed, friendly manner. He ushered me into the gallery and carefully locked up behind me. I noticed that he wore a little golden ring in one ear. When he spoke it was with the drawling long vowels of an upper-class Bostonian. The interior of gallery reminded me of the one in San Francisco. But even I could see that the objects on display were very different. When I said so, Wilson smiled. "Boston taste is a bit different from California. We have a range of stuff here."

He pointed to a small stone figure of a naked woman, wearing a classical head-dress. "That's actually European--- Greco-Roman and 5th century. Not tribal in the usual sense. But some of our clients like to see a wide range of material." He whisked me round the gallery. "This," indicating a large, badly eroded stone figure of a man's face, "is a rather rare Olmec head from Mexico. Their government has stopped the legal export of antiquities like that for cultural reasons." He made a face at me and smiled. "But things still get out." He shrugged and went on to a case containing several objects, elaborately carved and covered with a mixture of human and animal heads, "Inuit or Eskimo as you may call it; carved walrus ivory. Quite old and rare.

"Expensive?"

Wilson nodded. "Oh yes. Collectors will pay large sums for objects like these. Also some young professionals like to buy ethnic art partly as an investment. But also because it is chic at the moment." He gestured towards some larger figures. I guessed they were African masks, from the dark wood and the bizarre, inhuman features. He looked approvingly at me when I said so, obviously surprised at my knowledge. "Yes," he said. " From the Congo."

A sudden thought occurred to me. "Do you have anything from West Africa? Nigeria, for example?"

Wilson laughed. "That's strange. You're the third person to ask me that question today." I raised my eyebrows at him enquiringly. He went on, "Paul Friden called me from Brussels to ask if I had seen a Benin bronze head that Sylvia apparently took from his stock some weeks ago. He thought I might have it here."

"But you don't?"

He shook his head. "No." He sneaked a sideways glance at me.
"Why do you ask?" I told him it seemed to be missing. "Jesus!"
Wilson looked amazed. "How do you lose something like that?
It could be worth a fortune if it's genuine. The early ones are
very rare and very valuable."

"So I'm told," I said, "but do you mean that some are fakes?"

"Well, copies. Later copies were made." He smiled, "Whether
they are fakes depends on your point of view and of course
your motives." He frowned. " You'll find this is a kind of
strange outfit at times. Letting valuable objects move around
with very little security. And I wonder sometimes where all the
money comes from."

I smiled non-committally. "Who was the other enquiry from?"

"Well, it was most unusual, but Mrs van Eck called me later.
Asked me if I had anything of special significance from
Nigeria. She wants something very special as a gift for an
important Nigerian politician she's doing business with."

"Does that happen often?"

He shook his head. "Very seldom. Usually it's a temporary loan
for her husband's collection in that lovely house in the
Netherlands."

I spent another hour with him, going over his records and the
simple set of accounts he seemed to be keeping. What emerged
was the familiar picture of a business full of expensive stock
and with a low level of sales; occasionally a big item but

usually relatively inexpensive. It was a pattern that did not seem to justify the investment that had been made. In terms of cash-flow, I guessed the sales just about covered Wilson's salary and the outgoings of the gallery in Newbury Street.

But Wilson impressed me as a sharp, well educated man who clearly knew his field and probably was very good at charming the well-heeled Boston Brahmins and their wives at receptions in the Museum of Modern Art. But he was no businessman, even less so than Paul Friden or Jerry Prescott. He didn't seem to realise that the business was barely viable.

It was almost midnight when I arrived back at the club and the cavernous entrance foyer and bar was deserted. The uniformed porter on duty at reception gave me my room key and with it two message slips. I read them as I climbed the broad staircase. They were both from Tom Ambrose. He had called at nine o'clock and again at ten thirty. The last message said he wanted to speak to me urgently. He would call me again in the morning.

When he rang, I was half way through my exercises. He was calling from the coffee shop at the harbour and he sounded relieved to hear me. "Mr Lennox, you said to contact you if anything happened here," he blurted out as soon as I answered the bedroom telephone. "For a start I thought you should know that crazy girl has got me fired," he said bitterly. "Can you imagine? She told Mr di Giorgio that I had been pestering her! After the way she's been throwing herself at me--- or anybody, come to that." I winced slightly at that. He paused, "At least that's what he said when he fired me." Then he went on angrily, "But I think it's an excuse--- I'm sure he just wanted to be rid of me. I'm pretty sure he suspects me of helping Sylvia--- or at least of knowing more about it than he likes."

"Why is that, Tom?"

""The two men--- the ones I told you about. The big man and the one with the weird hair-do? They've been snooping around the marina. Asking about me at the coffee shop. Trying to find out where I stay. Luckily the guy who runs the place is a pal."

"Raoul," I said.

"That's right. He knew there was something wrong. Didn't like the look of them." He laughed, "Who would? Anyway he didn't tell them I had a room down on the harbour side. Said I lived at college. They hung around for two hours, sitting in their car, watching the place. Fortunately I didn't turn up. But I'm kind of worried."

"Yes, I can see why you would be," I said slowly. "Look Tom, is there someplace you can move out to for a while? Maybe for a few days? Until things get cleared up." I hope I sounded reassuring.

There was silence at the other end of the line. "Maybe," he said. "I could share for a couple of nights with a guy I know at college. But sooner or later they'll find me. If they really want to, they'll find me." His voice faded away. I realised he was scared at the prospect.

"Then that's what you should do," I said firmly. "Lie low. But keep in touch with me. Also this might be the time to contact the police. See if they can put the frighteners into these men."

Tom gave a short laugh. "After being fired by Carlos di Giorgio for annoying his step-daughter? And then complaining

146

about his hired hands. They wouldn't want to know." I guessed he was probably right. We needed something more specific than that.

"I wish I could do more to help you, Tom. But just lay low. That's all I can say for now. There are some things about Carlos I'm beginning to discover that may make him vulnerable. I think he can be made to back off. But I need more time."

Tom interrupted me. "Yes, Mr Lennox. But that isn't all. I've heard from Sylvia." That really woke me up. At last something definite. Now maybe Helen van Eck would show more interest now.

"A letter from her arrived yesterday. Only a short note, saying she's safe and well. But it was her handwriting, for sure."

"Did she tell you where she is, or what she's doing?"

Tom shook his head. "No, there was no address. But the letter is from abroad. Somewhere in Europe. The stamp has two words on it, in French I think. I have it here." He read it out to me, "Belgique, and Belgie."

French and Flemish! Sylvia was in Belgium! She's gone back to Belgium for some reason. Most likely to Brussels, a place she knows well. But maybe Brugges or Antwerp or any one of a dozen small towns and villages where, with her language skills she could blend in easily. Still, it was a genuine lead at last. "Tom, I'm going to be in Florida tomorrow to see some business contacts. Tell me how to find you." He explained how to get to the harbour and where his room was on the quay. "I'd like to see that letter, Tom, if that's OK with you."

"Sure, Mr Lennox. If I'm not around when you arrive, Raoul at the coffee shop will know how to contact me."

I hung up. 'Brussels,' I thought, 'where I first met her. How very odd.' Then I remembered to call John Boyd to warn him that the head was on its way to him. John had a collection of fine classical busts and statues lining his grand entrance hall. But I was looking forward to hearing his reaction to Linda Polk's head of Sylvia. I got him right away and told him about the package.

"When it arrives, by all means open it. I'd appreciate your opinion." I said. "It's not quite your period. But I think you'll be interested." That intrigued him especially as I refused to tell him anything else. I knew he'd be appalled, not just at the style but also by the subject. He had never approved of Sylvia and had made that clear in his coded gentlemanly way.

He thought her unstable and neurotic. "Even for a woman," he had advised me gravely, shaking his head sadly. "Why do you keep doing it?" John had little taste for women. As things had turned out I had to admit his judgement had been pretty sound, as usual.

What state was Sylvia likely to be in after the latest traumas? Why did Helen van Eck seem to be the only stable woman in that family? I wished I knew what Sylvia was up to, and why. I finished dressing and looked at myself in the mirror. "Don't worry about it," I said to my reflection. "It will all come out in the wash." I sounded pretty convincing. No wonder clients were so impressed.

CHAPTER 22

My first stop was the reference section of the Public Library, near Copley Square. I wanted to know exactly how the Ethnic Art debt to Southern Commercial Lending really worked. In Palgrave's Dictionary of Money I found an explanation of securitization of assets as an alternative to bank borrowings. It was perfectly legitimate. I had just never come across it before.

It became fashionable in the 1980's, when some companies moved away from conventional, and safer, methods of financial management. One result was the wave of new commercial paper that the media christened 'junk bonds'. A thriving secondary market in these interest-bearing certificates of debt had developed, all driven by good intentions. But where had I heard that before?

Once upon a time a single institution, like a bank, would deal with every aspect of the transaction, find a borrower, check their creditworthiness, design securities to attract savers cash to fund the loan and then hold the loan as part of a portfolio. Now, with the process fragmented, several specialist organisations might be involved. Securities would be sold on to a separate trust or corporation which could then market the paper. Often the initial placement of the securities was done privately, to avoid having to conform with the regulations of the 1933 US Securities Act.

In theory, there were benefits all round. For the borrower the costs were lower than a public bond placement and the process faster. For the lender the returns were usually lower but predictable, with less risk. And the security of the loan could be almost any aspect of the borrower's assets. Property or stock that wasn't working effectively to produce profits could be 'securitized' by this means and turned into cash to fund the business.

Of course the loan, like all loans, eventually had to be repaid. It was usually 'callable' by the lender after a set period of time. As further protection there could be a covenant, to ensure that in the event of the borrower defaulting the lender had first call on the assets.

I strolled down towards the Public Gardens in the summer sunshine, across the little bridge over the Boating Lake and into the Common. I sat on one of the benches, looking up the slope towards the classical dome of the State Capital. Why, I wondered, had Carlos and Pantuliano created such a complex method of funding for a small business? Why not a straightforward bank loan and overdraft?

I thought I knew why. This way there was no need to involve a reputable bank in the finances of the business. They probably told Sylvia that interest charges would be lower; which was true. And provided the loan was repaid on time there was no problem. So why was I worried? I stared off into space. The possibilities dawned on me. Suppose the loan couldn't be repaid when it became callable?

I groaned out loud and some passing tourists stared at me. Was this why Sylvia had decided to vanish? She had never been good at confronting messes. To say nothing about what Tom Ambrose had told me about Carlos and the girl: if it was true. Linda Polk's story about Carlos and his criminal links started to make sense now. Yes, I could well understand her running away.

But why take the Princess head? To sell it for cash? That seemed unlikely. And what about the diary? It all had to fit together somehow. Get a grip, I thought, there has to be a logical connection.

But I just couldn't see it. I shook my head. There was not enough information yet. I looked at my watch. Enough time to get out to Fenway Park and catch some of the Red Sox game. Maybe I'd find inspiration there.

CHAPTER 23

I got back to the Harvard Club about six thirty, hot and thirsty after a day on the bleachers. The Red Sox had lost, something that didn't seem to come as a complete surprise to the few fans who had turned up. I showered and changed and went down to the bar to wait for Donald Lynch

He bounced into the club just after seven, like a carefully groomed cannon ball, his prematurely bald head gleaming and a broad grin across his plump face. He was clutching a large brown envelope to the chest of his well-cut Brookes Bros bankers suit. The suit was immaculate and he looked as if he was just about to start the day. But I knew he had probably started twelve hours earlier with a working breakfast somewhere. Since then he would have been analysing, wheeling and dealing, thinking on his feet and generally staying one jump ahead all day. Donald was ferociously bright and fiercely competitive. He lived for his career. That was why he was earning a very large six-figure salary at the age of thirty-two.

He spotted me at once and shot over to meet me. He threw himself down into an armchair beside me. "Lennox, you old cretin," he grimaced at me, "Where is that drink you promised me?" I signalled and the barman came over. We ordered two dry martinis, straight up and Donald slapped the envelope down on the low table between us. "Now, who did you say used to own this company, Ethnic Art Inc?" he asked, still grinning but the grin no longer reached his little brown eyes.

"Oh dear," I said, reaching for the papers, "is it that bad?"

Donald pulled a face at me. "Not good." The barman arrived with what looked like two fish bowls of bluish coloured liquid. There was a reverent silence as we took the first sip. The martinis were magnificent; ice-cold and bone-dry, almost pure gin with only a passing acquaintance with the vermouth bottle. Donald raised his eyebrows and sighed appreciatively. "This is what makes life worth living," he said. He motioned towards the envelope. "I'd better explain this stuff while I still can." He launched into a violent belly laugh, beaming across at me.

Then he took me quickly through his analysis of the Ethnic Art financial position, including a succinct account of what securitization of assets and covenanted collateral meant. "None of that is necessarily terminal," he went on. "But given the high operating expenses," he paused, "very high--- have you been charging them your fees up front?" He guffawed and gulped down half his martini. "So, given the expense level and the presumed poor cash-flow from sales--- because as usual you have only given me part of the information--- the company appears to be in a condition that is known technically as totally screwed."

He beamed at me. "I hope you did get your fees up front." Then he held up his empty glass. "You know, these things are really very good," he said thoughtfully. I ordered two more martinis.

While we sipped them and looked over the dinner menu, Donald went on. "You asked me about Southern Commercial Lending Corporation and these two guys." He laughed and shook his head. "You can certainly pick them, Lennox." He pulled a sheet of paper from his inside pocket and handed it to me. "There's a detailed description for you in the information pack. But this is an overview."

The paper was a chart showing a complex series of boxes, each with the name of a company or some other enterprise. At first sight there seemed to be no logical relationships, no natural hierarchy--- just a confused network of inter-connecting lines showing the nature and extent of the maze of cross shareholdings and ownership. I stared at the diagram for a couple of minutes in silence, trying to make sense of it.

The name, Southern Commercial Lending, appeared in one box. Then I saw Bay Financial Services. I was beginning to feel on familiar ground. Southern Lending had a 40% stake in Bay Services and they were both partly owned by what seemed to be an investment bank called Gulf Financial Holdings. This in turn was a subsidiary of something called Caribbean Enterprises, which had a series of other wholly or partly owned operations, mostly involved in trading, importing and exporting. One of them was a consultancy company called Export Advisory Services. Southern Commercial Lending seemed to have stakes in most of the operating companies.

I blinked at Donald. "What do you make of this?"

He grinned wolfishly at me, "Well old son, if there isn't something illegal going on someone is wasting a great opportunity--- and somebody has gone to a lot of trouble for nothing."

"I've met some of these people," I said quietly. "They're not the type to pass up an opportunity. What's your guess, Donald?"

"It's designed to make it hard to identify the ownership of assets. And make it easy to move cash around."

"Laundering?"

Donald shrugged his shoulders, "That's what it would be good for."

Given what I knew and what I had been told, it seemed likely that something of that sort was going on. An elaborate financial structure based on off-shore holding companies with a confusing ownership pattern would be perfect for shifting cash profits from illegal activities like drugs; moving the money around through a complex of more or less legal enterprises until it reappeared somewhere as legitimate profits.

Then there was Ethnic Art's heavy debt structure. That had to tie in somewhere. Suppose the company defaulted on its repayments to Southern Commercial Lending. What happens? That very expensive collection of tribal art built up by Sylvia and her colleagues reverts to the lenders. Once it had been sold off it would represent clean money for them. Even if they took a discount on prices, it still looked like an almost fool-proof way of turning bad money into good. Of course Ethnic Art Inc was wiped out and maybe Sylvia with it.

All you had to have was access to a company that needed cash to acquire assets--- and a management naive enough or trusting enough to be talked into the initial loans. I felt sorry for Sylvia.

Of course, Carlos was supposed to be helping her. Helen van Eck had other concerns and presumably bigger worries. She had simply left Sylvia to it. "It is really her baby," she had said to me that first day. Then there was the fact that the company's operating costs were so unnaturally high. I needed to find out why spending was so far out of line.

Donald and I split a bottle of Hermitage La Chapelle with our meal. Combined with the dry martinis it made it hard to keep up with his explanations about how the overall financial structure worked. "Whoever put it together was good," he said. "It's really very clever. Of course I could have done it just as well," he added modestly. "But it is good. I've included in your notes a list of directors and key executives in the various operations. You won't be surprised to see the same names--- Cuneo, Pantuliano and a few others--- appearing all over the place. And by the way, Terry, be careful. Cuneo seems to be well connected in political circles in Florida and the Caribbean. How do you know these guys, anyway?"

I flashed what I hoped was a carefree grin across at him. "Some of them are advisors to Ethnic Art. That's all I know or care about." Donald waved a glass of the deep red wine at me. "That's the spirit, old son." He took a gulp at the heady Hermitage. "But watch your step," he said. "I'd hate to lose your valuable business." We ate in silence for a few minutes. It was a sobering thought.

"Speaking of which," Donald went on blithely, "Let me tell you about Utrecht Construction Group." He beamed at me. "There may be something you can do for me." Donald and I lived by an elaborate and largely unacknowledged system of debts and favours that we kept more or less in balance.

"But strictly in confidence," he said firmly. "And I mean no-one; especially not your client, Mrs van Eck." I considered that for a moment, then nodded. "Understood," I said.

"We have some clients in Europe--- a consortium of financial institutions. Dolf Erhardt in Brussels has the lead on it for us."

I remembered Dolf. At first sight he was slow talking and rather lugubrious: an apparently amiable Dutchman with a heavy footed, slightly bucolic manner that hid a financial brain almost as penetrating as Donald's. In fact, if anything he was more astute politically than Donald and so more effective in certain situations. He was the perfect contact man; smarter than he seemed and not so obviously clever that he frightened less intelligent clients, as Donald sometimes could do.

Donald went on. "Since the old man, Jan van Eck, had his stroke the institutions have been increasingly worried about the long term direction of the business. Of course there is a chance he may recover and take control again. But meantime businessperformance is poor and investors are not convinced the right decisions are being made to secure the future." I looked at him enquiringly. "The feeling is that Helen van Eck is making too many mistakes."

"What kind of mistakes?"

"Key ones. Putting the wrong people in senior positions. And committing large amounts of resource to projects in high risk markets, some of them too speculative to be credible. Too many of them have died a death--- cancelled by customers or delayed indefinitely. That kind of thing."

"Well," I said doubtfully, "that can happen to anyone. This

recession---."

"Sure," Donald said, "Things are tough all over. That's why people get worried when big public companies seem to be taking a high risk strategy. Especially if you happen to own 20% of the equity, as our clients collectively do. Say forty million pounds worth."

That made Ethnic Art seem less of a pressing problem. "What specifically is worrying them?" I asked.

"There is a lot of concern about the Group getting in too deep with some rather dubious governments in West Africa. Most recently, a heavy financial involvement in Nigeria."

"Tell me more," I said.

"You probably know they have military governments there from time to time," Donald said.

"But I thought they had democratic elections recently," I intervened.

Donald threw back his head and laughed. "Sure they did. And the democratically elected President, Obasanjo, and his deputy, are still in jail. They were arrested immediately after the result! You can go horribly wrong there financially if you get into bed with the wrong people. Plus there are serious religious conflicts, muslim and Christian, that make Ulster look like Noddyland. So it's a place generally regarded as bad news."

"But not by Mrs van Eck?"

"Apparently not. She seems to have gone a bit haywire since

the old man gave up control to her."

"So why don't the institutions sell? Or use their influence to stop her?"

"Exactly!" Donald beamed at me again. "That is why they are talking to us. We're trying to put together a strategy for them. There are a lot of angles to consider. Our clients don't want a sudden share collapse. That could precipitate a hostile bid from competitors outside Europe. In the long run that would be bad news. Also it's a restricted market with the van Eck's controlling 55% of the shares, one way or another, so it's difficult for anyone to get a really strong position."

"And you're acting for the minority shareholders?"

"Well, the main institutional ones at least. They don't want to see a hostile take-over bid but at the same time they can't get Mrs van Eck to listen to their concerns. They can't piss about much longer. UCG definitely needs a change of strategy. A period of careful consolidation."

I thought for a moment."If the family is satisfied I don't see what you can do."

"That is just the point, Terry. We have reason to think the old man isn't at all happy about the situation. But of course you're right. The best thing would be an agreed series of changes at the top of UCG, to head off a share collapse and a likely full bid." He smiled, "I've done the figures. They have about six months before they hit big trouble. With or without the Nigerian work."

I thought for a second. "Why not sell off and then pick up the pieces?"

Donald nodded, "Normally that would be an option. But our clients don't want to see the Japanese or the Americans with a strategic foothold in the European construction industry. So if possible we want to keep UCG intact. But, like I say, time is short. We can't wait until the group is in serious trouble or our clients lose a wad of dough."

"And you lose a lot of fees?" Donald beamed again, "Right! And I need the money!"

"So how can I help?"

"Speak to Dolf when you get back home. You're going back soon?" I nodded. "He'll fill in the detail. UCG needs a new image and new leadership; a change of strategic direction; a new ethical approach to customers--- all that sort of crap." He laughed. "Anyway, I thought you might be able to influence some of the family to listen to what the minority shareholders are saying.

"Some of the family?"

"Yes. Didn't I tell you? There are various family holdings. The old man owns the most shares, and the wife has some in her name." He looked at me and grinned, "And the daughter has around 12% too. Held in a trust fund. Didn't you used to know her?" he asked me innocently.

"Sylvia owns that much?" I said with surprise. Donald grimaced.

"But the mother has the key to the trust. She and Jan are the

160

trustees.

"So in any vote the trust shares would probably support the status quo?" Donald held up one hand, "Except that Dolf thinks there is a way to break the trust, now the old man is incapacitated. But that would need Sylvia to play ball. It would be much better, though, if Mrs van Eck saw reason and saved everyone a lot of hassle."

I laughed and Donald looked at me, puzzled. "Donald, I don't think you have any idea how difficult that could be."

But I agreed to contact Dolf Erhardt and to meet him when I was back in Europe. The rest of the evening degenerated into a blur as we moved on to coffee and calvados in the lounge. I comforted myself with the thought that Mrs van Eck was picking up the expenses.

CHAPTER 24

At crack of dawn the cab deposited me back at Logan Airport
in time for the early flight to Tampa. To my jaded eyes Logan
was definitely beginning to look its age. But after the previous
night I expect the same could have been said about me. Still,
Donald's information had been priceless and his analysis, in
spite of the jokes and the ritual macho insults, had been
flawless as usual. Breakfast was a champagne mimosa, while I
tried to think through the problems facing Ethnic Art. What he
had said about UCG kept intruding into my thoughts. But I told
myself that was a separate problem. I couldn't see a solution to
that one. I smiled ruefully. Come to that I couldn't see a
solution to the Ethnic Art problem either.

What was clear was that Carlos and Pantuliano had completely
undermined my client's interest in the business by their
financial machinations. Also clear was the fact that behind
them was a complex financial organisation, in which Marcus
Cuneo played a key role. I could only guess at the extent of that
organisation and where its cash came from. The more I
guessed, the more worried I got. Yesterday on the telephone
Tom Ambrose had sounded scared--- and I had seen what
Carlos's hired hands had done to Linda and to Prescott, with
very little reason. If the cash they were using did come from

organised crime, which was beginning to seem likely, I was rapidly getting out of my depth. Get a grip, I thought. The golden rule. What you can't control, don't worry about. I decided to concentrate on what I could do. Mrs van Eck was the client. How did I give her what she was paying for? But Mrs van Eck was beginning to worry me. Her reaction had not been exactly unconfined joy when I told her that her daughter might be alive.

"So she's been in touch with you." It was almost as if she had expected my news. Being charitable however, it did sound as if she had serious problems at UCG, with the family control of the group under threat. Maybe she was distracted. I decided it might be useful to find out more about the situation at UCG and what if any bearing it might have on my assignment at Ethnic Art. I nodded sagely. Once I'd spoken to Dolf Erhardt I should be in a better position to advise Mrs van Eck. She might want to keep the two issues separate. But eventually she would understand and come clean.

First I had to do some ritual dancing with Pantuliano. Cuneo would want to find out how much I knew. Well, enough to make life embarrassing for Carlos at least. The way the loans had been arranged was unusual, if not unethical, and it didn't show my client's son in law in a very good light. But I was sure there was more going on than just a clever attempt to take over Ethnic Art. I had a hunch the bank statements and the record of cash-flow would tell me more.

I had to admit I had started with a prejudice against Carlos and nothing I had learned had made me like him better. If Tom Ambrose and Linda Polk were telling the truth Carlos had no hesitation about using violence to recover his diary.

163

But what could be so important about the diary? Well, it seemed that the diary had information about Pantuliano and possibly Cuneo too. Did they know how careless their colleague had been in allowing wives and ex-wives to run around with confidential information? Probably not, I decided. When I had first met them Cuneo had not appeared even to know that Sylvia was missing. I smiled quietly. Perhaps my next chat with Pantuliano would start a few hares running. Maybe it was time to put the skids under Carlos and see what happened. The thought cheered me and I ordered another mimosa.

I'd have a chance to check on Tom and to see how much information there was in Sylvia's letter. Why had she contacted him? I sighed and started to look through the papers that Donald had given me.

Southern Commercial Lending was obviously a small part of a complex network. There were savings and loans, holding groups and partnerships, consultancy and corporate finance firms and export/import trading companies, with enough cross shareholdings and off-shore accounts to keep a small army of tax accountants happy for months trying to figure out what was going on. No doubt that was the intention. It took me just ten minutes to fall into a deep sleep.

I was wakened by the stewardess telling me we were starting our descent into Tampa International Airport. Getting through domestic arrivals was easy and I took time at the Avis desk to arrange a pick up car from their downtown office. Then I headed for the cab rank. The heat and humidity hit me like damp sponge. But the cab was blissfully air-conditioned.

In half an hour I was sitting, in good shape, in the cool,

glamorous pink and grey waiting room of Bay Financial
Services. The blonde receptionist knew me this time. "Mr
Lennox." She gave me the Doris Day smile again. "Mr
Pantuliano is expecting you. One moment please." She
announced my presence in hushed tones.

Pantuliano's office was big enough to impress and sufficiently
workmanlike to inspire confidence. It was longer than it was
wide, running away towards a large grey desk at the far end. A
long boardroom table ran the length of the room, made up of a
series of interlocking smaller tables in a stylishly worked
pattern of grey and pink. The carpets were pale grey and the
walls panelled in strips of pink and grey. Some design
consultant had worked overtime to create the effect. By the
door was a low coffee table, grey, and two large grey sofas.

As I came into the room Pantuliano stood up immediately and
came out from behind the desk, his hand outstretched. He
strode towards me, a grin on his plump face, his eyes gleaming
behind the gold-framed spectacles. He was wearing a button-
down white shirt and a dark three-piece business suit again.
But this time no Brigade of Guards tie. Had someone said
something? He still looked as if he needed a shave. "Terry," he
said, "I really appreciate you coming down here like this. I sure
hope it wasn't too awkward for you fitting it in."

I indicated with a half smile and a shrug that said, yes it had
been awkward but that for him nothing was too much. It was
hard to tell if he was impressed. He waved me towards one of
the seats. "I've asked for coffee, Terry. I hope that's OK?" He
sat down opposite me. The blonde receptionist, or maybe her
twin, brought in a tray with a pot of coffee and real china cups
and saucers, a sugar bowl and a cream jug. No polystyrene
cups here. Pantuliano poured us out a cup of coffee each. I

sipped mine. It was strong and black and very good. This was not the standard American hot brown water. I commented on the coffee, watching him load sugar and cream into his cup.

"Yes," he said mechanically, "It's good stuff. Colombian. Pick of the crop." He glanced up at me. "Mr Cuneo has interests in coffee plantations, amongst other things. He has extensive business interests."

"So I gather," I replied, looking at him over the rim of my coffee cup. He shot me a look, tasted the coffee himself and leaned back in his seat, stretching out his legs in front of him.

"I understand you have some questions about the Ethnic Art accounts." He smiled at me. "What can I tell you, Terry?"

I smiled back at him. "Well Rich," I said amiably, "it seemed to me that you asked for this meeting, so maybe there is something you want to say to me." He shifted uneasily in his seat. His plump olive-coloured jowls drooped slightly in displeasure. But he caught himself in time and the practised smile reappeared. A wave of the hand,

"Sure." He took a mouthful of coffee. He glanced at it approvingly, "Good stuff. Now, Ethnic Art," he went on briskly. "As you know we do a bit of accounting for Mrs di Giorgio's company. Or is it Mrs van Eck's?" He gave a little smile. "Carlos di Giorgio is a very valued colleague of ours. Very valued," he repeated seriously, looking me firmly in the eyes.

I nodded. "I can imagine," I said.

Behind the gold-framed spectacles the dark eyes narrowed

slightly. "More coffee?" he asked casually. The caffeine was already zinging through my head. He went on. "Anyway, Carlos needed some advice on funding for his wife's business. We arranged a couple of tranches of loans; gave her some free corporate finance advice; that kind of thing. Sylvia wanted to grow the business rapidly, so that involved buying a lot of expensive stock. Some of these ethnic objects are very pricey," he explained. "There was no way that level of growth could be sustained from the shareholders funds or from operating cash flow."

"The high operating costs seem to be knocking hell out of the assets and the shareholders funds," I added.

"Start-up costs, "Pantuliano said smoothly. I nodded and he seemed to relax a little.

"But a bond issue with securitization of assets? And a protective covenant. That's pretty heavy for a small private company, isn't it?

He looked surprised. "I see you've done some homework. But that's just a routine transaction nowadays--- to protect the lender's interests."

I didn't like being patronised. I leaned forward and rummaged in my brief case. "By the way, has Southern Commercial sold the bonds on or are they still holding them?" I smiled at him encouragingly.

"Pantuliano gazed at me blankly."Gee, Terry, I just don't know. I'd have to check on that."

I smiled at him again and laid on the table the sheet of paper with the financial structure that Donald had given me. "That surprises me, Rich," I said casually, indicating the Southern Commercial Lending name on the chart."Because I understand you are one of the directors of that company. And Carlos di Giorgio is another. And Marcus Cuneo is on the board of the holding company." I looked at him reproachfully. "You know, Rich, I'm not sure this is entirely ethical." I shook my head. "Maybe not even legal."

"Hey," the smile vanished. "What are you saying? There's nothing wrong with anything we do. It's all strictly legal and---

I interrupted him, "and in the best interests of Ethnic Art? Rich, let me make my position clear. I only want to safeguard my client's interests. And my client is Mrs van Eck."

Pantuliano's face slowly reddened. "Listen Lennox," he snapped, "Marcus Cuneo is an important man in this state. He has a lot of influential friends and business connections. And he's very touchy about his reputation. He isn't going to like it if you try to slander him. You'd better watch your step!"

"You're not listening to me, Rich," I said patiently. "I don't care about Marcus Cuneo's business connections--- interesting as they seem to be." I added, tapping the piece of paper in front of me. "I'm only interested in Mrs van Eck's business--- and whether Carlos di Giorgio, a director of Ethnic Art, has acted in that company's best interests, and those of its shareholders. The advice he received from you or whoever, is not my immediate concern. Provided my client's interests are protected."

Pantuliano sat back in his seat. The dark little eyes assessed me for a moment. Then he smiled. "OK, Terry, maybe I over reacted. I'm sure you'll find everything is in order," he hesitated, "even if Carlos did cut a few corners." He drained his coffee cup and looked across at me. "He can be impulsive at times. Emotional; you know what I mean?" He shrugged. "Now you--- you seem a very cool customer, if you don't mind me saying so. Maybe when we have this misunderstanding all worked out we could find some ways of working together." I looked non-committal. "As I say, Mr Cuneo's interests are extensive, and we can always use good advice. We have businesses all over the world. If you are interested?"

I inclined my head, "Thanks Rich. I'll keep that in mind. But first I need to put this one to bed." He smiled at me, the light glinting off his spectacles. I think he thought we had a deal.

"But let's talk about Carlos, him being so impulsive and emotional." I had his attention now. "From what I hear he's very impulsive at times. And maybe just too emotional?"

Pantuliano raised his dark eyebrows questioningly. "What are you getting at, Terry."

"Well," I said, "I happened to bump into his former wife, Linda, recently. Do you know her?" He shook his head. "It seems that Carlos has the idea she has some documents of his. And he's being a bit, well, impulsive I think you said? Yes, impulsive. About trying to get them back from her, I mean." Pantuliano's sallow complexion darkened. "He even sent along a couple of rather nasty lads to put the frighteners into her. Ransacked her apartment and roughed her up." I made a face. "Very unpleasant. Very emotional," I said. "For a man in such a delicate business situation."

Pantuliano stared at me. "You know, Lennox, maybe you know

a bit too much about Carlos di Giorgio." He looked away down the long room for a moment. "But I hear what you say. I'll do what I can to quieten him down."

I smiled at him. "Thank you for that." I said, with sincerity.

Pantuliano looked at his wrist watch. "I appreciate the information," he said. "Is there anything else?"

I stood up. "Not really. Thanks for your time." As he was showing me out of the room he said, casually, "What is the document you say Carlos is missing?"

I shook my head."I couldn't say. And Linda told me she didn't have it anyway. So maybe Carlos is imagining it all." I smiled.

Pantuliano stopped and looked at me. "That could be a worry." We shook hands. Now it was my turn to think we had a deal. I hoped my deal was better than his.

With him on the back foot I decided to slip in another fast one. I said casually, "By the way, have you seen Sylvia di Giorgio recently?"

Pantuliano shook his head. "No. I hear she's in Europe. Visiting her mother." He looked at me sharply. "Isn't she?" he asked. I shrugged.

"She wasn't there a few days ago. Mrs van Eck hasn't seen her for weeks." I stopped at the door of his office. "Maybe Sylvia's emotional and impulsive too!" I laughed. "Her and Carlos! What a pair. They sound like a load of trouble." From the look on Pantuliano's face he was beginning to agree with me. At last I felt the assignment was taking shape.

CHAPTER 25

I collected a shiny new hire car at the Avis pick-up point and set off down the coast road past the romantically named Cockroach Bay to find Tom Ambrose's place. It was at a small working harbour, used by a few commercial fishing boats but also as a cheap berth for some of the smaller pleasure boats that proliferate up and down the coast of Florida.

I found it tucked away down the side of a disused semi-derelict warehouse, behind a recently built and only half occupied shopping mall. One day soon the area would become yet another flashy consumer paradise of shops and restaurants, and the harbour filled with floating gin palaces. For the time being it was still a genuine little harbour, scruffy but pleasantly so.

I parked my car in the shade of the warehouse and walked around the jetty. Two wooden wharves ran out into the blue waters of the gulf and pelicans perched on the old piles of the piers, or flapped slowly over the water. On one of the wharves were several ramshackle huts and storehouses. The other was clear except for the usual clutter of nets, dinghies and old cars that seem to collect around working harbours. There were a few boats moored quietly in the pool.

I watched the pelicans one by one fold their wings and vanish beneath the water, emerging with a pouchful of something squirming. That made me think of lunch, so I walked across to the little coffee shop, really not much more than another shack. By the edge of the water and in the shade of the warehouse it was relatively cool, with a light breeze off the sea. I pushed open the screen door and stepped in. It was dark inside after the shimmering glare of the water. I paused to allow my eyes to adjust and looked around.

At the rear there was a small counter, with a cooking area behind it. The walls had a collection of calendars advertising beers and soft drinks, a large plastic Mickey Mouse clock with "Welcome to Disneyland" on it, a couple of Tampa Buccaneers posters and a large stuffed fish in a glass case. I suppose you could say the place had character. Down each side were six or eight cubicles, with brown formica tables and two facing seats. There was only one customer sitting in a corner cubicle by the door. I glanced at him as I entered. From the way he seemed to fill the corner he was a big man.

Behind the counter stood a young latin-looking man wearing a soiled white apron, a stained blue work shirt and jeans. I studied the range of pies he had displayed under plastic covers. The air was hot with the smell of old cooking. I decided against lunch and ordered a cup of coffee. I drank it leaning against the counter while the young man slowly dragged a cloth over its surface, pretending not to look at me. The coffee wasn't in the same class as the stuff Pantuliano served. And it came in a polystyrene cup. At last, I thought, the real Florida!

I attracted the young man's attention by pulling out some

money. As I pushed the note across to him I said, "I'm looking for Tom Ambrose. Is he around?" He seemed to have trouble with English, or maybe it was my accent. "Tom Ambrose," I repeated. "He stays here. Where is his place?" He took my money and tossed it into a cash-box, fishing out some change for me. He shook his head. "He's not around."

"My name is Terry Lennox. I'm a friend of his. Are you Raoul?" He stared at me silently. I could see in his brown eyes that he was thinking it over. "I'd like to leave a message for him. Where does he stay?" He pointed towards the wharf with the shacks and storehouses. "He has a room over there, at the end of the wharf." He spoke with the sing-song rhythm of Mexico. "Upstairs, at the top."

I thanked him and headed for the door, leaving the change behind. He called after me, "But he's not around--- not around anymore." I should have paid more attention to him but I was on my way out of the coffee shop as he spoke. I walked round the cluttered little harbour and down to the end of the wharf. A flight of rickety steps took me up to a small landing with a rough railing. The whole of the building at this level seemed to consist of one large room, with windows on all sides and a flimsy door, held on a Yale lock. As I tried the handle the door swung open.

I spoke his name quietly, "Tom. Tom, it's Terry Lennox," and stepped inside. The room was big and brightly lit from all the windows. The walls were roughly panelled with cheap pine, just the way the wharf had been built, and they were covered with a variety of athletics and football trophies, an old movie poster, an icon of Marylene Munro, and a close up shot of Dan Marino poised to throw a pass for the Dolphins.

In one corner of the room was a bed and in the other, near the window, a plain table and a couple of straight-backed wooden chairs. Beside the bed was an old dressing chest. The centre of the floor was covered by a carpet, worn and patched. The place was scantily furnished, to say the least.

But what I noticed first was the utter mess of the room. The dressing chest drawers had been pulled out and emptied on the bed in a pile. Shirts, socks and underpants lay everywhere. There were books too, lying scattered around on the floor. Some of them had been ripped apart. There was a book-shelf hanging half off the wall. The bed had been pulled to pieces, its mattress slashed, the stuffing hanging out in places. It was all reminiscent of the house on Chavez. Carlos, you bastard, I thought.

I stood looking into the room, my mind a turmoil of growing anger. Then I remembered what Raoul had said as I was leaving and I started to turn away. There was the sound of light movement behind me and suddenly I felt a heavy hand grab the back of my neck. At the same time my left wrist was jerked up high behind my back. A sharp pain shot through my left shoulder. "Shit," I thought, "That's my shoulder gone again." Another small memento from my climbing days.

Then I felt myself being propelled across the room. I hit the ruined mattress face down. For a moment I could see or hear nothing. Then a hand patted over my back, shoulders and chest as I felt a powerful weight hold me on the bed.

Then suddenly the weight was released. I rolled over, clutching my shoulder and cursing. In front of me I saw the big man from the coffee shop. Standing over me he seemed even bigger. "OK mister," he said. "Tell me who you are and what you want with

Tom Ambrose." I sat silently, calculating my chances against him. He was about six four in height, with massive shoulders and a square, powerful chest that seemed to drop straight down to solid thighs and legs. His thick arms hung easily down by his sides as he watched me cautiously. Everything about him looked solid, his head and face square boned and rugged, topped by grizzled close-cropped grey hair. His nose seemed to have been broken at least once and his big ears stuck out from his bullet head. His eyes, strangely soft and brown, beneath bushy dark brown eyebrows were the only incongruous element. But even they didn't reassure me entirely. He was wearing a cream coloured, crumpled light weight summer suit, with a tan sports shirt open at the neck.

I decided it was time to assert myself. I stopped rubbing my shoulder and started to stand up. He leaned towards me and placed a hand as big as a dinner plate on my chest. I subsided back on the bed. "Who the hell are you?" I said, trying to sound assured. The big man looked bored. He pulled a billfold out of his hip pocket. As he did, I caught a glimpse of the brown walnut butt of an automatic in a holster clipped to his trouser belt. He flipped open the billfold and showed me an official looking badge and identification card. "Sarasota Police Department," he growled, "Sgt Oliver. Now who are you, mister, and what do you want with Tom Ambrose?"

I began to feel a lot better. "I'm a friend of Tom's. Well, an acquaintance really. I met him just a few days ago. I'm here on business. He called me last night." I realised I was starting to babble. Get a grip, I thought. I took a deep breath and cautiously reached into my jacket inside pocket, pulling out my passport. I handed it over to Sgt Oliver, who flicked it open and glanced down at it. He looked back at me. "A limey," he said. "What are you doing here." I explained the reason for my visit, briefly and without naming names. "So what is your business with Tom Ambrose?" the policeman repeated.

I shrugged, "It's complicated. I met Tom at the house of the di Giorgio's--- Mrs di Giorgio's mother, in Europe, is my client. I went down to see them a couple of days ago. That's when I met Tom Ambrose at the house." I paused, wondering how much to reveal. Oliver stared at me.

I went on."Tom and I discovered we had some interests in common--- we both do some rock climbing. And I agreed to keep in touch. Then he called me yesterday, to say he was in some kind of trouble. He told me he had been fired from his part-time job by Carlos di Giorgio and then threatened by a couple of toughs. Tom gave me the impression they were working for di Giorgio. I had to come back here on business anyway and I decided to look in and see how he was. That's when you arrived." I gave a grimace and held my shoulder. "Why so rough, anyway?" I asked. "And where is Tom?"

I was conscious that I had left out a lot of the story but Oliver seemed to be reasonably satisfied. He walked over to the table in the corner and sat down heavily on one of the chairs. He overflowed it in all directions. "Tom Ambrose is dead," he said.

I gasped, "But how---". Oliver looked grim. "He was badly beaten--- and then stabbed. We think it happened last night. His car was found in the parking lot of a bar down the coast. At first we thought it was a routine fight or a mugging. Then we found his place had been turned upside down. Someone had been looking for something. When we discovered he worked occasionally for Carlos di Giorgio," Oliver's soft brown eyes focussed on me from under the heavy brows, "we became even more interested. We are always interested in anything to do with Mr di Giorgio and his business contacts," he added pointedly. "Have you any idea what may have happened? And why he was fired?"

"I know what he told me. It seems that di Giorgio's step-daughter accused him of pestering her, making unwanted advances to her. But I think that's unlikely." I hesitated, "I believe there was something else that di Giorgio thought Tom knew about--- something important."

"Like what?" Oliver sounded interested.

"I'm not certain. But I think it has something to do with Mrs di Giorgio. She and the boy were close." Oliver raised his heavy eyebrows. "No," I said quickly. "It wasn't like that. At least I don't think it was. They were friends, that's all. Anyway, Tom told me he was being hassled by these two guys he had seen with Carlos." I described the men Tom and Linda had seen. I toyed with the idea of telling him about Linda Polk and Sylvia's disappearance. How did all this fit with Helen van Eck? How much should I say? "There's more."I said.

"I thought there would be," Oliver sighed. "Tell me about it."

"What sounds like the same two men attacked a woman and a man in separate incidents in San Francisco in the last few days. At least one of these attacks will have been reported to the local cops." Oliver looked puzzled. I imagine he often looked puzzled, but it didn't fool me. "The woman is called Linda Polk. She's the former wife of Carlos di Giorgio."

Oliver looked interested. "So there is a possible connection. But what?"

I smiled. "It gets worse. It seems as if Sylvia di Giorgio, his current wife, has disappeared and for some reason Carlos is trying to cover it up. But the main thing is that poor young Tom told me he helped her to slip away by faking a sailing accident. He thinks--- thought, that she had taken something with her. Something that Carlos wants to get back. Somehow Carlos suspected Tom of being involved. Hence the thugs."

Oliver was looking puzzled again. "And the ex-wife? How does she figure in this?"

"The two women seemed to know each other," I replied cautiously.

He shook his head and stood up. "Hey, I'm almost feeling sorry for the guy!" I sat silently on the bed. Oliver took a hard look at me. "And you seem to know a hell of a lot about Carlos di Giorgio's business. How come you're so well informed?"

I thought rapidly. Until I had spoken to my client I had better not say too much about the business situation. "Sylvia di Giorgio has been running the company I'm looking at. It's owned by her mother, who lives in Europe. I've been digging around for information to help her decide what to do with the business." I decided to throw in another snippet to keep him interested. "The reason I'm here today was to have a meeting with a man called Pantuliano. His company, Bay Financial Services, provides accounting services for the business."

There was a deep rumbling sound that I realised was Oliver laughing. "Rich Pantuliano?" he asked. "You really don't waste a lot of time getting involved, do you?" I tried to look like an innocent abroad; which in some ways I was. "Let me warn you,

Mr--- ", he looked at my passport, "Mr Lennox, if Rich Pantuliano has anything to do with your client's business you should prepare her for bad news."

I nodded. "Yes, I'm beginning to get that impression. There's another man who seems to be involved somehow. A man called Cuneo."

Oliver gave a low whistle and looked at me admiringly. "How long did you say you've been here? Marcus Cuneo is heavy stuff." He shook his head, "I can't touch Cuneo. But we can put the pressure on di Giorgio and see what we come up with. He's small beer."

We stared at each other in silence for a moment. "Poor Tom," I said sadly. "He could have confirmed a lot of this. Now the poor kid's gone."

Oliver nodded. "Don't worry. We'll pick up these guys if they're still around. They don't sound too difficult to identify. Then we'll sweat them and see if there really is a connection with di Giorgio. I'll circulate their descriptions and check with San Francisco P.D." He smiled grimly. "And I've got enough to have a talk with di Giorgio. That may shake something loose. I'll enjoy that."

I gave him my contact addresses, as well as my telephone and fax numbers. I also gave him the addresses for Jerry Prescott and Linda Polk in San Francisco. I stood up. This time he let me. "If there isn't anything else I can do right now I'd like to go. You know how to find me."

"Thanks for the information, Lennox. I'll be in touch with you." We made our way back towards the coffee shop. "By the way,"

I said casually, "if you find out anything about Sylvia di Giorgio, I'd appreciate hearing from you. I'd like to keep her mother informed," I said.

I hoped he would believe me.

CHAPTER 26

I drove out of the shopping mall precinct and stopped for a moment at the halt sign on the north-south highway. I had planned to turn left, back towards the airport at Tampa. But on an impulse I found myself turning right and heading to Siesta Key and the house at Pelican Cove. I wanted to hear what Carlos di Giorgio had to say. I wasn't sure how I was going to play it, but I felt a growing anger and frustration. It seemed as if everything I looked at, every stone I turned over, revealed another piece of cruel deceit that led me back to him. It was time some kind of retribution came his way. I drove on in a rage, not cooling off until I was on the island and nearing the big metal gates. Retribution? I laughed. It must have been my Calvinist upbringing.

The gates were open and the cameras didn't seem to be switched on. I drove straight up the driveway unchallenged. All very different from the previous visit. Then it occurred to me that the security had been for Marcus Cuneo, not Carlos. So what kind of man needs that level of security in another person's home? Then I wondered about the house. Who really owned it? Perhaps Carlos was only hired help, like poor Tom Ambrose. The cop had indicated that Carlos was within reach of the law, even if Cuneo was untouchable. Maybe I could scare Carlos into saying or doing something.

But what did I want him to do? Part of me was still working rationally and professionally. I wanted my client's interests protected and Ethnic Art in the clear. On a personal level I wanted Linda Polk left alone. And Sylvia? What did I really want to know about Sylvia? Painfully, I realised that my feelings were not as clear as I had thought; that somehow my emotions were still involved. I arrived at the front door still considering my options. Why hadn't I left it to Sgt Oliver?

I pushed the entrance buzzer. Why wasn't I at the airport, reading a trashy thriller? There was no answer but I heard the sound echoing deep in the house. I waited and pushed the buzzer again. Still nothing. I decided to walk round the veranda to the rear of the house. The sun was hot overhead, in spite of starting its long drop into the waters of the Gulf. I stopped at the little terrace that looked down on the swimming-pool and looked around. The garden, with its shady alcoves seemed deserted. I called out, "Hello!"

I heard one of the sliding glass doors to the sitting-room opened behind me. "Hello yourself," a cool female voice said. I turned round. It was young Sylvia.

She was wearing a white man's shirt, with the tails knotted at her tanned waist, and a pair of dark cotton slacks. Her white leather sandals had heels high enough to bring the top of her head to my eye-level. "Sylvia!" I said. As ever, she took me out of my stride. "I'm looking for Carlos. Is he around?"

She pouted at me. "That's not very nice, Terry. I thought you might be here to see me. Anyway, Carlos is out somewhere.

Aren't you glad to see me instead?" She took a step or two towards me in her familiar manoeuvre; a kind of half slouch, her head bowed slightly, looking at the ground like a little girl apprehensive of a reprimand yet certain that her charm would be irresistible. She came close enough for me to smell the scent of cedar-wood from her hair. I put both hands firmly on her slim shoulders. This time I stopped her. She pushed forward, squirming under my hands, a half smile on her lips.

"Stop it, Sylvia!" I said abruptly. "We've got to cut this out. This is ridiculous."

She jerked back in a sudden flash of anger. "You didn't say that last time." Her face was suddenly distorted, twisted and ugly. "Oh, go to hell!" she snarled.

"No, I didn't say that last time. But I should have done. And that was very wrong of me. I'm sorry it happened," I lied. "This is all wrong--- I'm too old for you, and--- ", I struggled to find plausible words. "I'm worried about your mother. Do you know she's disappeared? That she may be in danger? That's what I'm here about. That, and Mrs van Eck's business. We just can't get involved. You must see that."

She stared at me, her eyes narrowed. "I hope she has disappeared--- disappeared for good. I hope she never comes back." She stood in front of me, her hands clenched, rigid with rage. Her normally hazel-coloured eyes were almost yellow, like a young tigress. "And don't call her my mother," she screamed at me. "She's never been my mother. Helen is my mother--- she was always there, while Sylvia was away enjoying herself; screwing around with guys like you."

Her voice rose higher. "She's not my mother; she's not; she's

183

not; she's not!" Every sinew in her body was taut now. "And she's not even pretty any more. She's old and ugly, like you, you bastard!" I was shocked into silence by the fury in her voice.

Her lips drew back in tight grin and her white teeth clenched, her eyes staring. "And Helen never cared for her--- not like me. She told me so. I was her real daughter. I was the pretty one. I can get anything I want." In an uncanny moment I seemed almost to hear Helen van Eck's voice, calming and consoling a frightened little girl.

"Sylvia," I started to say, "You must realise," At that moment the tension in her snapped. Her right hand flew in a wide arc and slapped me powerfully across the face. I saw it coming but the unreality of the situation made me take it. I jerked back my head, softening the blow. Then she hit me again, with her left hand but this time with the fist clenched. It took me just below the ear. Then the right hit me again. I tucked my chin in instinctively, covered up and moved in to shut down the barrage of flailing punches.

That was a mistake. It might have worked with a man, but I had never fought a woman before. She grabbed my hair with both hands, yanking down my head, mouthing obscenities. I struggled to free myself, a livid pain shooting across my scalp, bringing tears to my eyes. "Christ," I shouted. "Stop it!" I was bent almost double now and could find no way to break her grip.

She showed no sign of calming down. Instead, she struck savagely upwards with her knee, hitting my lowered face again and again. Three, four times, the hard bone was driven into the unprotected side of my head. Part of me was still thinking calmly. I considered kicking her legs away, but the thought of Carlos or someone arriving to find me wrestling with her on the floor made me hesitate. I twisted sideways. She had stopped screaming now but I could hear her panting now with a fierce silent intensity. She still struck out at me with her knee, at the same time trying to rip off my scalp.

I decided that I had taken enough. I picked a spot that would do her the least damage, clenched my fist and, using what leverage I could, I punched her in the solar plexus. She gasped and stopped flailing at me with her knee. That was a distinct improvement. I concentrated, and hit her again, hard. She lost her grip on my hair and reeled back. As I straightened up she threw herself onto one of the big leather seats, burying her face in her arms.

I stood there panting, trying to tidy my hair and clothes. She lay sobbing, her face still hidden. "You bastard! You bastard!" she repeated, again and again. I heard the door open behind me and I turned to see Carlos di Giorgio standing there.

He looked, astonished, from me to the sobbing girl and back again. My heart sank. How do I explain this situation away, I thought? I could imagine the version Helen van Eck would hear, from one source or the other. "What the hell is going on?" di Giorgio asked in wonder, staring at me. "And what are you doing here, Lennox?"

Before I could think of a plausible reply the girl uncoiled herself from the seat. Almost in the same movement she seized a small ceramic pot from a side table and hurled it at di Giorgio. He ducked as it smashed itself to pieces against the wall beside his head. Then, before he could recover his wits, the girl had rushed past him and out of the room. As she went she screamed, "And you're a bastard too, Carlos!" I was only relieved she had changed her target.

Di Giorgio straightened up, his mouth half open in amazement. He looked across at me and slowly shook his head. "She's as crazy as a loon, that one," he said. "Jesus! I thought her mother was bad---." He stopped and for an instant our eyes met. It was a strange shared moment. It occurred to me that Carlos and I had more in common than I had at first imagined.

"I asked her about her mother," I said cautiously, "and she flew into a rage. Became very upset. I don't know why," I added ingenuously. Carlos shook his head again in a confused way. "Yeah," he said. "Crazy as a loon!" He sighed. "Fancy a drink?"

Things were turning out better that I had reason to expect. I smiled ruefully. "Do I?" I said. He went over to the bar in the corner of the room and produced two glasses and a bottle. He waved the bottle at me.

"Scotch?" he asked. I nodded, "Water, no ice." I looked apologetic, "I realise it's un-American and subversive, but no ice."

We settled down on one of the big leather seats at the pool end of the long low cool room. We each savoured our drink in silence. It had a rich, peaty flavour that made me think of the Scottish islands. "So why are you here, Terry?" This wasn't the way I had imagined the confrontation starting. I studied him for a moment and decided to play it cards on the table, to win him over with my sincerity, frankly and openly. Well, more or less. I noticed that his eyes seemed more than ever blood-shot and tinged with red; more watery blue than before. The sun-tan could not entirely conceal the deep shadows under his eyes or the sagging jowls. He looked like a man with problems and the way he gulped down the whiskey made me feel he wasn't solving them.

"To tell you the truth Carlos, I'm pretty worried about what I'm finding at Ethnic Art." I gazed at him innocently. "I still have some detailed information to study. But the picture is, well, worrying."

Carlos reddened slightly. "From what point of view?"

"From the point of view of my client, Carlos." His jowls seemed to sag almost perceptibly and he stared down at his half empty glass. I went on, "That's one issue and I felt I should raise it with you before I have to report back to Mrs van Eck." He stood up, walked to the bar and mixed himself another drink. This time he didn't offer me one. He stood in the middle of the room and gestured towards me with his arm. The dark amber liquid splashed in his glass.

"Don't worry about the business," he said unsteadily. "Everything is OK. It's all in order."

"Well, Carlos, I'd like to think so." I paused, "Although there are some aspects of the advice it received from Bay Financial Services and its associates that does bother me." I stressed the associates, watching him carefully as I spoke.

He blinked at me. "Hey," he said angrily, "you better go carefully, Lennox, if you're planning to give them any trouble. You're out of your league if you try to take on people like that. They have all kinds of connections--- all kinds," he repeated, with a sneer. "Anyway," he went on, taking another gulp at his drink, "everything was done nice and legal."

I eyed him calmly. He stood defiantly in the middle of the room, swaying slightly. "I certainly hope so, Carlos. It would be a shame to cause trouble in the family." He shot an uneasy glance in my direction and finished off his drink in one mouthful. "And speaking of trouble in the family, I ran into a lady by the name of Linda Polk when I was in San Francisco."

Carlos threw himself into a chair and glared at me. "What are you up to Lennox? Why are you so interested in my personal life? What's your angle?" He gave a nasty little laugh. "Stick to your brief, Lennox. No one will thank you for interfering in private matters. No one! Take my word for it."

"Probably true, Carlos. Probably true," I said sadly. "I never expect to get my rewards in this world." Before he had the chance to reply, I went on. "Did you know about what happened to young Tom Ambrose?" He sat there silently, staring at me. "It seems he was badly beaten and then stabbed by a couple of thugs."

Carlos shrugged indifferently. "It can happen," he said.

"The thing is Tom seemed to think the men who did it were known to you. So it wouldn't surprise me if the cops want to speak to you about it. Especially since you've just fired Tom."

"You mean the kid is still alive?" Carlos blurted out.

"What made you think he wasn't, Carlos?"

He was on his feet again, pacing up and down the room. "I--, I don't know. I just assumed---. You said stabbed ." He glared at me defiantly. "Anyway, the kid was causing trouble with young Sylvia. I had to get rid of him." He stopped and stared at me, shaking his head slowly. "Listen Lennox, I don't like the way you're getting involved in our affairs. I have to warn you. And Marcus Cuneo won't like it either--- and he's a bad man to upset."

I tried to look surprised. "Marcus Cuneo? Do you mean he's involved in this too?"

Carlos fought back his anger. "OK Lennox. What is it you want?"

I sighed. People kept asking me that. "It's very simple Carlos. I want my client's interests looked after. So whatever arrangements have been made need to be--- ", I paused, "adjusted to ensure that." I finished my drink. "That's my primary concern. On a more personal level I want to feel sure that Linda Polk has no more trouble. Because she has nothing to do with any of this."

"You can't threaten me, Lennox. I've got friends. Powerful friends. You should know that," he muttered. His eyes were big and watery now. I decided he had enough to think about for the moment. When I stood up he remained sitting and he let me walk out of the room alone. When I looked back he was still sitting there, gazing out of the window into the darkening western sky. There was no sign of young Sylvia as I got into the car and drove away. I wondered what kind of family evening they would have together. Terry Lennox, catalyst and change agent. No home complete without one. I looked at myself in the car mirror and grimaced. At least I was on my way back to Europe, where life was simpler and more straightforward. Maybe.

CHAPTER 27

I arrived at Schiphol Airport about breakfast time on the Thursday morning after a more or less sleepless overnight flight. But at least I had finished 'A distant Mirror' and I was glad to be done with the 14th century; it was beginning to depress me. Or perhaps I had simply reached the point in an assignment when the inevitability of it all is depressing. I called the house at Vinkiveen and just had time for a cup of good Dutch coffee before I met Mrs van Eck's driver. I didn't ask for decaffeinated.

The driver was the same man as on my first visit, looking if anything taller, blonder and just as immaculately turned out in his double breasted blazer. As I climbed into the Mercedes I was uncomfortably aware of my own wardrobe. It was beginning to sag after a week of almost non-stop travel. And aircraft seats were playing hell with my back, in spite of the morning exercises. Why is virtue so rarely rewarded in this life?

I thought longingly about getting home; sleeping in my own

bed and having a decent work out at my gym. I was feeling more and more sluggish each day, as muscles slackened and atrophied. Was the same thing happening to my brain? That was a worrying thought. And how would I know? I decided the question was too difficult to deal with in my condition. Instead I fell asleep in the back of the car.

When the tall driver woke me we were outside the front door of the van Eck's house. I got out and patted the little stone lion on the head. "Good dog," I said, "Remember me?", and rang the door bell. The housekeeper didn't show me into the big sitting-room this time, but instead I was left in a small side room off the entrance hall. It was arranged as an intimate library or study, panelled in modern style with some pale coloured wood and with high windows that looked out at the side of the building. My feet sank into wall-to-wall carpet, dark green with a rich deep pile. Two walls were lined with books. The third was filled by a large stone fireplace with an artificial gas fire, not lit on such a pleasant summer morning. In the centre of the room were two leather armchairs and a low coffee table in a 1930's Art Deco style.

I wandered around, looking aimlessly at the books. After a few minutes Mrs van Eck appeared. "Terry," she said, "I'm so pleased you came." Before I could respond she went on, "But you'll have to forgive me if I don't spend too much time with you. I'm expecting some overseas visitors for lunch. Some business contacts. We may have to be very brief." She looked at me regretfully, her elegant head on one side, a sad little half-smile on her lips. She was wearing a sand coloured short jacket, with a long fluted skirt and a fringed sash tied at her slim waist. Round her neck hung a pendant on a gold chain, a single emerald, long and rectangular and about as big a stone as I have ever seen. "But when we've had our chat perhaps you'd join my guests for a glass of champagne." It didn't seem as if I had a choice.

She settled into one of the chairs and waved me towards the other. "Now tell me everything about Sylvia. Has she spoken to you?" I wondered again why she should think that.

"No," I said. "But I believe she has been in touch with friends of hers in the States. And if what I hear is true she is alive and well. And probably here in Europe by now." I paused. "But what she is doing, I have no idea."

Helen van Eck stared at me, her dark eyes impenetrable. "No," she murmured, almost to herself. "But she is back. How interesting."

It was an odd response but I let it go. I was getting used to odd reactions from this family. I decided to concentrate on Ethnic Art and what I had discovered so I explained the financial situation and the danger of losing control of the company if the lenders chose to call in their loans. I said nothing about the role Carlos and Pantuliano had played in creating the problem. That could wait.

Mrs van Eck took the news calmly. She nodded her head. "I see," was all she said. "Well, I expect that can be taken care of. Now tell me, who should take over from Sylvia."

I stared at her. "But Mrs van Eck, if Sylvia is alive and well surely you don't need anyone to take over?"

Her lips narrowed and a frown appeared. "And do you consider that Sylvia has handled any of this sensibly?" she asked me icily. "If what you tell me is accurate." She broke off and gave me a thin smile. "Of course I am sure you are correct in your assessment of the situation. But if so, I'm afraid Sylvia will have to be brought under tighter control." She looked at me sadly. "I'm afraid I have been too lax with her. I blame myself." She gave me appealing look. "But I thought she had changed. Improved. I hoped she had finally matured; that I could trust her to act with some responsibility." She stopped. Her face hardened. "You have no idea how difficult things have been since Jan became ill. I thought Sylvia might be a help to me at last." A flare of anger appeared in her eyes. "Instead, all she has done is to cause more problems."

I tried to intervene. "Mrs van Eck, I have to say that I think she has been very badly let down by her--- advisors--- over there."

But she was in no mood to listen to me. She waved aside my words. "Oh this Ethnic Art mess is bad enough. But that isn't all," she said bitterly. "She has been more and more difficult in recent months--- selfish and thoughtless. She has deliberately defied me!" Her features were pinched and pale with fury. Suddenly she did look her age. "And so unreasonable about young Sylvia. After all the trouble I took to bring them together again." She glared at me, "I should have known better."

"What has she done that is so awful?" I was astonished at her outburst.

Helen van Eck shook her head violently, the emerald pendant swinging. "That doesn't concern you, Terry. It has nothing to do with your assignment. Just tell me who you think should run Ethnic Art. I'm clearly going to have to get that situation under control."

She sighed and her saddened maternal look re-appeared. "Poor

Sylvia has never been able to cope with responsibility. Not even the child. It has always been the same, if I am honest with myself. Poor Sylvia!"

I said nothing, wondering how poor Sylvia could ever have handled a mother like Helen van Eck. And I understood a little more about the daughter too. Perhaps if Sylvia had been allowed to deal with her own life? But that was an old story that took me nowhere. I forced myself to concentrate on the assignment. "Mrs van Eck, I'll give you my final report as soon as I can. There are still a lot of details that I need to study--- the bank statements mostly. But if you need someone to run the business---."

"I do, Terry. I do." she interrupted. "How can I trust Sylvia after what has happened?"

"In that case you need someone close at hand. Someone you can see and speak to easily. I think you are going to face major problems, Mrs van Eck, and I'll try to spell them out for you in my report, as well as what you can do about them. But if Sylvia is no longer playing a major part in the business--- and it sounds as if you've made up your mind on that--- then the case for running it from the States will vanish. I'd recommend appointing Paul Friden in Brussels. He could do the job. But he'd have to be backed up by improved financial systems, proper stock-control, monthly accounts and reports." I paused, "I have to warn you that you may need a substantial injection of cash if the business is to continue in its present form. I'll know more once I understand the high expense levels."

She leaned forward and patted my arm. It was quite like old times suddenly. "Thank you, Terry. That will be a great help." She smiled one of her social smiles. "Now come and join us for a drink. I'm sorry you can't stay for lunch." I didn't remember being asked but I took the hint.

As we walked through the house she said casually, "I had a very pleasant surprise this morning. My little girl is arriving today from Florida. You did meet her there, didn't you?"

If I looked disconcerted she didn't seem to notice. I followed her into the sitting-room, with its wide open view across the lawn and the watery expanse of the polders. At the far end of the room there was a small group of men in business suits, some white and some who were clearly African. "Come and meet my new Project Development Group," Mrs van Eck said to me. She led me over to three men, white with Dutch accents, and introduced me briefly to them as a family friend. Well, I thought, that's a more accurate description than it would have been this time last week. But would it stay that way if young Sylvia turned up?

For the most part, the white men seemed ill at ease and awkward, a bit like hired help in for their Christmas drink. But it was clear that one of them, a man called Peter de Vries, was the boss. "My team is responsible for developing new markets for the Group," he explained. He spoke excellent English, with only a slight guttural accent indicating his nationality. A tall well built man, he had longish fair hair, strong good-looking features and a neatly trimmed moustache. His dark suit was expensively cut, his shirt front was immaculate and from his top pocket flowed a coloured handkerchief. I was all the more aware of the state of my own outfit. But at least I didn't have a handkerchief in my top pocket

I asked him how the business was going. "Great," he said breezily. "We're concentrating on Africa; mainly Nigeria

195

because of the oil industry."

"Yes, I heard you had landed a big new construction project there. Congratulations. Can you tell me what it's all about?" I said casually.

De Vries looked at me sharply. "It's part of a major infrastructure programme to support the oil industry in that country--- roads, bridges, harbour facilities. Very good business for us."

"Well done," I said admiringly. "I bet it's tough doing business in countries like that.

He grimaced and dropped his voice, turning away from the others. "It's a bugger. The whole place is as corrupt as hell. I don't know what the old man would think if he knew what we are doing." He shrugged. "But I have to say, Mrs van Eck seems to have them eating out of her hand. And she's convinced we'll be paid."

"And get your money out of the country?"

He shrugged again. "She's the boss now," he said and gestured across to where Mrs van Eck was in rapt conversation with the Africans. "There are our new business partners." He paused, "Or at least contacts who can help us. We find you really have to know the right people. And keep them all on side, if you know what I mean. They really appreciate meeting the owners of the business once discussions gets to this stage."

I took a good look at them. One was a dapper young man in an elegant three-piece business suit, with a white shirt and a formal red and black striped tie. The tie had its colours running diagonally downwards from left to right, indicating that he had probably bought it in the United States. The bar sinister must have different connotations in the New World.

But it was the other man who dominated the room, and just by standing there. He was a big man in every respect, tall and powerfully built, with a strong handsome head and an air of calm authority. By contrast with the other's dark suits he created a splash of colour. On his head he wore a close fitting patterned skull cap, and he was dressed in a set of flowing robes of brightly coloured woven cotton; a long loose apron, wide legged trousers and across his shoulders a kind of short cape with loose sleeves.

I decided to find out more and moved in his direction. Mrs van Eck introduced me to him. His name was Christopher Okigbo and it seemed he was well connected with the new Nigerian government, with some kind of role in economic development. The younger man was one of his political advisors. Okigbo beamed at me, "He also happens to be my sister's son," he boomed. "Very well educated and reliable."

It was clear from the way the UCG men acted that Okigbo was important. Obviously he could deliver something they needed. Or they thought he could. And if he was well connected with the new military leaders he could probably do a lot for them. Okigbo exchanged a few pleasantries with me but his shrewd dark eyes quickly appraised me. Then he excused himself politely, switched his attention to de Vries and lead him off to one of the windows, where they stood deep in conversation.

I finished my champagne and started to think about making my farewells to Mrs van Eck. Suddenly I wanted to go home. At that moment the younger Nigerian appeared at my side. He smiled at me. "I understand from Mrs van Eck that you are helping her with her collection of ethnic art." Before I could reply, he continued, "Did you discuss this with Mr Okigbo? You may know that he has set up a Trust with the objective of establishing a new Museum of African Art in Lagos. It's a very exciting time for us."

I tried to look interested but I wasn't quite sure who he meant by us. He went on enthusiastically, "It will be a focus in our drive to repatriate our great cultural heritage from abroad. To repair some of the damage inflicted on our traditions by colonial exploitation." His eyes gleamed at the prospect. "We believe it is important that our people can see their history and culture--- see the achievements of their ancestors. It will make them proud--- and strong."

"That's fascinating," I said. "But I'm afraid I know nothing about the cultural side of Mrs van Eck's business. I'm just a boring management consultant."

The young man looked crestfallen. "Ah, a shame," he said sadly. "Mrs van Eck has been so supportive of the Okigbo Trust. She has made some---," he hesitated, "some commitments. Some commitments that could be very helpful for all concerned. I had hoped you might be able to throw some light on when we might see the bronze head from the Oba's shrine. All we have seen so far are photographs. We are most anxious to see the real object. It could be very important to us." He glanced at me meaningfully.

Light began to flood into my jet-lagged brain. "You mean the Princess Head?"

"Yes," he said. "It will be a great honour for Christopher

Okigbo to bring such a rare and beautiful object back to his people."

"And Mrs van Eck has offered to sell the Princess Head to the Trust?" I asked.

The young man hooted with laughter, rocked back and struck me lightly with his hand on the shoulder. "No, no," he said. "Not sell. Not sell," he stressed. "Donate it, as a gift to our nation. To the Christopher Okigbo Trust. Very important. Such a gift would make her very popular with our people."

I'll bet, I thought. But before I could think of a sufficiently bland reply a door opened across the room. There stood young Sylvia, tall and slim and elegant, looking wonderful in spite of her overnight journey from the States. She was wearing an orange coloured trouser suit with a long loose jacket and a pale cream shirt with a high rounded neck. Her dark hair was knotted casually at the back with a short silk scarf that matched the colour of the suit. She seemed a lot more composed than when I had seen her last.

Her eyes met mine across the room. She raised her elegant eyebrows a fraction, then turned away towards the group standing around Okigbo. Helen van Eck had been engrossed in conversation with him but now she broke off to greet the girl. The two women embraced with what seemed to be real affection. I could see the pride and pleasure in the older woman's face. She hugged the girl and put one arm round her slim waist, looking up at her.

"Now, everyone," she announced, "I want you to meet Sylvia, my most beautiful girl. She's just flown in from America especially to meet you all."

Without a trace of embarrassment the girl coolly smiled and surveyed the group of men. "Oh Mummy," she said, "what a flatterer!" She kissed Mrs van Eck on the cheek and glided away in the direction of Okigbo, collecting a glass of champagne from a side table as she went. Instantly she had his attention and whatever he had been discussing with Mrs van Eck was forgotten. Young Sylvia stood close beside him, looking up into his face and swaying ever so slightly towards him.

"What a double act," I thought. "Helen and the kid--- Scylla and Charybdis. Poor Sylvia." I found Mrs van Eck and started to make my farewells. She took the news that I was leaving quite graciously.

"Of course Terry. My driver will take you to the airport." She looked across the room to where young Sylvia was holding Okigbo and his young friend enthralled. "Isn't she quite lovely, Terry?" I indicated that, yes, on balance, I thought she was. Too much enthusiasm, I decided, might have been misunderstood. Mrs van Eck sighed, "She's such a comfort in this difficult time. Especially with so little support from Sylvia." She shook her head sadly. Then, more briskly, "Terry, if you do feel that I should appoint Paul Friden I will of course agree. But in that case I wonder if you would see him again, for me. Speak to him about the job. If you still think he's right, and if he seems to want the position then I can offer it to him formally."

I nodded, "Of course. I'd be glad to. It will be useful to have another view of him." I looked her straight in the eyes. "But I must repeat, Mrs van Eck, there are serious financial issues that need to be addressed before you can make any appointment."

"Well," she repeated, just as she had done earlier, "I expect they can be dealt with."

I shrugged, "I hope so, Mrs. van Eck. By tomorrow I expect to be able to clarify the situation for you. I'll call you when I've studied the rest of the information."

We walked towards the front of the house. She stopped and took my arm. "It occurs to me, Terry, if it would be helpful." She smiled up at me. "That you might like to stay at our company flat in Brussels when you come back to see Friden. In fact, why don't you stay on over the week-end and enjoy a break. You've been travelling so much. It will do you good." She patted my arm maternally. "I'll give you the address when we speak on the telephone tomorrow. The apartment is free and fully equipped."

"That's very of you, Mrs van Eck." Had I misjudged her?
"There is one other thing. I wonder if it would be possible to pay my respects to your husband before I leave. If he is well enough to see me for a few minutes."

She hesitated fractionally, then she smiled her practised smile. "I don't see why not. He's been resting and at times he seems a little stronger. Of course I do try to keep the socialising--- and the business worries--- away from him." She frowned. "Although some people insist in trying to involve him. Still, I'm sure he'll be glad to see you, Terry. But do take care not to tire him." She left me and made her way back to her guests.

I found the long corridor with the Dutch seascapes and went through the swing doors and into the intense light and heat of the plant filled room at the end of the house. Jan van Eck was seated in his wheel-chair with a rug over his thin legs. His eyes opened blue and clear as I came into the room and he smiled at me, moving his emaciated great head slightly in greeting.

I sat down in the chair beside him. In the summer heat the room was like a sauna. I took off my jacket. "Mr van Eck, I know you are tired. But I need to talk to you." He moved his head slightly again to indicate he understood. "I have some questions to ask you. Just nod or shake your head. Don't try to speak unless you feel you must." He sat very still, his eyes fixed on my face.

I leaned towards him. "When I was here last week you tried to tell me something." He nodded "I think you said it was not her company. Did you mean Sylvia?" He shook his head firmly. I sighed. "Did you mean Helen?" He nodded and I sensed a new light in the blue eyes. "You were talking about UCG, not Ethnic Art, weren't you?" A look of relief crossed his pale features and he nodded again, more strongly.

I sat back, sweating quietly into my already limp shirt. It was beginning to feel like playing some strange game of charades in a steam bath. He was very weak, but I needed to know where he stood. "Mr van Eck, are you happy about the way UCG is being handled? About the overall strategy?" He shook his head slowly but firmly. "Could Sylvia--- your daughter, help. If she was willing?" The old man nodded, and sank back in the wheel-chair, his eyes closed.

I waited for some sign that he had recovered but he seemed to have gone to sleep. Then as I rose to leave he opened his eyes. "Find Sylvia," he whispered hoarsely. "Tell her I need her. Explain it to her." His eyes closed again.

I made my way thoughtfully back to the front of the house. the big driver was waiting there with the black Mercedes, holding open the rear door respectfully. I paused in the entrance and patted the little stone lion oh the head. "Keep an eye on things for me, there's a good fellow."

I was about to step out when, from behind me I heard young Sylvia's voice. "Terry," she called softly. As I turned she glided up to me and reached up to give me a little peck on the cheek. To an onlooker it must have seemed an informal farewell. But instead she whispered, "I want to say I'm sorry. Can you ever forgive me?" She looked up at me through her dark lashes for a moment, and then looked down, hanging her head. "Mummy says you're going to be at the flat in Brussels. May I come and see you? If I promise to be good?"

Before I could think of a reply to that one, she gave a giggle and whisked away across the stone-flagged hall to rejoin the others.

CHAPTER 28

The trip home went smoothly. When the airport taxi dropped me outside my flat in Edinburgh's so-called New Town there was still light in the sky, although it was well after 10pm. This far north summer days seem never to end. I climbed the familiar flight of stone steps, unlocked the heavy Georgian front door and pushed aside the piles of mail that lay behind the door.

There was one bulky envelope with a Miami postmark. I heaped the rest of the mail onto a side table, promising myself to look at it in the morning. I opened the Miami envelope and took the papers up to my little office area at the front of the house, glancing at them as I went to make sure they were what I wanted. There was a lot of detail. I thought about starting to assess the information. But the journey had taken its toll and the figures I was looking at had stopped making sense. I decided the best thing I could do was go to bed. For a long time I lay awake, trying to figure out why Sylvia might have wanted to keep the Princess Head away from her mother. Then I spent a while trying to work out what time my body thought it was.

Then I must have gone to sleep.

It was almost nine o'clock when I woke and the sun was streaming into my bedroom. I showered, shaved and exercised, and then went through my coffee making ritual. As I waited for the boiling water to work on the decaffeinated grains I stood by the window, smelling the aroma of the coffee and watching the routine movements of the people in the quiet formal street below. The New Town is a kind of semi-exclusive village of 18th and 19th century houses and flats laid out with a precise geometry that pleased me, in a series of streets and crescents broken at regular intervals by delightful tree-filled gardens. In time, like any village, you came to know your neighbours and tune in to the rhythm of the place. This was home.

The sun shone brightly. It seemed an ideal day to wander around the familiar streets and to restock my empty kitchen cupboards. I sighed. "But I have promises to keep," I thought. I dressed and carried a cup of coffee into my office. Then I called Dolf Erhardt. It was clear that Donald had prepared him and he was expecting my call. We agreed to meet for lunch next day in Brussels. He said he wanted me to meet someone, an investment banker by the name of John Grossman, who represented one of the big international merchant banks.

"That's fine, Dolf," I said. "By the way, do you know anything about a man called Christopher Okigbo?"

"Ah," said Dolf, "I see you're well informed, as usual." I decided not to disabuse him of the idea. After all, it's not a bad reputation to have. "He's a half brother of the military leader of Nigeria." I recalled what Donald Lynch had told me during our alcoholic dinner in Boston. The present head of government had seized power in an army coup a few years earlier,

205

frustrated by years of incompetence and corruption. Or maybe because he wasn't getting his share. He had of course promised democratic elections and, in time, he held them. Unfortunately the people chose the wrong man as President and the military refused to hand over power. Instead, the winner had been arrested. As far as I knew the legally elected President was still in jail, held in atrocious conditions if the western media was to be believed. I knew that civil liberty organisations were pressurising their governments to do something to help. The problem was that Nigeria is an oil-producing country and no-one seemed anxious to alienate them.

Dolf went on, "He's also related to the Minister with responsibility for oil and economic development." He laughed. "It's very much a family affair. Just like UCG. But let's leave the rest until tomorrow." He asked me to meet him at Le Cygne, a restaurant on the Grand Place. I was impressed. Le Cygne was a stylish place, so expenses were obviously not being restricted on this one. It sounded like a best suit job.

I called Paul Friden to say I wanted to see him at the gallery next morning. Then I called Helen van Eck. She wasn't available, of course, but her secretary gave me the address of the apartment. It was in the Boulevard de L'Empereur, near the Grand Sablon and the gallery and only a short walk from where I was to meet Dolf and Grossman. She told me that the concierge would have the key waiting for me and that the place would be clean and stocked with all I might need for the week-end. I was beginning to feel like a management consultant again, so I decided I'd better do some work.

I thought it was time to do some background checking and rang the woman I knew slightly at the local museum. I asked to speak to Jean Morrow. She was an expert on tribal art and she seemed to remember me. But maybe she said that to everyone who phoned up looking for free advice. I explained I needed educating rapidly on some aspects of tribal art and suggested we meet for lunch. As luck would have it she had just had a lunch meeting with her Director cancelled, so we arranged to meet at my club in Princes Street. She sounded brisk and efficient. "I can't make you an expert in an hour," she said bluntly. "It's a huge field. But I'll do what I can help you." I told her I was looking forward to seeing her. As I hung up I realised that it was true.

Then I turned to the banking information from Miami. I groaned. This was the part of my work I liked least; the detailed analysis, plodding painfully through pages of figures. That was why people like Donald were so valuable. He saw things at a glance in a column of figures, things that told a story. I started to work my way through the monthly bank statement.

An hour later even I could see the picture. Several large payments had been made into the Ethnic Art account from Southern Commercial Lending Corporation. I presumed these were the proceeds of loans secured on the stock of Ethnic Art. But in addition there was a series of equally large cash deposits from undisclosed sources. These could have been customers paying for expensive objects, but it seemed unlikely they would all have paid in cash. Of course, they might have been wealthy individuals trying to avoid paying tax. But the payments were unusually large and remarkably regular. In all, about three million dollars had appeared in the account from unidentified sources.

The expenditure side it was equally strange. There were large monthly payments out of the account, ranging from one hundred thousand to two hundred thousand dollars. They amounted to more than two million dollars over a twelve month period and appeared to be payments to different consultancy firms. However, most of the payments were to a company called Export Advisory Services. I checked back on the organisational chart that Donald had given me. Sure enough, there it was. Export Advisory Services was owned by Caribbean Enterprises, which was the parent company of Southern Commercial and also Bay Financial Services, Pantuliano's company, the one that was supposed to be advising Ethnic Art.

I guess that I had known for several days what was going on. Certainly Donald had known instinctively when he saw the figures in Boston. But now that everything was drawn together it was obvious and elegantly simple. Ethnic Art had a pattern of expenses way beyond its trading potential. If the mysterious cash injections ceased; well, I felt a chill of apprehension. Somehow I would have to deal with this. It was all very well for Mrs van Eck to say blithely that it could be handled. But it wasn't just the loss of money if the company went down. That would certainly put a dent in the resources of the van Eck family, even without the other problems at UCG that Donald had described.

The real problem was the kind of people who were involved. This was money laundering on a massive scale; with illegally earned cash moved around until it could be made to reappear as legitimate profits. Or legitimate assets, I thought grimly. That was the real danger from my client's point of view. I assumed Donald had been joking when he asked me the question, "Who used to own this company?" But the truth was that when Commercial Lending called in its loans, Ethnic Art and its costly stock would belong to Marcus Cuneo and the people who stood behind him. Carlos, you bastard, I thought

It was a neat scheme--- too clever for Carlos to have put together. But without him it wouldn't have worked. Not only was he able to siphon the illegal cash out of the business in the form of extortionate fees, turning it into legal earnings in the process, but only he was in a position to persuade Sylvia to agree with the loan arrangements. When the business failed and was unable to repay the debts, it would be taken over by whichever part of Cuneo's empire held the securities. The valuable stock of objects, built up with illegal cash, would be sold off and then, even if big discounts were taken, the money would be back in legal circulation. I smiled grimly. Even Ethnic Art's trading losses could then be set against legitimate profits from some other part of the network, to save taxes. It was beautiful. Donald would love it.

I shook my head. No, Carlos di Giorgio had not master-minded this. There were some clever and dangerous people involved and as Donald had said, I had better watch my step. But equally, Sgt Oliver was right. Carlos was only middle management. My problem was how to deal with the high command. I made more coffee and sat staring out at the sun on the grey roofs opposite. The germ of an idea was forming. But I was still missing a few pieces of the puzzle. I looked at my watch. It was time to meet Jean Morrow for my lesson in tribal art.

CHAPTER 29

I met her at the porter's lodge, before she could penetrate too far into the Club. It was taboo to have a woman wandering around the Club on her own at that time of day. At least, I thought, she should understand the need for these tribal traditions. I had of course seen her from time to time but this was the first time we had actually chosen to be together. I found her instantly attractive. She was small and well built, with a mass of fairish brown curly hair, a plump round face with a glowing healthy complexion. Her looks would have been merely pretty had it not been for her eyes. But they overwhelmed me on sight. Large, blue and luminescent, they held me like a rabbit caught in a car headlights.

She shook my hand firmly. The gaze was confident, open and frankly curious, rather like the head girl being introduced to a school governor. She spoke easily and well in classless English tones, with just a hint of some regional accent underlying the careful received pronunciation. We went into the Club's charming Ladies Bar, looking out onto the great bulk of the Castle on its ancient rock.

We exchanged platitudes and admired the view. Then I offered her a drink before lunch. She looked at me solemnly, her eyes wide. "I thought you would never ask," she said, and a broad grin transformed her face. I liked her more and more.

Over lunch she came to the point with typically engaging frankness. "Why did you ask me to lunch?" I explained I was interested in tribal art and in particular the background to Benin bronzes. She looked at me with new interest. "Why Benin?" she asked. I said something vague about it coming up in the course of an assignment.

Crisply she covered much of what Paul Friden had told me. "In the 15th century the Portuguese found well developed societies in West Africa, societies that seemed to have been there for hundreds of years. Benin was one of them--- and one of the most powerful and successful." She paused to tackle her shrimp cocktail. "It was part of what we turned into modern Nigeria. It had its own king, or Oba, and royal family, its own religion and priests, cities with paved streets that were better than any in Europe at the time. And they had mastered the art of metal casting. Some of their important buildings were clad in large, elaborately decorated panels of cast bronze. Very intricate and technically difficult."

I decided to impress her with my metallurgical knowledge. "So they had access to copper and tin?"

She hesitated, "Well, we call it bronze. Actually the early castings appear to have been more like brass--- a copper and lead alloy." She dismissed the topic with a wave. "That's not my field," she said firmly. "I have a colleague who specialises in that sort of thing, if you want to talk to him." She laughed, "He knows all there is to know about dating these bronze alloys, using chemical analysis and so forth. The information is useful in tracking medieval trading patterns. For example, how was it that tin reach the people of Benin so early? Some academics think the Phoenicians traded it down the west coast of Africa. It's interesting, but highly specialised. My field is more to do with stylistic developments, especially in the way figures were portrayed over time."

I nodded and poured her more wine. "Tell me about the Princess Heads," I said.

Her blue eyes lit up a fraction more. "They are quite rare. Basically they are representations of members of the royal family placed on an Oba's altar when he died, so that he was accompanied by his nearest and dearest after death. Some of them came to Europe in the 19th century, after the British mounted a punitive raid on Benin to punish them for the murder of a couple of officials. The basis of the Benin civilisation was wiped out in a few days. And a lot of loot was brought back."

"Including some of the Princess Heads?"

She nodded, "A few. But not all of them were early ones. The tradition was kept up over a long period. But the heads are quite rare and valuable, depending on age, rarity and condition. And also the provenance of the object. For example, can its history of ownership be established? That way we stand a chance of knowing what we're dealing with."

"If these objects are so important, don't you think they belong in their own country? Rather than here in Europe?"

She looked at me doubtfully. "That's a big question---and

currently a rather burning issue. Some items have been repatriated or even gifted to their country of origin only to reappear on the international art market after a year or so, for sale again to the highest bidder." She shrugged, "It is difficult to know the right thing to do in every case."

"So there is the potential for someone to make a nice profit?"

She nodded and looked at her watch. "Almost two o'clock. Lunch had gone in a flash, it seemed and she made a disconsolate face. "Time to get back to the coal face," she said. I did my best to detain her as long as I could. I didn't want her to go. But I had run out of questions on Benin bronzes. "Is there anything else you would like to ask me?" she said, looking me straight in the eyes.

I smiled. "I think there is. In fact I'm certain there is. Can I call you next week when I think of it?" She laughed delightedly. "I'd better go. Thank you for the lunch, Terry. But next time I'll expect you to do most of the talking. I want to know what this is all about."

I walked with her out of the Club and we stood together in the bustling crowds of Princes Street. I was still reluctant to let her go. I had only known her for an hour or so, but already I was half in love with her. Her simple, matter-of-fact charm was a delight after the neurotics I had been dealing with. Eventually I ran out of even flimsy excuses to keep her from leaving. I watched her small figure darted away into the crowd, still smiling at my transparent attempts to delay her. Always, I thought to myself, leave them laughing.

CHAPTER30

I had spent an exciting evening in Edinburgh, catching up with my laundry and listening to some music on the radio, a lively piece that turned out to be by Purcell; 'Incidental Music to the Virtuous Wife.' It was sub-titled "Good luck", which struck me as a touch cynical. Then I had looked through my mail in a desultory way. There was a telephone bill, a printed circular telling me I had won a villa in the south of France, and three invitations to invest in new unit trusts. I threw them all away. Then, as an afterthought, I retrieved the bills and put them in a file marked 'pay'. After that I worked for a couple of hours on my report for Mrs van Eck.

The findings were simple. My biggest problem had been to find some careful phraseology, just in case Carlos survived the forthcoming holocaust as her son-in-law and decided to sue me. That seemed unlikely. But you never know with clients--- especially families. The key phrase had to be a clear warning that highly irregular financial transactions had taken place, possibly illegally, which seriously jeopardised the shareholders equity.

My recommendations had taken longer to work out. Paul Friden was to take over the management of the business in Sylvia's absence---if there was a business. There had to be better accounting and stock control systems--- my hook for a follow-up assignment if I wanted one. Just at the moment I wanted no part of it. In fact I was filled with a growing distaste for the whole messy affair. God, I thought, post- assignment tristesse and the assignment isn't over yet. Pretty bad!

I sighed and looked around. Saturday morning--- it must be Brussels, I thought. I remembered Jean Morrow. After our lunch, to take my mind off her I had visited my gym and a heavy work out had left me physically exhausted but in better spirits. But why was I in Brussels when she was in Edinburgh? Well, that was one of the few questions I could answer.

The UCG apartment was located in a plain fronted utilitarian-looking 1960's block down the Rue d'Escalier, in a particularly dreary part of Brussels. But it was handy for the Gare Central and the second floor flat was comfortable, if not stylish. There were two equally sized bedrooms at the rear, looking down into the quiet grounds of the local primary school. One of them had an emergency exit that opened on to a rickety iron staircase running down the back of the building. The rest of the apartment consisted of a very large rectangular sitting-room which included a dining area. The furnishings, functional and impersonal, made the place feel like the hotel it was pretending not to be. At one end of the sitting-room there were big sliding doors, opening on to a tiny balcony above the main boulevard. In one corner was a small, well equipped kitchen with everything a lonely man might need, including a bottle of malt whisky.

The outer door of the apartment opened straight into the sitting-room from a dimly lit landing, with a flight of crude concrete steps leading down to street level and up to the floors above. A rather basic elevator was the alternative to the dark stair-well, the only illumination being provided by institutional-looking wall lights set head high behind metal grills.

I discovered when I arrived that the lights were set on limited time switches. Impatient, I decided not to wait for the painfully slow elevator and pressing the button to light up the stairs I set off for the second floor. Half way between floors the lights cut off. I was stranded in total darkness, cursing quietly and groping about from one light switch to the next. Bastards, I thought. And they say the Scots are mean.

After I dumped my case in the apartment I walked up to the Grand Sablon to see Friden. He seemed a touch less frenetic this time and I was convinced that he could make a reasonable job of running the company. "But what about Sylvia?" he asked me. Good question, I thought. I told him that Mrs van Eck wanted someone closer to hand, now that she was so tied up with UCG. That seemed to satisfy him.

"Still no sign of the Benin Princess," I asked him.

He shook his head gloomily. "Mrs van Eck has been creating hell. I'm sure she blames me."

"Don't worry," I said confidently. "It will all sort itself out." I hoped I was right, but at least it seemed to satisfy him.

I strolled down to the Grand Place with its splendid medieval architecture, the complex stone tracery of the Maison du Roi like solid lace and the succession of tall narrow sober town houses. On the south side of the old square stood the Gothic towers of the Town Hall and a series of stately facades, gilded, decorative and each one distinctive. These were the ancient guild houses, some of which had been converted into stylish restaurants.

Le Maison du Cygne was one of these; one of the most fashionable and probably the most expensive. Thank you Dolf, or whoever the client is, I thought as I mounted the four or five stone steps up to the front door. I stopped to admire the painted stone swan, wings outstretched, above the door. Inside, Dolf was waiting for me. He was about my height, possibly just below six feet, with the solid build of a countryman. His hair was dark and straight and just starting to grey slightly. His face, sturdily Dutch, was long and rectangular and pleasantly ugly, and marked with deep creases beside his mouth and nose. His soft brown eyes had a look of perpetual good-natured curiosity, rather like a happy but puzzled spaniel. When he spoke, his voice was surprisingly deep and strong. His English was perfect, with a strange transatlantic clip that overlaid his slightly guttural Dutch accent.

He greeted me warmly. Like a Dutch uncle, I thought, as I always did when Dolf and I met. He struck me as a man to trust. And he was, always provided you were a friend. But the homely style hid a sharp mind and a ruthlessness that had accounted for quite a few of his business opponents. I liked him--- and had reason to trust him. He took me up to the dining-room, its antique wall panelling glowing warmly in candle light.

John Grossman was already at a table beside a window that looked down on the cobbled square below. He rose and shook my hand as Dolf made the introductions. Grossman was of medium height and stocky build, with neatly trimmed brown hair brushed straight back from a high forehead. His face, square jawed and strong featured with wide set brown eyes, was tanned and fit looking. He wore a three-piece suit made of a light tweed, in a pale russet colour, and a countrified cotton shirt with a large, faint brown and green check. He looked as solid and reliable as English roast beef. His tie had the yellow and red diagonals of the MCC and they were not in the bar sinister direction. When he spoke it was with the tones of the best public school. "Terry," he said with a smile that signalled real pleasure. "I'm so glad you were able to join us for lunch."

The meal was superb. Nothing as sordid as business or money was allowed to distract us from the food. Dolf and I recalled people and places we had in common. We laughed together about Donald Lynch. Grossman and I exchanged views on the future of English cricket while Dolf looked interested but puzzled by that particular English ritual.

It was all very civilised. I chose a warm lobster salad to start and a lightly grilled sole. Dolf ordered the wine--- a good premier cru Chablis that went well with our food. Eventually, I knew the cost of the meal would find its way back to Grossman and his colleagues, whoever they were.

When we came to the coffee Dolf came to the point. "I think Donald Lynch outlined our problem in relation to UCG." I indicated that I knew a little of the background. "John here has been asked by three or four of the institutional shareholders, including his own investment house, to seek a dialogue with the van Eck family about the future of the construction group. To explain the concerns there are in the market place."

Grossman spoke up, "We are worried about the direction of the business--- in particular about its possible relationship with unstable regimes in West Africa."

"You mean Nigeria?"

Grossman nodded. "The military government is in bad odour with the international banks.

"In spite of the country's oil reserves?" I asked.

"Yes," he said. "In fact, the regime has made a big mistake by trying to use the international oil companies to put pressure on the British government. You probably know that there is a move to expel Nigeria from the Commonwealth. Obviously, expulsion would really shake their credit rating."

"Which would be bad news for anyone doing business with them," Dolf added.

"And presumably the oil giants are not too happy to be treated like that, either," I said. "Well, I would have thought the dangers are clear enough."

"Right," Grossman said crisply. "My problem is that I have made no progress in convincing Mrs van Eck of this. She seems determined to go ahead with major contracts in that part of the world. If they go sour they will almost certainly bring down the whole group."

I looked at him thoughtfully. "So why not just sell out? And try to pick up the pieces cheaply afterwards, if it's worth doing?"

Grossman smiled."Frankly Terry, that would normally be an option. Or something of that sort. But there are a couple of competitors, American and Japanese, that for long term strategic reasons we want to keep out of Europe. We would like to avoid a collapse of share price, if it is possible to do so."

"And Mrs van Eck won't listen?"

Grossman sipped his coffee. "She is a charming lady. But---"

"But she told you to piss off?" I said. Dolf guffawed.

Grossman looked pained. "Well, let's say she seemed to feel there is an implied criticism of her leadership of the group." He looked around for a waiter to ask for more coffee, "But in effect, yes."

"How do you think I can help you,?" I asked.

Dolf picked up the cream jug and slowly stirred a drop into his coffee. "We think the daughter, Sylvia, who lives in America could be the key to the whole situation." He glanced across at me innocently. "We understand that you know her. When Donald told me you were working for the family---" He paused. "We thought it might be worth having a chat with you." I sat quietly, waiting for the rest.

"Sylvia owns a substantial block of shares in the group. Shares that are held in a trust fund controlled by her father and mother," Dolf went on. "Effectively, for the moment at least, that means her mother."

"But our lawyers think the trust could be broken," said Grossman, "if Sylvia chooses to exercise a right she has had since she reached her fortieth birthday. However our impression is that she is still very much influenced by her mother, particularly now that Jan is ill."

I nodded silently.

Grossman went on, "And we are by no means convinced that the mother is necessarily an influence for the good; certainly not in this case." Amen to that, I thought. "We, our associates, would simply like to feel that the daughter understands the issues. And ideally of course that she is sympathetic to our aims. We don't expect her to sell out to us or anything like that." He smiled at me, as one who would appreciate the niceties of family affairs.

Quickly I ran through Grossman's options in my mind. He wouldn't risk precipitating a messy take-over battle. So he'd want it done quietly and confidentially. Although if one of the competitors waiting in the wings was willing to bid up the share price there was a good chance the institutional shareholders would sell out at a better profit. I didn't buy entirely their desire to keep the group European. The institutions always have a fall-back position and an escape route. But maybe I was overly cynical. For some reason I did believe Grossman when he said their objective was only to change the direction of the business, at least at this stage.

"Tell me exactly what you want Mrs van Eck to do."

"Simply to understand the need to reassure the minority shareholders," Grossman said.

"Which would take what?" I persisted.

Grossman sipped his coffee and studied me for a moment. "She would have to agree to some changes we have in mind--- at board level, I mean. Bring in one or two people who would make the other shareholders feel more comfortable. And agree to review the current commercial strategy. Especially the risks involved in going heavily into places like Nigeria at the moment."

"Wouldn't that more or less kill off the contract for them? I doubt if the military government would be happy about the delay, under the circumstances."

Grossman smiled blandly at me. "Possibly a little time to reflect would be no bad thing, under the circumstances."

Got it, I thought. "But I understood from Donald that UCG was desperate for new business."

He inclined his head. "It is possible that with the right people in place there are other business opportunities somewhat closer to home that could be brought forward to the advantage of UCG. Smaller projects certainly, but much, much safer. Enough to keep the group intact--- albeit perhaps slimmed down to its core activities. The current uncertainty about UCG---, the changes Mrs van Eck has been making, have rather tended to hold up decisions in a number of cases. If we felt that we were able to reassure the market place---." He left the sentence hanging. So Grossman seemed to think that the group could be turned around. Maybe it was the MCC tie. Or perhaps Dolf. But I believed him.

"I'm still not sure what you expect me to do," I said.

"We'd like you to arrange for us to meet Sylvia van Eck," said Grossman. He looked across at Dolf. "We've been trying to contact her but we seem to be unable to get in touch."

I smiled ruefully. "That doesn't surprise me. I was told by Mrs van Eck that her daughter vanished weeks ago in a sailing accident." The two men exchanged glances. "Yes. We had picked up that story. But we've been unable to confirm it. We rather thought it was Mrs van Eck being difficult."

I sat back, toying with my cup. "Do you know anything definite?" Dolf asked me bluntly.

"Definite?" I shook my head slowly. "No. Nothing definite." I looked across at the two of them. "But I have a feeling she's around, somewhere. It seems she has a lot of problems. Personal problems mostly. Knowing her, it's perfectly possible that she has simply run away from them and gone to ground somewhere. She can be unpredictable at times."

Dolf pursed his lips. "Is it possible you could find her for us, Terry? Get her to talk to us about UCG?"

Grossman leaned forward. "Or alternatively use your influence to persuade Mrs van Eck to speak to us again." His voice tailed away as I started to laugh.

"Frankly," I said, "I doubt if Mrs van Eck is the sort of woman anyone could persuade to do something she doesn't want to do. And as for Sylvia, I have no idea where she might be." As I spoke I recalled the letter she had sent to young Tom Ambrose. "Although," I added thoughtfully, "it is possible she's back in Europe now."

Dolf put his heavy head on one side and looked at me like a wise old owl. "What do you think, Terry? Can you help us?"

I promised to do my best and to keep them informed of

developments. Grossman looked at his watch. "Many thanks, Terry," he said. "If you can help us we shall of course be glad to agree some kind of introductory fee; to cover your costs and time."

We walked down together to the Grand Place in the warm summer afternoon sunshine. He gave me his card as we parted, and shook my hand. "We really would be most grateful if you can be of assistance, Terry. We seem to be in a cul-de-sac on this one at present. It would be nice if we can settle things amicably with the family. Some of us have fond memories of old Jan. But if not, " he shrugged his shoulders. "It could become messy. I suspect some of our fellows wouldn't mind overmuch if the whole house of cards came down." He glanced at Dolf and then smiled at me, "So if you can help---."

As we watched him disappear in the direction of the Amigo Hotel Dolf turned to me. "You see the situation, Terry. You'd be doing everyone a favour if you can persuade the family to talk seriously to John. And remember, money will not be a problem."

We went our separate ways. For the second time in a week a client had told me that money was not a problem. I must be doing something right. The trouble was I didn't know what.

CHAPTER 31

I walked across the cobbles towards the tall guild houses on the north side of the square. Quite illogically, I felt vaguely irritated that Dolf and Grossman had tried to involve me in their schemes. A few days ago I thought I had seen the last of Sylvia and the van Ecks. Now I seemed to be embroiled in their problems more than ever. Why should they expect me to influence the family--- especially Helen van Eck? Even if I could find Sylvia, why would she listen to me, given the way we had parted? Especially if young Sylvia told her what had happened at the motel in Florida; which seemed highly likely.

I threw back my head as I walked and silently cursed myself for being so stupid. I remembered the girl's parting words at the house at Vinkiveen. Oh God, I thought. Will she appear at the apartment? Any kind of relationship with her now would be bad news--- for all sorts of reasons. The girl was a spoiled brat, with a severe hang-up about her mother. OK, maybe in time she'd grow up. And then she would be a hell of a woman. But I didn't have the time to invest in that process; or the emotional energy to see it through.

That was the logic speaking. But if I was honest, I knew that part of me half-hoped she would appear. After all she was a beautiful young girl. Then reason intervened again. Get a grip, Lennox, I thought. Imagine the complications that would create with Helen van Eck. And with Sylvia, were she to put in an appearance.

I wandered around the old part of the town for an hour or two and then made my way back to the apartment. A quiet week-end was beginning to appeal. Rather than run the gauntlet of darkness in the stairwell I took the slow old elevator up to the second floor. The apartment was as silent and impersonal as an empty coffin and about as welcoming. I looked around the place. Why had I accepted Mrs van Eck's offer to use the place? I decided I didn't like Brussels well enough to spend a week-end there. Quickly I changed into some casual clothes and started to pack. I'd decide where I was going when I got to the Gare Central.

The sound of telephone shattered the silence. I answered it, half expecting to hear Mrs van Eck or perhaps young Sylvia. In spite of everything I felt a growing sense of excitement. "Hello," I said, without identifying myself.

At the other end of the line I heard a low gasp and a pause. "Terry?" the voice said, in a hoarse whisper. "This is Sylvia." For a few seconds my mind was awash with unfocussed thoughts. Sylvia, I thought dully. Before I could reply, she spoke again. Her voice sounded thin and weak. "Are you alone? Can you speak?"

Then I knew. It was Sylvia--- not the girl. Like Dolf, she retained a trace of the accent she had grown up with during her school years. There was just a hint of Dutch guttural under the polished tones of a typical middle-class English girl.

"Sylvia?" I said. "Where are you?" There was silence and I heard the sound of voices and a noise like glasses clattering in the background. Then without waiting for her to reply, I went on, "Yes. I am on my own. But where are you, Sylvia?" I repeated. "What's going on?"

In the space between us I could sense her struggling to control herself. "Oh Terry," she sobbed, "It's been so terrible. My God, it's like a nightmare." She hesitated and then stammered on, "Terry, I must see you. Can I come and see you?"

My mind was still in a whirl. Sylvia was alive. Tom Ambrose had told the truth. I thought of Carlos and his friends, Linda Polk, and young Tom. "Where are you, Sylvia?" I asked again, trying to grasp on to some solid information.

When she replied she seemed desperate, close to tears, her voice strained and slightly slurred. "I'm here in Brussels. Terry, I need to see you." Her voice rose hysterically. "Terry, I'm so afraid. I've just heard about Tom--- he's dead. Murdered!" Her voice broke again, "And it's all my fault. I know it is. Help me Terry. There's no-one else I can turn to now."

I tried to calm her, while I considered the various options. "Do you know how to get here?" I asked. "Yes, yes," she blurted out. "It's not far. I'm in a cafe just round the corner In the Rue Haute. I know the apartment." Of course she would, I thought.

"Right," I said. "Come round right away. Tell me about it then." Then a thought occurred to me. "How did you know I was here, Sylvia?"

As she rang off I heard her say, "Mummy told me you were staying at the company apartment. I hung up the receiver.

Good old Mummy, I thought.

CHAPTER 32

Ten minutes later she was standing on the darkened staircase when I opened the door of the apartment. For one brief moment I thought it might have been young Sylvia. With her flair for the dramatic it was just the sort of classic timing she would chose. But although the immediate impression; the dark hair, the shape of the face, the slim figure reminded me strongly of the girl, I knew it really was Sylvia who stood before me.

Then I saw how much smaller she was. Also her hair was darker, pulled back severely from her face and tied in a tight pony-tail. Her face under the remains of the Florida tan looked drawn and gaunt and there were lines around the eyes and across her forehead that I had never seen before. She wore a tan belted Burberry over a pair of jeans tucked into expensive looking Italian leather boots. Her mouth, thin and tense, opened in a desperate smile. "Terry," she whispered. She seemed to have trouble catching her breath. "Oh Terry!" She threw herself into my arms.

I held her for a moment and then pushed the door shut. "Come in," I said and led her into the sitting-room. She clung to me as if she was afraid I would vanish. Her body, always slender, felt thin and angular against me. She had lost a lot of weight. God knows how she had been living since she had vanished that night. We stood together for a while silently, her face buried against my chest. Then I eased her gently away from me. There was a strong smell of wine, or something stronger, on her breath.

I held her there, my hands on her shoulders. They felt painfully thin under my hands. She looked up at me, her dark eyes glittering. "You'll help me, Terry?" she gasped.

I smiled. "Of course." I released her and turned away. "I think we need a drink. Sylvia, I'm amazed to see you," I said.

She nodded eagerly and ran her tongue over her lips. "Yes, a drink would be good."

I went into the kitchen. There was decent malt in one of the cabinets and I poured out two good-sized shots. I took them back into the sitting-room, along with the bottle. Sylvia fumbled in her handbag and pulled out a pack of cigarettes. "Do you mind?" she said automatically, throwing back her head and drawing in the smoke. She glanced at me and smiled weakly. "Still all the same old vices."

We sat facing each other on a sofa. As I sipped my whiskey I studied her over the rim of my glass. It was the Sylvia that I had known. But there was a different kind of intensity in her face. Now I could see the lines, the dark shadows, the jaw muscles twitching, the touch of grey in the dark hair. "How did you know I would be here," I heard myself asking. I wanted to be certain.

230

Sylvia gulped down a mouthful of the neat whiskey. "Mummy told me you were staying here for the week-end." She looked at me, "I'd thought so often of contacting you. But somehow I didn't dare."

"Just a minute," I interrupted. "Tell me when you spoke to your mother."

Sylvia looked puzzled. "She told me you would be here last time I called her." She thought for a moment. "It must have been Thursday," she said. "She told me where you were all the time; in San Francisco and in Boston. I almost called you several times." She looked across at the whiskey.

"Another?" I asked. She nodded and reached for bottle. I noticed her hand shook slightly as the amber liquid splashed into her glass. When she stopped pouring the glass was almost half full. She swallowed a mouthful and lit another cigarette. I wondered if I had understood her. How much had she had to drink to night? "You mean that Helen knows you are alive and well? That she has known for some time?"

She nodded. "Oh yes," she said. Mummy knew why I had to get away. I--- I told her how I felt about everything." She laughed bitterly and took a gulp from her glass. "Not that she seemed to care about me."

"Sylvia, are you telling me you've been in touch with Helen since you left Pelican Cove?"

She gazed at me, her eyes dark and impenetrable. "Oh yes! She kept telling me exactly where you were all the time. Almost as if she expected me to come to you for help." She gave a little laugh again, "I think she hoped I would. Just so you could persuade me to go home to Mummy like a good girl. Do as Mummy says," she said bitterly. She was clutching her glass in both hands now, trembling as she drank. Then she glared at me. "But I wouldn't! I wouldn't!" It didn't seem the time to point out that she had.

She slumped forward. "But now young Tom is dead. And I know it's because of me." She looked at me. "It was Carlos, wasn't it?" She seized my hand. "Please help me, Terry. I've no-one else now."

If Sylvia was telling the true it meant that Mrs van Eck had deliberately mislead me from the start. But why? I smiled encouragingly at Sylvia. "Tell me about it," I said. It's a kind of meaningless phrase, but it's all most people need to spill out their problems.

Sylvia took a deep breath. "I don't know what came first," she said. Then she went on angrily, "Yes, I do. It was when I discovered what a crook Carlos is. When Linda Polk told me about him and I found out about some of the things he was doing."

"With Ethnic Art?" I asked.

She nodded miserably. "Yes. I put so much of myself into that business, Terry." She leaned forward and hid her face in her hands. "It seemed a chance to get something right at last. A chance to make Mummy see that I was alright again. That she could trust me." She looked up at me mutely. "You know what a mess I had made of everything else. Then I realised that there was a lot of money coming and going. Money that I didn't know anything about. At first I believed him when he said they were only routine transactions. But when Linda told me about him--- ." She went on. "And there were other things. When I discovered what he had done to Sylvia--- ." She couldn't finish the sentence, but simply shook her head in despair and took another mouthful of whisky. She held the empty glass out to me, in silence.

I splashed a little in the bottom of her glass. She threw it back in one gulp and then tossed her head, shaking her hair. For a moment she looked like the young girl I had once known. The mannerism reminded me of young Sylvia in the garden at Pelican Cove. "So I took his diary," she said defiantly " The one where he kept details of his meetings. All the deals and arrangements with Marcus Cuneo and the others." She looked at me, contempt for him in her eyes. "He must have been really stupid to do such a thing. God knows how I ever married him!"

I shrugged, "Perhaps he's not so stupid. Perhaps it was insurance, just in case he ever has to face the law. If he could incriminate some of the bigger boys in the set up, I expect he would be able to negotiate his way out of quite a lot. But it would certainly be dangerous if Pantuliano and the others ever found out he had that kind of record."

Sylvia nodded. "That's why I took it. I thought, oh I don't really know what I thought! I just wanted to protect myself. And to hurt him too. Hurt and scare him." She stared at me defiantly for a moment. Then she shook her head. "I must have been mad. I don't know why I did it." She began to tremble again, the empty glass rattling against her teeth. Tears filled her eyes. "And I've caused so much trouble. Poor Tom. I must have been mad." She kept repeating it. "I just wanted to hurt everyone--- to frighten everyone."

I took the glass from her and gently laid her back on the sofa. I lifted up her feet. "Rest here for a while, Sylvia. You're safe with me."

She murmured something I didn't hear properly and then she fell into a restless sleep. I realised I hadn't asked her about the Princess Head. I sat in silence for a few minutes, watching her. Then I got a blanket from one of the bedrooms and covered her with it.

I suppose I sat there with Sylvia sleeping beside me for about half an hour. I was just about to go and explore the kitchen, when I heard a noise, faint but unmistakeable. It was the sound of a key turning in the lock. I shot across to the door as it opened. It was deja vue--- or my worst fears realised. Young Sylvia stood in the doorway, tall and slim and beautiful. Like her mother she was dressed casually and stylishly in jeans and a short jacket but her hair flowing loosely on her shoulders.

She smiled her little girl smile at me. "Surprise!" she said. "Didn't I say I would come?"

I stepped forward and put my hand on her lips. For once I had thought of a suitable reply. "Hush," I said to her quietly but firmly. "I have a surprise for you. I'm not alone."

Her eyes widened and she looked beyond me into the darkened sitting-room. "My God," she said, half excited and half annoyed. "Don't tell me you have a woman with you. How embarrassing!" She started to push past me.

"Sylvia, your mother is here."

The girl wheeled round to face me. "My mother? You mean

234

Sylvia? Here?"

I nodded grimly. Sylvia stared at me in astonishment. "But why would she come here?"

"You can ask her yourself in a moment. But she seems to need help--- a lot of help. She turned up here out of the blue and she's not in good shape." I paused, "She seems to have been running away from Carlos for weeks. And she's been drinking. Sylvia, will you help me with her?"

The girl stopped and looked at me. I could see the doubts in her dark eyes. "But why did she run away? I don't understand. And she never drinks. You must be wrong."

I shrugged. "Your mother has been having a bad time with Carlos. She has lot of troubles. some of them to do with you." She flushed and looked away. "But mostly things to do with the business." I put my hand on her shoulder and led her towards the sofa where her mother lay asleep. "This would be a good time to start to mend some fences. She needs help."

As we approached, Sylvia stirred and half sat up, leaning on one arm. She pushed her hair away from her face and stared at the girl standing before her. "Sylvia," she whispered hoarsely. "Oh Sylvia. It's so good to see you. I've been so lonely."

The young girl stood looking down at her for a long moment. She seemed to be seeing her mother as she had never seen her before. She sat down on the sofa beside her and took her mother's hand in hers. Sylvia lay back on the cushions, clutching the girl's hand. "I've missed you so much," she said softly. From her closed eyes tears welled slowly out and ran down her face.

The girl stared at me in bewilderment, and then back at the thin, strained face of her mother. I decided a strategic withdrawal was appropriate and headed for the kitchen to make coffee. As I looked back I saw that young Sylvia had found a handkerchief from somewhere and was gently wiping away the tears on her mother's face. At one point in the coffee-making process I glanced in to see them. They were holding each other in their arms and I think they were both crying now. I rattled some cups and saucers around and tried not to get emotional. Get a grip, Lennox, I thought. This place is beginning to look like the last act of La Boheme.

I don't know how much Sylvia told the girl but when I took the coffee through, they seemed sombre but somehow more relaxed. "Sylvia," I said, "I can move out if you want to stay here with your mother tonight. Or you can use the other bedroom and I'll sleep here on the sofa."

The girl shook her head. "No. I have to get back to Vinkiveen tonight." She gazed at me frankly. "You know, I did come here to apologise to you for my behaviour. I don't suppose you can ever forgive me for such an appalling display." She shook her head sadly. "I must have been out of my mind." She looked down at her mother. "I think I have been for years in some ways."

She stood up and picked up her jacket. Sylvia lay back weakly, "Can't you stay a little longer. It's been so good to talk to you properly. And there is so much more I want to say."

The girl bent down and kissed her on the forehead. "I'll see you soon, mother." It was the first time I had heard her use the term. "But I have some things I need to get straight."

Sylvia gasped, "Promise me you won't tell anyone I'm here. I---
I can't go back to face things now. I couldn't face Helen!"

"It's all right. I understand," the girl said. Then she smiled at
me. "Take care of her, won't you. I don't want to lose her now."
For the first time since I saw her in the garden I felt that I was
dealing with a real woman.

I saw her to the door. She looked up at me and said "I've
learned something tonight." She gave a tight little smile, "First
it was about Helen. And then about Sylvia--- and about you
too." She stood for a moment and then reached up to kiss my
cheek. "About myself most of all." Then she disappeared into
the darkness.

CHAPTER 33

After the girl left Sylvia dozed off again. Then she awoke, slowly and painfully. She sat up and held her head. She moistened her lips with her tongue and made a half-hearted attempt to straighten her hair. "God, my head. What a mess," she said, with a groan. But then she smiled at me. "Did I dream it or was my girl really here?"

I told her she had not been dreaming and asked her if she felt well enough to go out to eat. My lunch with Dolf and John Grossman seemed a long time ago. Once she had tidied herself, we left the apartment and went to eat at a little restaurant near the Gallery St Hubert called the Sans Nom, , where they served steaks barbecued over a grill built into the old whitewashed stone walls. We drank a bottle of the house wine--- the only wine on offer and very good. At first I had wondered if I should let her have more to drink, but she was so elated by her meeting with young Sylvia that it seemed churlish to object.

"Tell me more about the diary," I said. "Where is it now?

Sylvia looked surprised. "I left it with Linda Polk. "I thought she could use it to get some of her money out of Carlos." She curled her lip. "I suppose I only wanted to cause him trouble," she muttered sadly. "And to tell the truth, by that time I wanted to get rid of it. I was pretty terrified. There were two men who seemed to be everywhere I went. They followed me to San Francisco." She glanced at me. "I suppose Carlos knew that I would go to Linda's."

"So you were in San Francisco? Were you ever at Linda's house?"

She nodded, "For a while. But only briefly. Then Linda found me a flat in the city. It wasn't much but I thought I could disappear there." She shuddered and poured herself another glass of wine. "But those men found me. I don't know how. Maybe they saw me with Linda and followed me. I'm not sure. They tried to make me give them the diary. They threatened me. Knocked me about." She pulled up the sleeve of her shirt. "Then they burned me with a cigarette." I saw a series of ugly red scars on the inside of her arm, still only half healed.

"I told them I had destroyed it. I think they believed me at first, because they left me alone for a while. I moved apartments. Then Carlos sent them back to look for me again and failing that to find Linda Polk. So I just ran. I got a car and took off. I kept thinking they were following me. So I kept on running." She shivered. "They were scary. Especially the one with the weird hair. I must have driven for days---, stopping at motels." She looked at me in anguish. "I was afraid to go into hotels or restaurants even. I bought food in supermarkets and ate in my room when I could. Not that I felt much like eating." She picked up her glass of wine and studied it. Then she looked across at me. "I suppose I started to drink too much. The way I used to. Remember?

I said nothing but nodded silently.

"Yes, of course you remember," Sylvia said sadly. "That was the real problem with us, wasn't it?" She reached across and grasped my hand, her eyes dark in the pale face. "I hadn't been drinking, Terry, I promise you. I had stopped. But I was so scared and lonely. The only person I could contact was Mummy. And she,." Sylvia stopped and shook another cigarette from the packet on the table. "She simply wanted me to go home to her. But I couldn't."

She stared at me intently. "I had my own reasons for not wanting to do that. Then after a while she tried to persuade me to contact you." She smiled thinly, playing with the cigarette. "That was a more attractive idea. But I didn't know what you might do if you knew where I was."

"Do?" I said, puzzled. "What do you mean?"

"I had to stay away from her." She shook her head defiantly. "For good reasons, Terry. Not just to prove a point, believe me. Though I suppose that was part of it."

"And Linda had the diary by this time?"

"Yes," she said. "I gave it to her. Of course she may have destroyed it--- or hidden it somewhere."

"But Linda told me---,"I started to say. Then I stopped.

Sylvia looked exhausted and I realised she was beginning to slur her words. It was all rather familiar. Fumbling to light the cigarette, she dropped her cheap disposable lighter on the floor. I picked it up and held it carefully to her cigarette. She slumped back and sucked in a mouthful of smoke. She looked more and more befuddled. I wanted to know about the Princess Head but I decided the questions could wait. There was a lot I didn't understand. But it had been quite an evening.

We left the restaurant and I guided her back up the hill towards the apartment. She half stumbled on the old cobbles and clung to my arm. "Oh," she muttered, "I'm so tired. I'm so very tired, Terry."

As we stepped out of the elevator I noticed that the stairs were illuminated. A man walked down the steps from the landing above us and I looked up at him sharply. Sylvia was still leaning heavily on my arm. I suppose somewhere in my mind I was thinking about the men who had harassed Sylvia and Linda Polk and killed Tom Ambrose. But he was nothing like them. Medium height, with a square ruddy face and a shock of fair hair and he was wearing a very European-looking raincoat.

I relaxed and fumbled for the key to the apartment door, holding Sylvia awkwardly propped up against the door frame. She was almost out on her feet, whether from the effects of alcohol or from sheer physical and emotional exhaustion I couldn't tell. The man in the raincoat walked past us, looking curiously at Sylvia. Hardly surprising but nevertheless I felt an irrational surge of annoyance. The apartment door swung open. At that moment the time switch cut off the lights in the stairwell and we were plunged into darkness.

The only faint light came from a street lamp shining through the big double windows of the sitting-room. "Damn," I said, reaching into the room for a wall switch near the door. At the same time I struggled to support Sylvia.

Then everything seemed to happen in a rush. There was a sharp blow on the back of my neck that stunned me for a moment. I fell into the open doorway and sprawled on the floor with Sylvia half on top of me. In the darkness and still dazed from the effect of the blow I had only a vague impression of what happened. I rolled over and caught a glimpse of the man in the raincoat. Behind him was another man, bigger and bulkier in the darkness. In that confused instant he looked vaguely familiar. Sylvia was still there on the floor, half unconscious.

Before I could react, I was grabbed and my arms forced up behind my back as I was pushed face down on the carpeted floor. I started to shout for help but a strip of cloth was thrust expertly into my mouth and knotted tightly. I heard the men exchange a few words in a language that sounded like Dutch or Flemish. Then there was a slight pin prick of pain in my wrist.

For a moment I wondered what it was. Then I guessed and I started to struggle. The two men held me down on the floor. Within a few seconds I felt myself slipping into darkness. I had guessed right.

Then there was nothing but oblivion.

CHAPTER 34

A jolt shook me back to consciousness. I opened my eyes slowly, still in a drugged, hazy half-world. I had been dreaming something strange, about a beautiful African princess who had lost her head. It was pretty weird. My eyes were open but still I saw only darkness. I felt stifled and I could taste and smell the musty odour of rough sacking. I realised that it was covering my head and that the gag was still between my teeth. Then in the darkness I felt myself being lifted bodily and carried between two men. At one stage my feet were dropped onto soft ground. But my body was held firmly and I could barely move.

I thought I heard a sound like the screech of rusty metal. Then I was half carried, half dragged across rough ground. I tried counting the steps the men took but it was difficult to concentrate. From time to time they stopped and I heard a few whispered words. I cursed myself for not knowing any of the language they were speaking. They seemed to carry me a long way. Counting slowly, I reached five hundred before I was dropped heavily to the ground and I realised that I was sitting half propped up, with my back against a rough stone wall of some kind. Nothing had been said to me throughout the entire process. I wondered about Sylvia. Then something faintly comical occurred to me. Was it now me who was missing? But then who would miss me? Who would care? The footsteps faded quickly away leaving total silence around me.

Slowly I started to check out the situation. My ankles were tightly bound, as were my wrists. But at least they were not tied behind me. I took a deep breath and strained against the cords that bound them together. The pain made me stop. They were meant to keep me in place, that was clear. I gave up as the cord cut deep into my skin.

Then I bent forward and began to tug at the sacking that covered my face and head. The men had tied it loosely around my neck but gradually I was able to ease it off. I spat stray fibres from my face. Now at least I could breathe. But where the hell was I? All around me was still total darkness.

But it was not the total suffocating blackness into which I had been plunged. Slowly my eyes began to adjust to what traces of light there were. I seemed to see, or perhaps sense, that I was in some kind of huge natural space, with rough walls like the one behind my shoulders. The place felt very cold and damp. The silence was complete. I tried to spit out the cloth gag but it was too tightly tied. I gave up the effort and started to think.

I turned my attention to the cords round my ankles. It was difficult in the darkness to get any idea of how they were tied. I tried to trace them with my fingers, blindly. These guys seemed know what they were doing. I hoped they had used conventional knots. I convinced myself that if there was a logic to the way the knots were tied, I should be able to unravel them

244

given time, which I suspected I had plenty of..

I twisted my wrists around and found the knots behind my feet. Slowly and painfully, dredging up memories of rope work from my rock-climbing days but my fingers numb and clumsy, I worked on the knots. After an age they gave a little and I felt the bindings slacken. Eventually, my hands and arms aching, I managed to free my feet. At least now I could move around. But to where?

I looked around. It seemed as if I was seeing more as my eyes adjusted to the darkness. I realised that I had been left in a small recess opening into a large open area. There were vague patches, not of light, but of what seemed to be less dense darkness. I felt my way cautiously across a rough stone floor, overcoming an irrational reluctance to leave the false security of the solid wall behind me. Looking up, I saw a faint glimmer of star-light, far above. Somewhere up there was an opening of some kind, presumably to the outside world.

Suddenly I tripped over something solid and crashed heavily to the ground with a curse, unable to break my fall. I lay for a moment, winded, while I collected my wits. Then, awkwardly I scrambled up. I felt around in the darkness with my feet and encountered something hard and bulky. I kneeled down and ran my hands over what seemed to be a pile of wooden crates, long and heavy.

Groping slowly along the edge of the boxes my numbed fingers encountered something cold and metallic. I felt a quick surge of hope and I moved my hands carefully around the metal. It seemed to be some kind of plate, possibly a hinge. At one corner there was the sharp head of a screw jutting above the smooth metal. I began to work the cords around my wrists against the sharp edge of the screw, praying that it was secure enough to take the strain. After about an hour of work the ropes frayed and parted under the pressure.

With a gasp I untied the gag and started to rub some feeling back into my hands and arms. Now at least I was mobile. I had a chance. I peered around in the darkness and started to explore the place. But I still had no idea where I was or which way to go and the light was still too poor for me to make sense of my surroundings.

I looked up again at the patch of night sky, above me. There would doubtless be more light as dawn approached. I decided things weren't so bad after all. Then I remembered Sylvia's plastic disposable cigarette lighter. I fumbled into my shirt pocket and found it, remembering thankfully how I had picked it up in the Sans Nom. Please God, I thought, let it have plenty of fuel.

Miraculously, it lit at the first attempt. I held the flame high and looked quickly around. As I had guessed, I appeared to be in a kind of large natural cavern with high rough lime stone walls that soared thirty feet or more above the floor. I studied the lay-out of the cave, trying to the shape of the place in my mind. There seemed to be several low passages which lead off in different directions. Some of them seemed to be natural but others looked as if they had been artificially widened and heightened. But in the flickering light there was no way of telling which tunnel had been used to bring me here.

Then at my feet I saw a number of wooden crates, some of which had roughly stencilled lettering on their sides. I held the flame closer. The signs on the boxes were in French and I realised that they belonged to a co-operative of mushroom

246

growers. The address on them was in Namur. I extinguished the lighter to save fuel and sat quietly in the cold darkness to think things through.

If I was guessing right, I knew now approximately where I was. The caves were part of a vast complex of limestone caverns south-east of Brussels, running right down to the River Meuse. Some of the more spectacular ones had been turned into tourist attractions but many, like this one, were used by the locals to grow mushrooms commercially. Apparently the mushrooms love darkness and a steady cool temperature. For me it was beginning to pall. I flicked on the lighter and checked my wrist watch. It was past midnight. Soon it would be Sunday morning. I wondered if anyone worked in these caves on a Sunday. I decided that was unlikely.

I stared upwards. The opening in the roof of the main cave was too high for me to reach, even if I could remember my old climbing skills. But what if there were other air shafts that were more accessible? I started to explore the side passages one by one, using Sylvia's lighter intermittently. Eventually one tunnel led me into a smaller side cave, hardly larger than a good sized room. The walls were soft and crumbling and they inclined steeply at the inner end, narrowing rapidly to form a kind of natural rock chimney.

Above, again I realised with a thrill I could see stars. This chimney also led to the outside world. I studied the walls carefully in the flickering light. If somehow I could get a start, I might be able to climb out using the sides of the rapidly narrowing funnel to brace myself. Quickly I made my way back to the main cavern and dragged half-a-dozen of the boxes into the side cave. The soft limestone walls of the natural chimney were worn and broken. A mixed blessing, I thought, looking over them carefully. Here and there were possible handholds that might have been carved out by ancient water flows.

From one of the crates I kicked off a short length of wood which came away with part of the metal hinge attached. Then I climbed up on to the pile of boxes. From there I could just reach the start of the chimney. I stretched out a hand but the walls were still too far apart to give me any leverage.

Balancing precariously on top of the pile of boxes I cut a foothold in the wall and then another higher up. I stopped for breath. Then, reaching up I grasped the rock with my finger tips, my feet anchored in the lower hole. I steadied myself for a second. Then, praying that I had judged the distances correctly in the darkness, I pawed out behind me with one hand.

With relief I touched the wall, reassuringly solid. Now I knew I would have some purchase as the chimney narrowed. I hung there, collecting energy and nerve for what lay ahead. Craning my head back, I see a dark patch of sky above. Perhaps twenty feet, I thought. Well, I had made that kind of climb before and more. But not recently, I grunted to myself. And not shot full of drugs.

The most difficult part came near the top. A moment of blind panic hit me as the shaft seemed to be narrowing too rapidly to let me through. By now I was drenched with sweat, exhausted, and half blinded by the falling dirt and sand that scattered down into my face at every move. What scared me was the thought of having to find my way down again if the chimney didn't go.

I squeezed myself further on, scraping my flesh on the rough walls. Then I glanced upwards. My heart sank. It couldn't be. But it was. A heavy metal grill shut off the top of the shaft. I clung there, twenty feet above the cave floor and only a few feet from the opening. I could feel the cool night air on my face. I rested for a few minutes, summoning up my strength. I anchored myself firmly, reached up with one hand and pushed as hard as I could. Nothing happened. The grill seemed to be set as solid as the rock.

I wriggled a little closer, holding myself in space by the pressure of shoulders and feet against the walls. Praying that I wouldn't slip, I grabbed the metal grill with both hands this time and took a deep breath. Imagine it's a simple 200lb bench press, I muttered to myself. I thrust upwards, steadily increasing the pressure. One of my feet slipped a fraction but I was able to catch myself in time. I re-set myself and pressed upwards again.

There was a sudden cracking noise and a flurry of dirt and debris slid down on me. The grill lifted free at one side. Now I knew I was almost free. I lowered the grill again and shifted myself into a better position. The chimney was so narrow now that there was barely room to move. This time I lifted the metal grill clear and pushed it sideways far enough to create a space.

In a moment I had levered myself up and out and lay gasping on my back in the middle of a grassy field. Above me the stars were fading and light seemed to be seeping into a sky broken by fast moving clouds. The clouds looked wonderful.

When I had recovered I looked at my watch. It was just on 4.00am. Not too bad for an old man, I thought. My physiotherapist would be proud of me. I checked the direction of the dawn and started to walk away from it. If my guess about the caves was right, I would be heading in the general direction of Brussels. Now that the flow of adrenalin had slowed down I suddenly felt weak, sick and light headed. I breathed deeply in the cool night air. Whatever they had shot into me was having an after-effect. Or maybe it was lack of sleep and the exhaustion of the climb. But a growing feeling of anger drove me on. At least now I knew where I was, more or less. And I was determined that pretty soon I would know what the hell was going on.

I counted on finding a road of some kind. After all, Belgium is a small country, thick with farms, small towns and villages and lots of people. If I was right about my general location the outskirts of Brussels would be no more than twenty or thirty miles away, depending on how long I had been unconscious in the car. Soon I'd find a road. And even on a Sunday morning, where there was a road I'd find traffic.

As I stumbled across the countryside I reached into my hip pocket. My wallet was still there. That ruled out robbery as a motive for the attack. So what was it about? As I walked through the silent early morning I began to work it out. I had an idea who the big man at the apartment had been--- and if I was right, I knew where I would find Sylvia.

For of course it was Sylvia they had wanted. But to get her, they needed me out of the way, at least for a while. Presumably they knew someone would find me in the caves on Monday morning, when the workers arrived. So they didn't mean me serious harm. That was vaguely comforting. But whoever sent the men knew that Sylvia was with me at the apartment. Who knew that? Had the girl told Helen van Eck?

Because now I knew who had been misleading me from the

start.

Well, practically everyone, I thought ruefully. But most of all Mrs van Eck. She had used me as a kind of lure to attract Sylvia within her reach. It was all beginning to make sense now; up to a point, at least.

Now I had a sudden desire to see my client again. I owed her a final report, whether she wanted it or not. And she owed me an explanation or maybe two.

CHAPTER 35

I was back in the apartment by eight o'clock. I had guessed right and found a narrow farm track and then a minor road. At six o'clock in the morning, tired and dirty, I waved down a surprised farmer in a small van. He turned out to be taking a load of cut flowers into the Sunday market in the Grand Place and he refused to take money for the journey. "Mais non, monsieur," he said with a shake of his head, "J'espere que vous pensez du bien des Belges." Somehow I was coming out of this one smelling of roses.

As I had feared there was no sign of Sylvia at the apartment and the place seemed to have been ransacked, drawers opened and beds pulled apart. Whoever the men had been they had obviously been looking for more than Sylvia. Now I was sure who had sent them and why. The girl must have told Helen van Eck about Sylvia. That bothered me. The two women had seemed so much closer the previous night. Sentimental clown, I thought. I should have known better.

I made myself coffee with lots of caffeine. Then I showered and shaved and changed into my business suit. I stood out on the balcony, sipping the coffee and looking down on the quiet

Sunday sunlight in the boulevard below while I considered my options. However unsatisfactory she might be I still had a client, at least for the next few hours. I decided to play it by ear to see how she reacted. Then I could make up my mind what to do about Grossman's offer. I sighed. The assignment had seemed so straightforward only a week ago. Now strictly speaking it was almost finished.

Except that is for Sylvia. But that was a big exception. From the very beginning it seemed the case had been about her. And in spite of everything I still owed Mrs van Eck my best advice. Whether she took it of course was up to her. Then I could walk away with the money and a clear conscience. Run away, more likely, I thought grimly.

Forget about Carlos, Pantuliano and Marcus Cuneo. Forget about the Princess Head. Sylvia had taken it and she must know where it was and sooner or later she would have to hand it over to Helen van Eck, who did after all own it.

Or did she? If Cuneo's scheme worked, the Princess Head of course would be his, along with the rest of Ethnic Art. That was why I couldn't just forget Cuneo and his friends. Besides, could I really forget about young Tom Ambrose, and what Carlos had done to Linda Polk? To say nothing of Sylvia. I shook my head.

I felt the sting from the patches of missing skin on my back and elbows. And how could I forget being man-handled, drugged, and dumped in the cave? Maybe that hurt most of all. But even worse was the thought of being taken for a fool; being used by Helen van Eck. No, I still had a few loose ends to tidy up. And a client to see, for the last time probably.

I arrived at the house at Vinkiveen just after lunch, after driving up the motorway from Brussels. My hire car rolled over the little bridge and I parked outside the front door. I had decided not to announce my arrival. That was the only thing I had decided. I was tired and sore from my night in the caves, my head seemed full of cotton wool and I hadn't thought through exactly what to do. All I knew was that I needed to confront Mrs van Eck with what I knew and to find out how Sylvia was. It was strange how I kept coming back to Sylvia. And I suppose that I still had an idea there had to be a rational way out of this mess, if only Helen van Eck would level with me.

I rang the door bell and waited. The little stone lion sat quietly in the corner. I ignored him this time. The darkly dressed housekeeper showed no surprise and ushered me into the small library room where I had met Mrs van Eck on my last visit. After a long wait she appeared. She didn't look pleased to see me. "Terry," she said coolly, "I didn't expect to see you so soon." I'll bet, I thought. "You should have told me you were coming."

"I have my report on Ethnic Art for you, Mrs van Eck," I said, ignoring her remark. I pulled the papers out of my brief-case and laid it in front of her. "You'll find all my recommendations in there. But I suppose now that Sylvia is back, some of it will be redundant."

"Why Terry, what do you mean?"

"Mrs van Eck, I was with Sylvia last night. I know she's alive and well--- and I'm betting she's here with you now."

"As a matter of fact she is here. But how on earth did you

know?" She looked at me calmly.

With difficulty I controlled my anger. "I was attacked by two men last night at the apartment." I told her how I had spent the night pot-holing. She tried to look shocked, "My goodness, Terry, what an experience! I hope you weren't injured." Then she smiled. "But what a strange end to the story."

I looked at her enquiringly. She went on smoothly, "Sylvia was found wandering in Brussels last night, in a dazed and confused condition. Some friends identified her. You mean she had been with you? What a pity you hadn't let me know, Terry." She smiled benignly at me, the gentle mother figure again. "But at least now we have her back. I can't tell you how much of a relief that is."

"I can guess," I said. "May I see her?"

The smile faded fast. "That would be a little difficult, Terry. She's still very--- mixed up." She looked sadly at me. "I'm afraid she seems to have slipped back to some of her old habits." She paused. "It looks as if Sylvia has been drinking too much again. It was a problem at one stage." Tell me about it, I thought.

"It seems that running the business was just too much for her. She must have felt under more strain than I realised." Mrs van Eck shook her head regretfully. "I blame myself. I should have known. I was rather afraid something like this would happen." She brightened up. "But now our family doctor has seen her and given her something to make her sleep. That's what she needs now. Rest, Terry. Lots of rest."

I knew the feeling. "Still," I insisted gently, "I would like to see her before I leave. I feel so responsible."

She looked at me sharply but the irony seemed to escape her. Then she relaxed. "Why not," she smiled, "perhaps for just a few minutes. Now Terry, is there much more you want to discuss? There is so much for me to deal with here at the moment." The sad little smile again.

I told her the bad news about the Ethnic Art business. "There are serious issues to confront, Mrs van Eck."

She flicked through my report. "Yes," she said absently. "It's very worrying." She pushed my report to one side and stood up to indicate that the audience was ended. "But that is not my immediate concern."

I remained seated. "What is your immediate concern, Mrs van Eck?" I asked her quietly. "The Princess Head? Do you really think that is going to pull UCG out of the hole it's in?"

The calm facade vanished and she went white with fury, her lips tightened, her eyes wide. The serene poise was gone in an instant and suddenly I saw where young Sylvia had acquired her tantrums. "That has nothing to do with you," she spat out. "Nothing at all. You've done what I wanted you to do. As far as I'm concerned your assignment is finished. I will not have you interfering in UCG or anything else. If there are other problems I can deal with them."

I stood up now. "Yes Mrs van Eck. What you mean is that I led you to Sylvia and now you think she will lead you to the Princess Head. That's what this whole thing has been about, isn't it? To enable you to buy some high risk business from those Nigerians. Don't you realise how dangerous it is dealing with these people at the moment?"

The facade re-appeared as quickly as it had vanished. "I have no idea what you mean, Terry." The dark eyes were inscrutable. "It is true that Sylvia appears to have lost a very valuable object on her escapades. And in, well, let us call it her present emotional condition she seems quite confused about where it might be." She stared at me as if it might be my fault. "I suppose she said nothing to you?" When I didn't answer she went on. "Gross irresponsibility," she said. Then she leaned forward slightly towards me. "But Terry, perhaps if you were to speak to her she might listen to sense. She seems to trust you."

I had the distinct feeling she didn't know why. "Explain to her how vital it is for me to get the Princess Head back," she said confidentially. "You seem to have such a good grasp of our business problems," she added icily. "I'm sure you do know how important it is."

I took a deep breath. "Mrs van Eck, let me tell you what I know. I know you are under pressure to change the direction of the UCG business and to restructure the board. One contract may or may not keep you afloat for a while. But what you really need to do is talk to your institutional shareholders and make sure they are comfortable with the situation. One way or another they can make or break the group." She glared at me and her mouth opened. I cut her off, "They can help you, Mrs van Eck. Or sink you. At least talk to John Grossman about it."

Her anger exploded. "No," she spat out again. "No, no, no. This has always been a family group and now Jan isn't fit to run it, I intend to go on as before. These people didn't try to interfere when Jan was in charge. And I won't let them do so now. I know exactly what we need."

I didn't think it was the moment to tell her why the institutions hadn't intervened when UCG was being run by someone they trusted. Instead I shook my head. "Mrs van Eck, I think you are making a mistake. Possibly several." Such tact, I thought to myself. "These people don't want to take control of the business away from you. But that's how it will end if you don't cooperate with them now," I want on rapidly, "Besides, are you sure this Nigerian deal is what your husband would want to do in this situation?"

That did it. She switched off and stared at me coldly. "I said it earlier, Mr Lennox. As far as I am concerned your assignment is over. Send me your account. Now please go."

I started to gather up my papers. "I'd like to see Sylvia before I leave," I repeated.

Mrs van Eck, having made her point, seemed prepared to relax. "Of course." She gave me a fixed stare. "In spite of everything, Mr Lennox, if by any chance you should find out anything from Sylvia about the Princess Head, I will agree to pay you a bonus." She turned to leave the room. "Otherwise consider our relationship at an end." She paused in the doorway, "I'll ask Marie to show you Sylvia's room. Please don't stay long."

Now I knew for sure I didn't have a client. Unless of course it was John Grossman.

CHAPTER 36

The housemaid took me up a flight of stone stairs I had not
previously seen and into what seemed to be a floor of guest
bedrooms. From the position, I judged we must be almost
directly over the sun lounge where I had seen Jan van Eck on
my previous visits. Here the floor was wall-to-wall carpeting in
a deep blue colour, with a pile rich enough to silence our
footsteps. She tapped on one of the half-a-dozen dark teak
doors and then slipped into the room, leaving me standing
outside. When she re-appeared she motioned me to enter and
stood for a moment in the doorway, looking vaguely
disapproving. Then she reluctantly withdrew, silently closing
the heavy door.

Sylvia was lying in a big double bed, half of her face
illuminated by the light that filtered in through drawn shades
covering the long window. She turned her face towards me as
the door closed. She was pale, paler than when I had last seen
her at the apartment and her eyes were clouded and lifeless,
with no trace of the feverish brilliance of the previous night.
She had clearly been heavily sedated.

I sat down awkwardly on a chair beside her bed. The blankets had been tightly tucked around her shoulders so that I wasn't able even to take her hand. After a moment she focussed and recognised me. "Terry?" she whispered. "Thank god you're all right."

I smiled at her, "I'm fine," I said gently. "But how are you?"

"Fair," she said. She sounded weary. "Just fair." Her voice was so weak that I had to lean forward to hear her.

"Sylvia, I know you're tired. But I have to ask you some questions."

"Oh, not you too," she said brokenly. Her eyes filled with tears. "Mummy keeps on at me!"

"Trust me Sylvia," I said, "I'm trying to help you." I hoped I was right. "You told me you gave the diary to Linda Polk. But what did you do with the Princess Head?"

She struggled to half raise herself from the bed. "Please, Terry, please! I don't want to talk about it. I mustn't let Mummy have it. Terry, I promised---." She collapsed back on the pillows.

"I understand," I said gently. "I know what your father thinks about what is being done with UCG. But Sylvia, maybe I can help; just maybe. I mean, help you both. But I need to know where the Princess Head is. Sylvia, please trust me."

"I knew the Nigerian contract depended on it," she whispered weakly. "I knew it had to be kept out of their hands and that Daddy disapproved of the whole thing and thought it was too

260

dangerous. But Mummy wouldn't listen. So I took it away."
She lay silently staring up at me.

"Yes," I said quietly. "But where is it now?"

"I left it with Linda when I gave her the diary. She said she
would keep it safe for me. Hide it somewhere safe. In a bank
vault or something. I told her it was valuable." She gave a faint
smile. "But not how valuable. So she promised she would take
care of it until I send for it."

Linda Polk! I thought back to her house on Chavez. But there
had been no sign of the bronze then. And certainly she had
nothing with her when I saw her get on the train to Denver. Of
course, I hadn't actually seen her get on the train when I
dropped her at the station in Oakland. Suppose it had been
waiting there for her? Or suppose she didn't actually get on the
train? Linda and the Princess Head could be anywhere by now.

The situation seemed to be more confused than ever. But
maybe there was a way forward. "OK, Sylvia. Let's forget
Linda and the Princess Head. I don't see how that can help us
now. But there is something important you can do to help;
something I know your father would want you to do." She lay
quietly looking up at me.

I drew a deep breath "If you chose to, you have the right to
vote your shares in UCG in support of some people who want
the same things as your father. I know them--- some of them at
least. I believe you can trust them. The problem is your mother
won't listen to what they say. With your support--- .

Her eyes widened and started to fill with tears. She shook her
head weakly. "No, Terry. Please don't ask me to do anything

261

like that. What I've done is bad enough. I couldn't face it--- I just couldn't cope with that. Not now. I'm---, I'm not strong enough. Mummy won't let me. And I need her so much now. I have no-one else to help me."

I watched her silently. The tears were welling in her dark eyes and it seemed cruel to press her. This was not the diamond hard Sylvia I had known; and once loved.

"I can't go back to Carlos," she whispered. "That's finished. And he knows I took the diary. He'll never stop until he has it back. He won't believe it's been destroyed, or that I don't know where it is. So I have nowhere else to go. Terry, I have to depend on Mummy. There's nowhere else I can go. You must see that, Terry. I have to stay here."

I bent forward and kissed her forehead. "Don't worry," I said with a confidence I didn't quite feel, "I can take care of Carlos. He may not be a factor for much longer." I hoped she was hearing me and believing. "Suppose I take him off your back, Sylvia. I mean permanently. Will you at least speak to the people I'm talking about--- these people who want to help UCG? A man called Dolf Erhardt?" She sank back, exhausted now. But she nodded her head almost imperceptibly.

I decided that meant 'yes' and left while I was winning. It was a small success but it was a start. All I had to do was figure out how to take Carlos out of the game.

CHAPTER 37

I tottered into my flat in Edinburgh late that night and stood looking around vaguely. Then, pulling off my jacket and tie I kicked off my shoes and flopped down on top of my bed.

When I awoke the sun was streaming into the room through the wooden shutters. I rolled over and looked at the digital clock on the radio beside the bed. It was eight o'clock on Monday morning. And I was still wearing last night's clothes. I groaned and sat up. Everything was going to hell and every muscle ached as the climb in the cave began to take effect. I stripped off and headed for the shower. A long hot soak helped to clear my head as well. No exercises this morning, I decided. My physiotherapist would understand. There, I had made a decision. Perhaps things weren't completely out of control. I decided that Mozart's Requiem Mass was the most appropriate music as I made coffee.

I was sitting looking morosely at my Capricorn coffee mug, and considering alternative careers when the telephone rang. It was John Boyd. "Good morning, good morning," he boomed.

"Terry, I have some good news for you. And some bad news. Which would you prefer first?" He went into hoots of laughter at his own old witicism. I winced and waited patiently for him to subside.

Then I said quietly, "Just the good news, John. I can supply enough bad news myself." This struck him as incredibly amusing, judging from his response.

When he quietened down he said, "The good news is that your bust has arrived from America."

"Ah," I said. I had forgotten about Sylvia's bust. "And the bad news?"

"The bad news," John solemnly said, "is that it is damaged. I hope you had it insured."

I shrugged. There were worse tragedies. "That's a shame," I said. "You could recognise it, I suppose?"

"Oh yes," he said and gave a short laugh. "Very sorry, but it has cracked round the base. You'd better pop round and have a look at it. You may want to claim or something. Come and have coffee." Before I had a chance to reply he had rung off.

I got round to John Boyd's house in mid-morning. The big airy Georgian kitchen was full of light and the aroma of fresh coffee. Some of his best china cups and saucers with the family crest were laid out on a silver tray. Just a cup of coffee in the kitchen with an old friend. John liked to surround himself with beautiful things. Things with a pedigree to match his own; Eton, Balliol and the Faculty of Advocates.

He stood there, tall and dark, distinguished looking, with long patrician features and a small neat moustache. He beamed at me and gestured towards the window. There, on the kitchen draining board stood the bust of Sylvia that Linda Polk had given me. It was a slightly sad sight now, lurching sideways on its base. "Seems to have broken away from its support," John boomed in his cultured tones. "But easy enough to repair, I should think."

I nodded and walked over to the head. I took it between my hands and moved it gently. Particles of clay fell from the lower part of the neck, where Linda Polk had fitted it into a slot in the wooden base. "Didn't want to touch it until you had seen it," John went on. "Not a bad likeness, as I seem to recall. Bit unstable though." He gave a guffaw and then quickly coughed, shooting a glance at me to see how I had taken it. "Sugar?" he asked and poured out two cups of coffee.

"Just milk," I said absently. Seeing Sylvia's likeness again, as she used to be, brought me face to face with a question I suppose I had been evading since that very first morning Mrs van Eck called me. What did I really still feel about Sylvia? Could it be that I was still in love with her, in spite of everything? It was a question I had never dared to ask myself in the years since we had split.

Carefully, I lifted the head away from the base and laid it on the draining board. That was when I realised that the figure was hollow and that the cavity was filled with some kind of loose stuffing. Gently, I eased out a length of cloth. It came away easily when I pulled. Then it seemed to catch on something.

I reached inside with my fingers and tugged. It came free, revealing itself to be a woman's silk head scarf. But it seemed

265

to be wrapped round something solid and rectangular. In a surge of excitement I realised what it was. This was really why Linda had wanted me to have the bust. I took the small parcel over to a table and unwrapped it, spreading out the scarf.

There it lay. We were looking at a simple red leather-covered notebook; the very private diary of Carlos di Giorgio!

"How exciting," said John. "I hope this isn't something valuable and illegal you're smuggling into the country." He gave one of his nervous laughs. "I might have to report it."

"Don't worry, John," I replied. "I'm only an innocent bystander." I looked across the table at him. "This is not of real value," I said. "But it could be very useful."

I grinned and started to turn over the pages of the diary. It covered the current year and seemed to be a record of meetings that Carlos had attended with Marcus Cuneo, Pantuliano and others whose names meant nothing to me. I had a feeling they might mean more to Sgt Oliver. There were several references to Ethnic Art, as well as Southern Commercial Lending and also to Bay Financial Services. Here and there the name of Caribbean Enterprises appeared. There seemed to be details of dozens of meetings scattered throughout the year, with dates and locations and the names of those present.

I whistled in amazement. Some of the entries included brief notes about decisions and even sums of money. I flicked rapidly through the diary. It was packed with detail and every page was potential dynamite. I could see why Carlos had been so desperate to recover it. But why did he keep a record like this in the first place? Well, either Sylvia was right and he was stupid. Or it was a kind of insurance policy, in case he ever needed to do a deal with the law. That seemed most likely. I sat staring at the page before me. Either way, Marcus Cuneo wouldn't approve, that much was certain. The question was, how best could I make use of it?

John had been examining the head more closely. I heard him cough politely and looked up. "This is interesting Terry," he said. "Most strange." I joined him at the kitchen sink. "The clay appears to have been moulded round some kind of metal framework. Look here." He pointed to where the clay had broken around the neck and pulled at a piece that was almost hanging off. It came away easily in a large triangular lump. Underneath was a dark brown material.

He picked up a spoon and tapped the freshly exposed area. There was a sharp metallic clang. He bent down and studied the surface carefully. Then he straightened up and stared at me, his eyes wide, his eyebrows raised. "Are you quite sure you're not smuggling something valuable? This looks like a bronze casting, with some fine detailing on it."

I stared back at him. Suddenly I knew what I had--- and what I had to do. "John," I said. "Rejoice! For the Lord has delivered the Philistines into our hands."

"Ha!" he said, carefully teasing away the clay from the bronze beneath, "I always thought you were one of the Philistines." As I watched, first in small pieces and then in entire sections, the clay fell away. It was a strange sensation to see Sylvia's image crumble before my eyes. And even stranger to see another woman's face and head emerge from the wreckage. In less than half-an -hour the Princess Head stood on a side table in John's elegant sitting-room.

The bronze was about nine inches in height and a dark chestnut colour, with a deep rich patina of age on the polished metal. It was the head of a young woman of nobility, that much seemed clear. She wore a close fitting skull cap of some open weave and a high necklet around her throat and lower neck. The eyes were large and wide spaced. She had a strong, broad nose and rich full lips and the craftsman had artfully sculpted the whole figure into soft curved lines that radiated serenity and a special kind of beauty. Her hair dropped straight beside her face, in front of delicately shaped ears. At once I knew I was looking at not a ritual object, made to strike fear and obedience into primitive people but the face of a real woman; someone once loved and remembered.

Rapidly I reassessed the situation. This changed the game completely. First I had to get the bronze into safe hands, at least temporarily. I used John's telephone to ring Jean Morrow. She took my call almost immediately and she seemed glad to hear from me again. I explained to her what I thought I had. "So that's why you were so interested at lunch," she said briskly. "Bring it in. Let's have a look at it. If it is really Benin we would love to see it." I sensed a note of scepticism in her voice. I packed it carefully back into the box that Jerry Prescott had used and then ordered a taxi to take me to the museum.

When I arrived she came down to reception to meet me. I watched with growing pleasure as her small strong figure approached me across the wide main hall. She was simply but elegantly dressed in a stylish black skirt and jacket, with a severe white high necked shirt that never the less emphasised her figure. As she drew near to me, her soft mouth curved into a wide smile that was warm and genuine. Her wide blue eyes shone. "I didn't expect to see you again," she said. "Especially after I had bored you to death with African art."

She showed me into a small meeting room and I unpacked the box. Her scepticism seemed to diminish. She placed the head in the centre of the table and examined it thoroughly, being careful not to handle it. "The surface has been slightly damaged," she remarked, looking at me accusingly.

I shrugged and tried to look innocent. It was just too complicated to explain at this stage. Perhaps, one day, I'd get a chance to tell her the whole story. I had a feeling I'd like to do that. She carried on with her examination. "Who does it belong to?" she asked me in her direct way.

I laughed, "Ah! That is the 64 dollar question." She looked enquiringly at me. "At the moment it belongs to a client of mine. But its ownership may be in dispute quite soon, especially if I can't sort out some boring business problems." I paused, "I think the present owner has in mind to donate it to a private collection in Nigeria. For what I can only describe as indirect financial advantages."

Jean looked at sharply. "Oh dear," she said. She scowled at me, her pretty face darkening.

"You don't approve?"

She hesitated. "Well, I have no problem with objects like this going back to their place of origin. In some ways it's right that they should be seen as part of their own culture."

"But?"

Her lips tightened a fraction. "It's a question of the security of the object--- whether it will be looked after properly. And I think I told you what can happen if it gets into unscrupulous hands. Some of them simply reappear in the West for sale in expensive show-rooms to the highest bidder, often a wealthy private collector. Then it will disappear from public view forever." She stared at me."And I doubt if ordinary people in the country of origin would see any benefit."

"You mean, it's a jungle out there?" I said. She stared at me again, clearly not amused. I hastily changed the subject. "So what do you think of it?" I asked her.

"Well, what you have is certainly a Benin bronze casting. Probably a Princess Head; an ancestral object from the shrine of an Oba." she said brusquely. "Stylistically it could be quite early. It is certainly heavily patinated," she glared at me again, "where it hasn't been damaged."

"What sort of date?"

"Could be 16th or even 15th century. But without a proper provenance it's hard to be certain. They were made for a long time. Right up to the end of their civilisation. And even afterwards!"

"What do you mean?"

"Well, it's not unknown for people to make modern copies of them. And they can be done remarkably well."

"You mean fakes?" I said sharply.

"Depends how they're explained," she said calmly. "It would only be a fake if it was presented as something it was not."

I told her what I knew about the head, as Paul Friden had explained it to me. Jean looked unconvinced. "It's possible," she said shortly. "There were a lot of Europeans in the coastal trade in the 19th century, when Benin was destroyed."

She seemed to come to a decision. "If you are prepared to leave it with me I could have one of my colleagues look at it for you. He makes a special study of Benin material." I remembered her telling me about the metallurgical research into trade patterns. I told her I was more than happy to do that, and I was sure my client wouldn't mind a small sample of the metal being taken from the interior of the head to test its composition. "Anything to assist academic research," I added gravely.

Leaving the Princess Head with her in the Museum meant that it was as safe as the Bank of England. Safer, probably. Jean Morrow was all formality and efficiency as she wrote me out an official receipt and sent me on my way, But as I looked back from the top of the steps leading to the big front door I saw she was watching me go. I waved an arm to her and she beamed at me. I could see that smile all the way across the width of the Museum and in my mind all the way down the street.

CHAPTER 38

I went back to my flat in the New Town and searched the place for something to eat. I sighed. There wasn't much. That is the price one pays for a peripatetic life style. However in the freezer there was a brown sliced loaf and a packet of frozen corn and at the back of the kitchen cupboard I found a tin of tuna. I defrosted the corn and mixed it with the tuna and the remains of an elderly jar of mayonnaise from the fridge. Then I toasted the bread and spread the mixture on it.

I set a place at the kitchen table and opened a bottle of Beaujolais Villages that some forgotten guest had left me. Red wine with fish? Well, things were tough. I didn't even know if I still had a client. And I had just given away a half a million pounds worth of African art.

I drank the wine and ate the sandwiches while I thought about my priorities. Two of them were professional. Which were how to save my client's assets from Cuneo and also how to persuade her to cooperate with John Grossman and his friends. I might actually be paid to achieve these.

The third one was more personal. How was I going to even the score with Carlos di Giorgio? How to make him pay for Tom Ambrose and all the rest of the trouble?

The irony was that as it turned out I didn't like Mrs van Eck any better than I liked Carlos. After all she had mislead me right from the start. She had simply made use of me to get her hands on Sylvia and the Princess Head. Then there was the small matter of sending her boys round to rough me up and dumping me in some god-forsaken cave to give her time to work on Sylvia. But in spite of everything she was still my client; as far as I was concerned the job wasn't finished yet, whatever she said. There was the old man to consider, too. And then there was Sylvia.

Yes, Sylvia. I seemed to keep coming back to her. Rapidly I put that thought out of my mind. Mrs van Eck clearly wanted nothing more from me and she wouldn't appreciate my continued interest. But that was irrelevant at this stage. I thought through each of the three priorities. There was no escaping it. Logically Sylvia was the common element. Fleetingly I wondered again what I really felt about her. But the question didn't seem helpful, so I shut the idea out again. I sipped the wine. It seemed to have developed nicely in the glass. But then most wines taste better the more you drink of them. If only people were the same.

Three priorities however, like three dry martinis, are too many. What I needed was a neat solution that would wrap up all my problems. Then from nowhere the idea came to me and I smiled. It had an elegance that appealed to me.

I went through Carlos di Giorgio's diary and carefully photocopied any pages which refered to Ethnic Art. Then for good measure I copied any interesting looking notes on his meetings involving Marcus Cuneo. I didn't recognise all the other names of individuals and organisations. But I was sure Cuneo would.

I glanced at my watch. It was early afternoon. Allowing for the time change, it was about time for Pantuliano to be arriving at his office. First I found the card in my wallet on which I had noted Sgt Oliver's telephone number in Sarasota. He'd be at work early for sure. My call went quickly through to his desk. "Oliver," I heard the gruff voice say. I told him who I was. "Oh yeah, the limey."

It didn't seem to be the time to remind him about the difference between the Scots and the English so I asked him how he was making out with Tom Ambrose's murder. "We have a good description, Mr Lennox, thanks to you. We think we know the men we're looking for now. They are from around here as it happens and it's only a matter of time before we pick them up."

"You think you will be able to find them?" I asked.

Over the line I heard Oliver laughing loudly. "Sure we'll find them! That's what we're good at! We find people! That's what we do for a living! And when we do we'll tie them in with Carlos di Giorgio."

"What about Cuneo?" I asked.

"Well," Oliver said slowly, "that's more difficult. I can try. But there is only so far I can go with a guy like Cuneo."

I thanked him and told him I thought American policemen were wonderful. But he didn't seem to catch the irony. Then I rang off.

Of course, if I had been a proper public-spirited citizen I would have sent the diary to Oliver. But I had what I hoped was a better idea. I called Pantuliano's office and was put through promptly by what sounded like the blonde receptionist. On the telephone her welcome sounded even phonier than her smile. But at least she seemed to know me.

"Terry," Pantuliano boomed across the ocean. "Great to hear from you. How's it going? What can I do to help?"

"Rich, I think this time I can do something to help you." I paused. "Or just maybe we can help each other."

"Shoot," he said, sounding more cautious.

"Tell me, Rich, do you have a secure fax line I can use to send you some papers? I mean, really secure? This is not something I would want anyone but you to see."

"Sure," he said. "I have a personal fax right here beside me." He gave me the number.

"Stand by, Rich," I said. "Don't think about leaving your desk for any reason. I'm about to send you some sensitive documents and I don't think Marcus would want anyone else to see this stuff." I gave him my telephone number. "You may want to call me back, once you've had a look." Then I began to fax him the pages I had copied from the diary."

I had given him half an hour to react and in exactly twenty minutes my telephone rang. But it wasn't Pantuliano. Instead it was Cuneo. I had hit the jackpot.

He didn't waste any time. "Lennox, I told Pantuliano you were a clever son-of a -bitch. You seem to have got hold of some interesting information. I'd like to know if you have the original documents." I told him I did. "And is it what it appears to be?" he asked, choosing his words carefully.

"Mr Cuneo, you will know how accurate the information is." I said. I drew a deep breath. "But what I have is a diary belonging to Carlos di Giorgio."

There was a moment of silence. "Mr Lennox, I'd like to have the originals--- and of course any copies that may exist. What do you want in exchange? I assume there is something you want."

I liked that. No messing around. No wonder Cuneo was doing so well. I decided straight talking was the way to deal with him. "You can have the original diary, Mr Cuneo, although I want to keep copies of some of the most interesting pages. But I promise you they will be kept in a safe place. They won't be made public unless anything unfortunate happens to me."

"And what do you want, Lennox," he snapped. "What is it I can do for you?"

"Ethnic Art," I said. "I want to know that the debt to Southern Commercial Lending will be extended to allow settlement over the next," I hesitated, wondering how far to push. "Three years."

"Hold on," he replied. I listened while he spoke to someone in the background. "Agreed. Anything else?"

I picked my words carefully. "Carlos di Giorgio has been responsible for some--- let us say, irregular--- cash transactions concerning the company. I want that to stop. And I want him to resign as a director immediately."

This time there was no hesitation. "Agreed." Then, "Send the diary to Pantuliano."

I decided to turn the screw. "You know your own business, Mr Cuneo, but it seems to me that Carlos has become a bit of a liability." There was silence at the other end of the line. "I feel you should know that his attempts to recover this diary have linked him with the death of a young man in your own backyard. And also to a couple of assaults in San Francisco."

For the first time Cuneo sounded rattled. "What are you talking about, Lennox?"

"The victim was a young man who worked for Carlos at his home. One of the assaults involved a former wife of Carlos. The other was against an employee of Ethnic Art. The men who are suspected of these crimes have been identified and are known to the police. I think they will easily be tied back to Carlos. He hired them and I imagine they will say so."

There was another long silence. I went on breezily, "I suppose he had a reason to keep a record like that. And I imagine he was anxious to make sure no-one else knew about it. And especially that it was floating around loose."

Cuneo finally broke his silence. "OK. I understand what you are telling me," he said briskly. "I think Rich once suggested to you that we might be able to use you in our organisation from time to time. Are you interested?"

"Thanks you, Mr Cuneo," I said."But I really don't like big organisations. Can I take it that Carlos will be removed from the board of the company?"

Marcus Cuneo's voice was cold and hard. "Yes, Mr Lennox. He'll be removed from the board." I had a sudden image of a pawn toppling from the table. Cuneo spoke again," You don't like Carlos, do you Lennox? Is there something personal?"

Good question, I thought. Why did it all keep coming back to Sylvia? I stayed silent and after a moment or two Cuneo spoke, his voice calm and business-like, "Do we have a deal, Lennox? Or do you have any more surprises for me?"

"We have a deal, Mr Cuneo," I said. I hoped I didn't sound as relieved as I was feeling."

"Remember, Lennox," he said. "No more surprises. I don't like surprises." The line went dead.

I rang Dolf in Brussels and told him to alert John Grossman to the fact that he might receive a call about UCG the following day. Dolf wanted to know more.

"Be patient, Dolf," I told him. "That's what you Dutch are supposed to be good at, isn't it? It's all that sitting about with your fingers in leaking dykes."

He said something in Dutch that I didn't understand.

CHAPTER 39

Next morning I was on my way back to Schiphol Airport. For some reason it had been difficult for me to get Mrs van Eck on the telephone the previous evening. The third time I called, I left a message with Marie, the housekeeper. I was beginning to feel I might be making progress with her. "Tell Mrs van Eck I may know where to find the Princess Head."

I had a feeling that would probably do the trick.

Sure enough, that brought her to the telephone. She sounded cold and suspicious. When I refused to discuss it with her and insisted on seeing her face to face she sounded even less happy. But I wanted to be certain that any deal I made would stick. Cuneo was one thing--- there is a certain honour among thieves. But Mrs van Eck was something else. At least Cuneo had never lied to me.

The big fair-haired chauffeur was waiting for me with the black Mercedes at the airport. I studied him carefully. Seeing him again in daylight I had no doubt he had been one of the two men who took me from the apartment. "Vinkiveen," I said to him, "and don't stop at any caves on the way." He didn't even smile. The Dutch don't have a terrific sense of humour.

We sped south towards the van Ecks house beside the inland sea. The little stone good luck lion was still standing guard by the front door and Marie showed me into the big sitting-room where Mrs van Eck had originally briefed me. She rose gracefully from the writing-desk where she had been sitting that first day.

"Terry." She held out her hand and gave me her practised smile. She was wearing a dress of apple green silk, wide skirted with a neat waist and a broad white belt. Her only jewellery was a single strand of pearls. As ever her hair was meticulously arranged. "I'm so glad we are not going to leave any unpleasantness between us." She smiled at me again. "I've been so worried about the way we parted. Now tell me your news." She motioned me towards one of the large armchairs and sank into a seat opposite me, discretely tucking her dress beneath her as she sat down. "What have you discovered about the Benin bronze?"

"How is Sylvia?" I asked her. A fleeting glimpse of irritation flicked across her face. "Oh much better," she said. "But still very weak. She has clearly been neglecting herself on her travels" She smiled wanly at me. "But I simply cannot get any sense out of her about what she did with the missing bronze." She leaned towards me eagerly. "Tell me what you have discovered."

Again I didn't reply immediately. I looked at her steadily, "Can I clarify something first, Mrs van Eck. Do I still work for you? When I left here on Sunday I was under the impression--- "

She brushed my words aside with an impatient flap of her hand. "Oh, do be quiet Terry," she snapped, the lovely mouth suddenly tightening. Quickly she recovered and smiled at me coyly. "You mustn't pay any heed to me when I'm upset. If you knew the pressure I've been under--- and for Sylvia to behave as she has done! It's all been such a disappointment."

Her eyes turned an even darker hue. "Her behaviour has so bad! Threatened everything I've worked for. And now young Sylvia is being almost as difficult. It seems there's no-one I can really trust. No-one!" Some of the gloss faded again. She glared at me, "Terry, you know perfectly well why I want that bronze for Christopher Okigbo," she said peevishly. "You know how much we need the Nigerian contract--- don't pretend to me! If you know anything about the Princess Head I demand that you tell me."

"Yes," I said to her quietly. "That is why I'm here."

She leaned forward and put her hand on my arm. "Tell me what you know, Terry. Don't beat about the bush. If it's a question of money I'll pay you a bonus. I'll double your fee, whatever it is." She stopped, struggling to recover her composure. "Terry, I have a right to know. I need that bronze. After all it does belong to me."

"Well now, Mrs van Eck, technically it belongs to the Ethnic Art Company. That is exactly what I've been trying to explain to you. If you read my report you'll realise that the company could soon belong to someone else. And that includes all the stock. Which means the Princess Head."

She sat back bolt upright, her lips thin and hard. "I must have it," she said intensely, almost desperately. Then she looked at

281

me. "What do you advise me to do?" Her voice was quiet and composed and I felt as if I had a client again.

"I think I know how to save Ethnic Art," I said, "and how to keep it under your control. Which would help you to recover all the stock."

"Including the Benin bronze?" she persisted.

"Including the Princess Head," I said carefully. I think it's called being economical with the truth. Or was that another small deceit?

"Tell me what you want me to do, Terry."

"I want you to agree to meet John Grossman----." There was a sharp intake of breath. But she remained silent. "Just see him and consider his proposals. That's all you have to do. Just listen to what he has to say. And remember he is speaking for people who have the interests of UCG at heart. Whatever you may feel at the moment, please take my word for that."

She considered me for a moment, her glittering eyes fixed on my face. Then slowly she nodded. "All right," she said quietly. "It doesn't seem that I have much choice. But I can agree to that. How soon will I have the bronze?"

I wrote Grossman's telephone number down on a card and pushed it towards her. "Call him now, Mrs van Eck. Call him and say you're willing to discuss his proposals." She flushed and for a moment I thought I had pushed her too far. But she fought down her desire to tell me to go to hell, picked up the card and walked across to a telephone table by the long window.

"I'll speak to him. But I expect you to deliver the Princess Head." I nodded my agreement. "And I don't promise to agree with what he has to say," she snapped out as she dialled Grossman's number.

I listened, thinking rapidly as she spoke to him. She sounded charming but guarded and I was under no illusions about how far I could trust her. Once she had her hands on the bronze there was no reason why she shouldn't tell Grossman to go to hell. And me too, I thought. Did I care?

I remembered the old man in the sun lounge, who did still care about the business he had built up over half a lifetime. I remembered Sylvia, frightened and lonely, back under her mother's thumb. She had been so close to getting it together this time. Perhaps she would recover from this latest disaster, with a bit of help. I thought about the girl and I wondered where she stood in all of this. I decided the end game did matter to me. There was one more move I had to make.

When Helen van Eck replaced the telephone receiver I stood up. She had agreed to meet Grossman in Amsterdam in two days time. Before she could say anything I told her I wanted to see Sylvia. She nodded. "In the sun-room. She likes to sit with her father." She caught hold of my arm. "Terry. I've done what you asked me. Now I must have the Princess Head."

"In a few days," I said, "when you have heard what John Grossman has to say." I smiled at her, cheerlessly. "Trust me," I said.

Her mouth tightened. "It seems I have no choice." She spat out the words. My client wasn't enjoying this part of the assignment.

I found my way down the long corridor to where Jan van Eck and his daughter sat side by side in the intense heat and light of the sun lounge. He seemed to be asleep, a rug over his legs and his head back, his thin hands clasped across his chest. Beside him was a table with an ice-bucket and a few bottles of beer. Sylvia was reading, stretched out on a lounger, a pair of huge sun-glasses obscuring half of her face and dramatically contrasting with the pallor that had wiped away the Florida suntan. Her dark hair was swept tightly back and tied in a tail at the back. She wore only a light cotton halter top and a pair of tennis shorts that revealed how painfully thin she had become. I had never seen her like this, not even when she had been hitting the bottle really hard. She had always been slim and elegant and it seemed that the Florida sun had fined her down to a lean hardness. But now her arms and legs were angular and bony. God knows what she had been doing in the weeks since she and Tom Ambrose organised her disappearance. All the colour and excitement that I remembered, that I had seen in her daughter that night at the motel, seemed to have been leached out of her.

She glanced up as I came in. When she recognised who I was she removed the sun-glasses and smiled. The eyes were still Sylvia. But the fire had gone and there were dark shadows beneath them. "Terry," she said. She sounded surprised but she held out her hand towards me.

I went across and kissed her lightly on the cheek. In spite of everything she did seem better than when I had last seen her. I sat beside her, keeping hold of her hand. "Sylvia," I said quietly, "I need to talk to you. Do you remember me speaking to you about your voting rights in UCG? About supporting the proposals to change the board?"

I felt her stiffen. "I couldn't do anything like that, Terry," she said pleadingly. "Please don't ask me. I--- I couldn't face upsetting Mummy again. I wouldn't be able to cope with it. Not now."

I nodded understandingly. "I want you to know that everything is going to be all right as far as Ethnic Art is concerned," I said gently. "You have nothing to reproach yourself about. And don't worry about Carlos; not ever again. I'm sure that Carlos has been---" I hesitated, "well, eliminated as far as you are concerned. The diary is no longer an issue now. You will have no more trouble from Carlos, believe me."

"How---," she started to ask.

I held up my hand to silence her. "Don't ask," I said with a smile. "Just trust me." It was a phrase I was using a lot. This time, though, it was better received.

"Terry, if only I could believe that," she whispered, clutching my hand. "It might change everything. Little Sylvia and I could start again." Tears started to well in her eyes again. She stared at me helplessly, "It's such a mess, Terry. I've made such a mess of everything. Do you really think I could? Can I really do it?"

I was aware that Jan van Eck had stirred beside me. When I turned to him his eyes were fixed on his daughter and his lips were moving slowly. "You must do it," his hoarse old voice said. "Your mother---" he struggled to find the strength. "Your mother needs help. She's wrong on this." He gave his head a barely perceptible shake. "Just trust Terry." He lay back exhausted.

I took a beer from the ice-bucket and held it up enquiringly. Sylvia nodded and I poured out a glass of the cold beer. I raised the glass to the old man in a silent toast and watched as a small smile of satisfaction touched his lips. I savoured the bite of the cold beer. Then I raised my eyebrows at Sylvia. "Well?" I asked.

She chewed her lip for a long moment. Then she looked at me. "All right, I'll do it." Her voice was stronger. She put her sunglasses back on and gave me a tentative smile. "I'll speak to these people. If you and Daddy think it's right it must be OK." She shrugged her shoulders weakly.

"No," I said firmly. "You have to think it's right, Sylvia. But I think you will, when you hear his story." I swallowed the rest of the beer and stood up to leave. Looking down at Sylvia I wondered if I was expecting too much from her. Carlos and the past few months had taken their toll and the glue that held her together hadn't been very strong in the first place. Thanks to your loving mother, I thought.

But if she handled this, if she stood up to her mother for once, Sylvia might become her own woman. She'd need time of course and help. Could I do anything for her? Or was it too late for that? I leaned forward and she raised her face to me. I kissed her on the mouth this time. But the old electricity was missing.

I was leaving the house, probably for the last time, when I heard my name being called. I turned to see young Sylvia coming towards me; tall and dark and beautiful. As usual she looked like a million dollars, in nothing more expensive than shorts and a cotton sweatshirt. "Terry, I need to speak to you. I never did apologise to you properly, did I?"

"Apologise?" I said angrily. "Isn't it your mother you should be apologising to? Why the hell did you tell Helen where she was that night?" The girl stopped in her tracks, confusion in her eyes. Her eyes widened. She looked for a second like a puppy smacked on the nose by a rolled up newspaper.

"But Terry, I didn't tell her anything! Believe me! I promised you and I didn't tell her anything."

I thought quickly. She might just be telling the truth. Helen van Eck could easily have had the apartment watched, knowing I was there. The girl started to turn away, dejected. I caught her arm and she turned back to me, stepping into my arms and pressing her face into my chest.

"Terry," she whispered, "I have to get away from here. I think Helen is going mad. And she's treating my mother so strangely. And--- and---." She stopped and looked up at me. "That awful man Okigbo has asked me to go with him to Paris." She pulled back angrily. "As if I could! But when I told Helen she acted as if she wanted me to accept! She actually seems to want me to go with him. I can't believe it. What is she thinking about?"

There is a crude word for it, I thought. But I decided against saying it. Instead I held her in my arms for a moment. It felt good and I knew I could easily have got accustomed to the feeling. Instead, I stepped away from her. She gazed at me. "Terry," she said simply, "Can I come to see you? I want to do that."

I decided it was time to be sensible. I shook my head. "No,

Sylvia. It just isn't possible. There are too many difficulties. You should forget me. I certainly intend to forget you." I hoped she believed me.

The hurt look appeared in her eyes again. "It's Sylvia, isn't it? You're still in love with her, aren't you?" Suddenly I felt like one of those characters in a comic strip, when a bulb lights up over his head. It was the question I had been evading for weeks or maybe even for years.

Now I knew the answer. I smiled at her. "No," I heard myself saying. "No, I'm not in love with Sylvia." I kissed her lightly. "But she loves you and she needs you now."

I watched her walk slowly away into the house. Then I reached down and patted the little stone lion for the last time. "Good luck," I said. I slid into the back seat of Mrs van Eck's black Mercedes. They'll certainly need it, I thought.

CHAPTER 40

I woke late next morning, back in my own flat. I showered and shaved and went through the exercises my physiotherapist had. recommended for my bad back. The ache in my muscles from the climb out of the cave had almost disappeared. But I knew I was approaching another of my periodic lows so I decided it was coffee time. I headed for the kitchen, still in my bathrobe.

What I really needed was a trip to the gym and a solid work-out. Maybe later in the week I thought, as I watched the kettle slowly come to the boil. I poured the hot water over the coffee grains and wandered off to find some suitable music. I knew I should give Dolf a call and tell him that Sylvia was willing to back his clients if her votes were still needed after her mother had heard what Grossman proposed.

Instead, I was looking aimlessly about for some music. And none of the orchestral pieces seemed right. I needed something to lift my jaded mood: something to jolt me out of the depression that was setting in now that everything seemed to be falling into place. "Ah yes! Cosi fan tutti! The very thing!"

'They all do it' or is it, 'Everyone is the same.' I never did know the correct translation. But the charmingly cynical story of the opera appealed to me; all about a series of small deceits.

Mozart's overture, with its buzz of barely suppressed excitement had just started when my telephone rang. It was Jean Morrow. I told her how pleased I was to hear her voice. And I meant it. The day began to seem brighter.

"Well," she said, "you had better wait till you hear what I have to say." I waited. "I'm sorry to have to tell you that the Benin bronze you left with me is not exactly what it seemed to be." She was obviously struggling to find the correct words.

"Meaning what exactly?" I asked, curiously.

"Meaning that when my colleague ran his metallurgical tests," she hesitated, "he found that the chemical analysis isn't consistent with the head being as early as it seemed to be stylistically." She paused. "That's about it."

"Listen," I said. "I haven't had my coffee yet. And I'm a slow starter anyway. What exactly does that mean?"

"It means the craftsman used a 19th century alloy. It is mostly copper and tin, but with some other metals added."

"A 19th century alloy," I repeated. "You mean it's a fake?"

Jean hesitated. "Well, that depends what you mean by a fake. What we have is a very good 19th century copy of an earlier Princess Head. Whether it's a fake or not depends on how it is presented to a prospective buyer."

I started to laugh. "That's wonderful!"

She sounded amused too, but she was laughing at my reaction. "I'm glad you are taking it so well," she said. "I was nervous about telling you. But you do realise that its value will be much lower than we thought?"

"Of course it will," I said and I went off into another peal of laughter. "Tell you what, I'll explain it all later." Then I made arrangements to collect the head from the museum.

I still had to keep my bargain with Helen van Eck. But I was loving the idea of how Okigbo and his relatives would feel when after a decent interval they tried to put the Princess Head back on the international art market.

"By the way," I said. "I would very much like to see you again. Socially, I mean. You don't happen to be free for dinner tonight?"

"I thought," Jean Morrow said solemnly, "you'd never ask."

EPILOGUE

After that things went very well. I sent the Princess Head to Mrs van Eck. She must have made enough concessions to satisfy John Grossman and his friends because he sent me a big cheque.

Later I heard from Sylvia. It seemed that Grossman hadn't needed to call in her votes after all. Just the threat of losing control had been enough to make Mrs van Eck back off and agree terms with him. As for Sylvia, it sounded as if just knowing that she could actually act independently was restoring some of her confidence. Also, it seemed that she and young Sylvia were getting along fine. I just hope the kid never tells her about Florida.

Mrs van Eck also sent me a cheque; for the exact amount of my invoice. She seemed to have forgotten about the bonus she offered me for the bronze Princess Head. Along with the cheque was a newspaper cutting showing her presenting the bronze to the Christopher Okigbo Trust, which the paper described as a private trust dedicated to the furtherance of Nigerian national culture. A smiling Okigbo was pictured shaking hands with her. I deduced from this that UCG got the contract. I only hope they were paid for it. But that would be Grossman's problem. After all, every problem was once a solution to another problem.

Sgt Oliver phoned me one evening later that summer. The Sarasota Police Department had picked up the two men and charged them with assault and murder. Oliver said he would have gone after Carlos di Giorgio too.

But it seemed that his body had been washed up somewhere down the coast, south of Siesta Key. It looked as if he had gone out sailing alone after dark and had fallen overboard. His skull showed serious injuries, which could have been the effects of the sea and the heavy surf. Oliver said the death had been put down as just an unfortunate sailing accident. I thanked him and hung up the receiver.

Then I smiled. Who would have imagined that Marcus Cuneo had a sense of humour? But it was just another small deceit, I suppose.

THE END

www.ingramcontent.com/pod-product-compliance
Lightning Source LLC
Chambersburg PA
CBHW062127170626
46813CB00002B/588